LILO MOORE

BEER FEST

Chapter One

If there's one thing you learn when you spend a lot of time alone, it's that there is nothing more human than a hug.

The bad ones are those uncertain clasps, where you jerk a few times on the way in, petrified that the other person didn't actually mean for you to hug them – or worse, that they're going to try to kiss your cheek. Then you don't know if you're supposed to close your arms around them completely, or keep your hands clear in a kind of plausible deniability, leaving them to wonder if they were the one wanting the hug more.

The good ones… they might be tight and apologetic or warm and soft, but they're always a deep breath out, a little tear, a meeting of souls and bodies and… smells – I mean that in a good way.

This was one of those hugs. His arms were draped around me – everywhere, somehow. There was a slight tremor in him; he squeezed just a little too tight, but that was okay, because it made me feel as though I could hold on as hard as I wanted, tuck my head into his shoulder and just breathe. He'd grown sturdier since I'd last seen him, but he was still so *Max*, that hugging him was like clutching a little piece of myself.

I'd missed him more than I thought.

'Are you crying?'

'I'm not falling for that,' I mumbled into his hair. I was a smidgen taller than Max – not unusual for a woman who was an inch shy of six feet. What *was* unusual, was that I still felt tucked up into him. He was gathering my lonely soul and it manifested itself in an enormous hug that should have been physically impossible. 'You're just trying to make me let go.'

I felt his laugh against my chest – inside my chest. At least the wonders of technology meant that laugh was as familiar to me as it had been after a year of sharing a dorm during our study abroad semesters at the University of Freiburg fifteen years before.

Fifteen years. It wasn't quite half my life, but it felt like all the most important bits had featured Max.

'Does it feel like I want you to let go?'

'Nope,' I said, breathing in deeply, one more time. I pulled back only far enough to peer at him.

He smiled – a signature Max grin that made me want to blubber all over him. With his crooked tooth, he always looked as though he was telling a joke. He usually was.

'You know what I think about masculine affection,' he said.

'I'm not a man.'

'*I'm* still showing affection.'

My face hurt, I was smiling so hard. 'Cutting off my circulation, too.'

One eyebrow lifted – an eyebrow the same shade as his hair, making it also improbably white. 'Four years, Fi. *Four years*! It's definitely too soon to let go of you.'

'Fine, if I'm going to lose a limb, I'm taking you with me.' I tightened my arms around his shoulders. 'I hate adulting.'

'No, you don't. If you hated adulting, you wouldn't have your fantastic career and you'd live here in Munich and spend your days being bohemian with me.'

It was way too early in our reunion to be talking about my 'fantastic career' and the work dilemma that still had me by the guts. I'd travelled halfway around the world and felt like I'd gone back in time. Work could take a back seat for once.

'Bohemian my arse,' I scoffed. 'I hate to break it to you, but getting high occasionally does not make you a free spirit. Which of us recently started a business?'

His answering smile was a small, self-deprecating number. He reached behind his head to grasp my hands, pausing briefly to squeeze them, then unravelled my arms from around his neck. 'A struggling business is very bohemian. I'm eking out a living until I can die of consumption.'

'Did you just make an opera joke? Who even are you?'

'I had a boyfriend who made me sit through *La Bohème*,' he said with a chuckle. 'But *you* dragged me to the opera once in Riga.'

'That was ballet and it was much less boring. Which boyfriend was that? Xaver? Kai?'

'You know all the names of my former boyfriends and girlfriends,' he quipped, smacking a kiss to my cheek and looking around for my suitcase. 'It was Kai.'

Since he knew about the romance vacuum in my life recently – well, forever, really – it was a relief to think I still knew just as much about him. We usually saw each other twice a year, took off on a crazy trip when I visited, ticking off ten cities in eight days – stuff like that. But a global health crisis and my stupid career had made the absence longer this time so video call oversharing had been a necessity.

'I missed you too much, Fi!' He punctuated this sentence with another rough hug, giving a worked-up sigh. My face landed in his neck and the warmth, the smell of him made me woozy with tiredness and relief.

'Have you forgotten that the planes fly in both directions?' I said, my words muffled in his collar. 'And Australia isn't like Narnia, where the portal only opens up a few times before you get too old – not that that would apply to you. If either of us never grew up, one hundred percent it's you.'

'You don't want me to grow up,' he muttered, but his scowl was wobbly and he was somehow grinning at the same time. Only Max. 'If there was a magic portal, you can believe I would have come through it. Unfortunately there are only expensive airfares and we brew beer and not money.'

'I can't wait to see the place. You actually run a microbrewery. After all the times we joked you should do it.'

'Perhaps it was fate, after all. But if I became a brewer because my surname is Dutch for 'brewer', what are you supposed to be, Miss Butkus?' He grabbed the handle of my suitcase and wisely darted away after that one. He knew the rule: the only one who was allowed to make 'butt-kiss' jokes was me. 'But I don't know,' he threw over his shoulder, 'now you've got your big promotion at BJ Williams, maybe your name is apt, too!'

My scowl was a lot more acidic than his had been. 'The global team was kissing *my* butt to get me on board!'

'Lucky them. Are you coming?'

After our study abroad year, I'd returned to my marketing degree at the University of Sydney and got a boring, well-paid job at BJ Williams – affectionately known between Max and me as Willi's Blow-Job or simply 'the Beerhemoth', since it was one of the largest drinks conglomerates in the world.

Max had loved his taste of freedom too much and had never

gone back to Holland after his year abroad. He'd lived in Munich for over ten years, now. Eek, how were we old enough for this fifteen-year reunion?

It was the middle of September and it turned out global marketing VPs were required to schmooze and get drunk at Oktoberfest once a year. I would take that, as it meant an extra trip to see Max. The rest of our friends from Freiburg had decided to come, too, since we'd always meant to hit Oktoberfest together, but the university term dates back then hadn't allowed it.

We had planned an unofficial University of Freiburg 2007-8 international student reunion and I had planned three weeks of reconnecting with my best friend and trying to gain some perspective to make a decision about my career.

Although I'd been to Munich airport at least five times, finding my way out to the suburban train station always threw me. But when I saw the wide, red carriages and the rows of carpeted seats, memories of all my previous trips flew back.

Max parked us at the end of a carriage and squinted at my suitcase. His albinism meant his eyesight wasn't entirely correctable, but he did okay with his glasses. I guessed he wasn't studying my luggage to admire it, though.

'Is this Louis Vuitton or something?' he asked.

I bit back a laugh. Max, in brown corduroy trousers that were furry like a bear in some places and worn to dirt tracks in others, saying the words 'Louis Vuitton' didn't quite compute. I hadn't seen him in four years, but I recognised his old Adidas sneakers. They could be called 'vintage' by now.

'It's not Louis Vuitton,' I said dismissively.

'It's a bit different from your turtle backpack.'

'Yeah, because it's not going to wrestle me to the floor,' I said drily.

'It's probably just as heavy, though, right?' He threw me a smile, his pale eyes twinkling, and it completely disarmed me. I grasped his arm and snuggled in, resting my head on his shoulder. But he sat up suddenly after only a moment, giving me a pat of apology, and rummaged inside his ancient backpack.

'How could I forget?' He produced two cans of beer and pressed one into my hand. 'A tinny for the road,' he said in a passable Australian accent. Max was amazing at languages. It had driven me crazy that year in Freiburg when his German improved so quickly, while I'd been slaving at the stupid language for years in Australia and still sounded like a bad actor in a World War II movie.

He popped the can and tapped the bottom against mine, sprawling back in the seat. I nursed my unopened beer with an odd tingle of nostalgia that was disturbingly bittersweet.

Shaking off the feeling, I pulled on the ring with a little too much force and my beer spurted foamy mess, making me flinch. Shooting out his hand, Max cupped the can and lifted it to his mouth – my hand and all. I stared, frozen in place, as he licked up the spilled beer, his tongue swiping hot along my knuckles.

He had a crease in his bottom lip, right in the middle. I hadn't forgotten. I knew every nuance of Max's face. But that day my eyes fixed on that crease and I had a lot of questions about his mouth.

Whoa, that hadn't happened before.

'I see your hygiene hasn't improved in four years,' I ground out, ignoring the gravelly quality of my voice. 'Did you shake it on purpose?' *So you could lick me?* Crap, I hadn't meant that.

I knew – had always known – that Max was bisexual, but I had never been included in that spectrum.

Back in Freiburg, he'd had one of those messy, seminal relationships with his boss from the restaurant where he'd been a dish-pig. Although I'd seen him hook up with a girl or two over the years, he'd always seemed a little less fussed.

Both of us were late bloomers in the romance department – or *never* bloomers, in my case. Watching my parents chip away at each other's self-respect for over a decade – even *after* they'd got divorced – had kind of killed my appetite for anything that started with an 'r'.

Max gripped my wrist to hold it still and licked once more along the base of my thumb. I ignored the enormous whump in my stomach. It was just a symptom of this weird funk I'd been in ever since I'd realised my dream promotion would require swallowing my pride and holding my tongue and that sounded quite nauseating, actually. I still didn't know what to do.

'Me? Do it on purpose?' he asked with studied innocence. With a jaunty shake of his head, he produced a fresh pack of tissues and a little bottle of sanitiser. He plucked the can out of my hand and wiped it down while I cleaned up, trying not to think about his mouth on my skin. 'The only time I shook it on purpose was—'

'Dubrovnik,' I said, forcing a frown, while I was laughing inside.

'It was for your own good! You picked up that guy after you soaked your shirt.'

'With hindsight, anyone you pick up with a shirt soaked in beer isn't going to blow your mind in bed.' I said drily.

I scrunched up my nose at him, but settled back in the chair, my shoulder against his. It kind of sounded like I hooked up a lot, but it wasn't like that. When a casual hook-up is all that's going, sometimes you take it. That, and Max was the best wingman you can imagine. It's easier to pick someone up when you're in another country and your best friend has your back.

I lifted the beer to my lips and took a long sip. In combination with the light pressure of Max's knee against mine, in the harsh light of the Munich S-Bahn, with the gentle rock of the carriage, it tasted like every trip we'd ever taken together, like the years falling away.

'I cannot believe I live in a country that does not understand the appeal of public drinking,' I said with an emphatic sigh, lifting the can to my lips for another glug. 'It's good to be back.'

The four long years without travel felt like a lifetime. At least before the world had closed down for a few years – Australia especially – I'd had my trips with Max to reset my mind, remember I was a person outside of my testosterone-fuelled workplace.

I was here, now. I would rediscover the Fiona who used to roam Europe with nothing more than a turtle backpack and her best friend. We'd enjoy an enormous beer in a tent with the rest of the world and see our friends again and it would be *wonderful*.

I was jetlagged as hell. That had to be the reason for the weird hug craving and the philosophical effect of two sips of crappy beer. I glanced at the can, recognizing the Fuchsbräu label – it was one of the BJ Williams brands, one of my family of commercial assets to play with. I felt Max's gaze on me and glanced over to find him giving me a thoughtful look.

'I thought I'd… make you feel at home,' he said lightly.

'No, you didn't. You're having a dig at me for working for a big multinational while you slave away for your handcrafted, organic, free-range hops-containing, we-could-never-have-afforded-it-back-when-we-were-cool-enough-to-drink-it beer.'

He howled with laughter and the odd panic of nostalgia dissipated into relief. He looped an arm around my neck, which, given my height, kind of felt like he was trying to give me a noogie. He pressed a kiss against my hairline and, for a fleeting second, I had to ask myself whether he'd used to kiss me like that. But it was such a smacking kiss, that the question seemed stranger than the action that had precipitated it.

Max was just that kind of guy. It wasn't anything to do with being queer. He just loved affection and he wasn't going to apologise for it.

I shrugged him off and knocked back more of the beer. It did taste sort of like the idea of beer, rather than the actual stuff, but I wasn't going to tell Max that – right now, when he was shooting me amused looks. It went down extremely well and it would knock me out, given my current state of jet-lagged stupor, where my eyes felt as though they'd been scraped along the plane carpet and I'd left some of my consciousness back in Singapore when I'd got on my connecting flight.

'I would rather have tasted your beer,' I mumbled. 'I can't wait to see Snaketooth.' In my professional opinion as a marketing VP, Snaketooth was THE BEST name for a beer in history. I wasn't biased at all.

'Do you really think I'd let my beer be sold in cans?' he said with a snort.

'I take it back. You have grown up.'

'Are you too disappointed?' he asked.

That was a loaded question. If Max had changed, where was my conduit to the past? I was thirty-six. And even though I hadn't married or had kids like a lot of my friends, I was losing some shine – or life was. All I had was my career and that wasn't making me feel great about myself right then. I closed my eyes so I wasn't tempted to look at him again and worry about what might have changed.

'Fi?' His voice was unbearably gentle. His breath feathered my ear. I sighed deeply and snuggled in. I wondered if he'd been working out, because his shoulder was weirdly padded. I was annoyed about that, too. When I'd first met Max, he'd been a stringy little whelp with a shock of white hair and I'd loved that Max to bits.

'Moppie.' He nudged my cheek. 'We have to get off the train.'

I sat up with a snort, with no idea how long I'd been asleep. The rude bastard laughed at me as he grasped the handle of my suitcase in one hand and held out the other to pull me up.

Chapter Two

Jetlag was a bitch. At three o'clock the following morning – what day was it again? – I was wide awake and staring at the sleeping form of my best friend across the pillow. It wouldn't be so bad, especially since I hadn't seen enough of his face for my satisfaction, except I knew I'd crash out again that afternoon.

I'd fallen asleep before we could even catch up after getting home from the airport. Three AM anxiety made me feel guilty about that, but I reminded myself of the time I'd nursed him through a violent stomach bug in Vietnam and the guilt dissipated again.

His eyelids fluttered and he rolled over with a soft grunt, facing me fully. His hair was a bit longer than I remembered from last time, and stuck up on one side. 'You awake?' he mumbled, his eyes still closed.

'No,' I whispered. 'Go back to sleep.'

His lips twitched. 'What time is it?'

'Jetlag o'clock. I said go back to sleep, Dornröschen,' I teased him gently, calling him Sleeping Beauty and smoothing his hair over his forehead.

'I can't sleep with you staring at me like that,' he said, his eyes still closed. 'I can feel it.'

That was a disturbing thought. Was Max so in tune with me that he could feel the unexpected tingle on the back of my neck, too? 'I was just thinking about that time in Vietnam.'

'You're lying awake thinking about me shitting my pants? It's good to see you, too, Fi,' he said with a snort.

'I was remembering it fondly,' I insisted with a grimace. That sounded weird even to me, but all our history was precious – even more than I'd realised at the time. If I ever got the runs, he was the only person I'd allow to help me and I hoped it was still the same for him.

'I know, moppie,' he said softly.

Tears pricked violently behind my eyes. It must have been the lingering effects of recycled plane air on my eyeballs. Or maybe just this beautiful man, my friend, calling me the ridiculous Dutch nickname he'd picked out for me back in Freiburg. It meant something slightly condescending like 'babe', but it sounded so dorky that I had tolerated it then – and by now, I loved it.

'Sorry I fell asleep in the middle of a conversation when we got home yesterday.'

'You've done worse – and so have I, as you remember.' He lifted a sleepy hand to smooth my hair. It was heavy and clumsy, but I leaned into it like a cat.

'Do you think… I've changed?' Gargh, that was a leading question. 'Or you have? I don't— I hope not.'

'It's okay, Fi,' he said, weirdly not surprised by my questions. 'Things always change. You've been depressed, but it'll all be okay.'

I stilled. 'I have not been depressed.'

Max cleared his throat. 'Okay. I just… it was a figure of speech. What's up? The important things don't change.'

'You own a brewery, now,' I pointed out, trying not to sound petulant as I scolded him for growing up without me.

'I own a business loan from the bank and Jan-Philipp and I struggle to make the payments. Maybe we'll lose all our money and have to shut down.' His light tone struck me cold. I would sell my apartment and invest in his brewery myself before I'd let him shut down.

'Do you have a marketing strategy?' I asked.

'It's three in the morning. Shut up about marketing.'

'I want to help.' Marketing was the only thing in life I was actually good at, as my salary attested to.

'And I want to go to sleep. I only said it so you don't have to worry about things changing. I'm a waiter who brews beer on a small scale and has no money – same as always. And your best friend.'

'My best friend,' I repeated, hoping my voice only sounded unsteady to my own ears.

'I know you've been working too hard, moppie,' he said sleepily.

I tried not to take that as a criticism. Yes, I'd been working hard, covering a global marketing VP position on a temporary basis. Making that promotion permanent should have been everything I wanted: a full-service move to New York, the seniority to contribute to decision-making at a high level and compelling proof that I was a competent and valuable human being. Oops, that last one wasn't supposed to be something I had to prove any more.

But the promotion came with an enormous side-serving of arsehole boss and I was questioning whether any of it was worth it. I was at some kind of crossroads, although it felt like a dead-end street. At least I could run back the other way for the two weeks of Oktoberfest and pretend I was twenty-two again – in between my work 'meetings', which were going to suck.

'Are you saying all I do is work?' I accused.

'I still love you,' he murmured, as though that was the only answer I needed. Perhaps it was.

My nose stung. In a panic, I wondered how I could swipe at my eyes without Max knowing what I was doing. A choked snort emerged from my throat and the game was up. His eyes snapped open, reflecting the dim light of the clock. 'I'm okay,' I said with a gulp. 'It's just… the past few years. I don't know… I've been really lonely.'

The next thing I knew, I was squashed into his chest and his arm pressed me tight against him. He smelled familiar, a mix of musty midnight human and a hint of one of those man-soap flavours. His skin was hot against my cheek. The sudden physical closeness must have overloaded my synapses, because I was thinking about his mouth again, about his tongue stroking along the back of my hand.

Damn, I had to sort myself out quickly, before I started thinking I was genuinely attracted to him – the one relationship I couldn't afford to screw with.

'It was hard,' he crooned softly. 'I still feel tired, too. And I had housemates during the lockdowns, at least. You had a difficult time. And I know no one quite appreciates how much good work you do.'

He propped himself up on an elbow and reached for his glasses and I stupidly noticed the broader outline of him in the dim light. But it was Max. It didn't matter if he had biceps or quads or fucking rhombuses. I remembered when he was so weedy that *I'd* helped *him* to climb over a wall after we'd got locked in the Père-Lachaise cemetery in Paris.

'Is the promotion worrying you? Because that guy you told me about is a dick. I hate to see him hitting your confidence.'

'I don't want to talk about it. We've got three weeks to just enjoy ourselves like we used to. I'll work out the promotion crap afterwards.' And resent every minute I had to spend in a beer tent with my boss instead of Max.

'Three weeks to recapture your lost youth?' he said with a teasing grin. 'How's that single grey hair you found?'

I gave him a shove and he toppled onto his back. 'I don't know about *lost youth.*' I ground out the last two words. 'But I could let my hair down – celebrate that the world is still where I left it.'

'Thankfully, the world is still here and still full of beer and bratwursts,' he said with a chuckle.

'Don't joke about bratwursts,' I reproached him. 'Since you don't eat meat, I'll assume you're making a bad joke!'

'Since you've been telling me on video chat about your recent lack of… bratwursts, maybe I *was* making a joke.'

I groaned. 'I'm sorry for oversharing.'

His fingers ghosted down my cheek as his grin was illuminated in the dim light from the streetlamp through his blinds. 'I love your oversharing. It's… us.'

Warmth bloomed in my chest, so happy there was still an 'us', that he'd put up with me no matter what I did. 'I didn't come here for a bratwurst binge,' I insisted drily.

'But if one comes to you…' he began, his grin turning silly. We were so in tune – at least, we'd used to be – that he was probably imagining the same thing as me: a whole lot of hot dogs being thrown at my face like the gif we'd traded many times.

'Is Oktoberfest really a good place to pick someone up?'

He made a series of noncommittal noises which made me seriously doubt my beerfest romantic prospects. 'There are a lot of people mixing. Someone will probably try to pick you up.'

'Thanks for your confidence in my abilities to attract someone,' I said, even though it felt too early in the morning for the sarcasm that had grown a touch too habitual for me recently. 'To be honest, I don't think I can be bothered. And if I don't put in any effort…'

'The guy could put in some effort, you know,' Max said with an amused huff.

'To be completely honest…' I hesitated one final time. 'I told you my love life has been even more dire than usual lately, but the truth is, even when I've tried I haven't had an orgasm with another person in… years.' Yikes, it did sound like the problem lay with me, when I put it like that. 'It just doesn't seem to happen for me at the moment.'

His mouth hung open. 'You don't come at all? Those idiots mustn't be trying. What about fingers? Or oral?'

My face flushed, but Max was obviously more at ease with the subject, because he wiggled his tongue at me. At least it put me at ease again. It was just Max. He'd talked me through numerous hard lessons in sex and relationships over the years.

'It's not for lack of trying,' I mumbled. 'Usually, they have a good go, but I give up at some stage and fake it.' It felt strangely good to say that out loud.

'How many years?' Max asked, his voice high.

'It's not like I wrote down the last time someone else gave me an orgasm,' I snapped. 'Two years, maybe three.' From what I could see of his face in the dim light, he was looking at me strangely, like I needed help. I wished he'd laugh with me. 'It's fine.'

'Maybe you do need a prince charming in lederhosen. Or a few Oktoberfest-gasms.'

'Shut up,' I grumbled, giving him another shove, but I knew he was trying to make me feel better. That had always been his special skill. 'Maybe I will keep an eye out for… particularly appealing bratwursts.'

Maybe here, with my old friend as my wingman and the chance to turn back the clock, I'd be able to fix what had gone wrong with me. I just wanted to get on with life, *do* things so I wasn't thinking about all the choices that had started to feel final.

He rolled over and I stared glumly at his back as he stowed his glasses in their case and stilled. 'Do you think you'll be able to get back to sleep?' he asked. 'I've got a reading light somewhere if you can't.'

'Why do you have one of those?' Max needed a strong lamp and a magnifier to read – and large print if possible. His peripheral vision was okay, but his eyesight had never been good enough to drive, for example. These days we shared an audiobook subscription and chatted through the titles afterwards. He liked angsty romance, which figured.

'Ben has insomnia,' he muttered.

'Oh,' I said stupidly. I knew about Ben – a tiny bit. Max had always dismissed him as a fuck-buddy but if he'd stayed over enough that Max had bought him a reading light, maybe there was more to it. Maybe he'd got serious with someone and he hadn't told me. He'd tell me right?

The faintest tingle of something different in him was enough to scare me. I wanted to know what was going on with him but not if it meant something changed between us.

I tucked myself against his back and slung an arm over him. Max was the best hot water bottle. My thoughts scattered, leaving only the strong impression of how much I'd missed this guy – then the oddest impulse to press a kiss right between his shoulder blades.

Surely, my brain was just fuzzy from being exhausted.

Chapter Three

'Who's Dornröschen, now?' When I levered my eyes open, I wasn't surprised to see a familiar pair of sky-blue eyes and a shit-eating grin from the other side of the bed. He already had his glasses on, blinking at me through the lenses. 'I've been staring at you for about half an hour and you didn't wake up. I'm bored.'

I settled into the pillow, pulling the blanket around me in a puffy cocoon with a masculine tang. It was a shame he slept like a German, with two single blankets instead of a double – although he'd probably be protesting about me stealing it, if we were sharing one.

'These sheets smell like you,' I murmured sleepily. His smile faded and, as that snaggle-tooth disappeared, I listened back to what I'd just said. Was it weird? 'Didn't you even put fresh sheets on for me?' I grumbled to cover the awkward moment.

'I forgot you have an unnatural sense of smell.' I hated that he'd forgotten anything about me. 'The sheets were clean three days ago so I didn't do it.'

'You forgot I could smell pot at the convent we stayed at in Tuscany?'

'I remember you wouldn't let me buy some,' he said with a pout.

'I still say you can't take the pot the poor old nuns need for their arthritis.'

'You spoil all my fun.' His gaze flew to mine. 'Joking!'

'I'm sorry I was so weird last night,' I groaned, pressing my forehead to his shoulder. 'I know you're joking. You can tease me. I can tease you.'

'Right. And I stand ready to enact your sex plan: Operation Enormous Bratwurst,' he said, breaking into giggles. 'Oh, sorry. Operation Assisted Orgasm. It's not the size that matters.'

His grin was back and I had the sudden urge to grab his face and kiss that saucy smile right off it. *That* would shut him up – and freak both of us out.

'I take it back. No teasing,' I grumbled. 'And no sex plan.'

I threw back the blanket with a groan. It had taken me over an hour to fall asleep after our three AM heart-to-heart. At least I'd familiarised myself with the collection of new pink spots on his back and the dark Snaketooth tattoo on his shoulder blade. I wanted a better look at the tattoo in daylight. It looked badass and sexy and I was annoyed that he hadn't told me he'd got it. Max had drifted off again quickly, snuffling softly and smelling amazing, while I was restless and… kind of horny.

I didn't sleep as well in general since the lockdowns and I'd been worried Max and I would disturb each other, but I'd never imagined I'd lie awake with my face hovering near his bare shoulder, contemplating sinking my teeth into it.

It would pass. It was probably that time of the month. Stupid hormones insisting I get down to business.

Speaking of getting down to business, I hauled myself off the bed and padded to Max's wardrobe where I'd hung some of my clothes. He came up beside me and I nearly jumped.

'I have a dirndl you can borrow, if you want to get into the spirit.'

'You know my position on dirndls.' I rarely wore any kind of dress, as dresses only ever seemed to invite snide comments from my colleagues – or open criticism from my mother. 'I don't want every Tom, Dick and Hannes chatting up my boobs instead of my face.'

Max gave me a considered look, but said nothing. I understood anyway. He knew I was above-average height and occasionally sensitive about my above-average boobs. He also knew that saying anything to me about it was pointless.

He leaned past me to fetch a pair of coarse brown shorts, embellished with stitching reminiscent of antlers and alpine flowers. The bloody great flap at the front was unmissable. Undo two buttons and dick's out ready to go. No wonder guys liked wearing them.

I tore my eyes from the flap. 'In what way are lederhosen vegan, my friend?' Max had been vegetarian since he was a teenager and he'd gone completely vegan about ten years ago – before it was cool, as he claimed.

He grinned at me and I realised I'd missed the mark. 'You think I'd wear leather? Do you know me at all? I run a vegan pub, Fi.'

I rubbed the cloth between my fingers. It was thick and malleable, but clearly woven material, now I looked closely. 'Hemp?' I guessed, hiding my guilt at thinking he'd wear leather.

'You do know me, after all,' he said with a laugh and nudged me with his elbow.

He retrieved a forest green dress on a hanger and held it up with a flourish. The pretty bodice was satiny and patterned with tiny white flowers. The neckline plunged, of course, designed to be worn with a white blouse underneath. The ruched hem would probably press right against my nipples. The attached, mid-length skirt shimmered green-grey and a shiny, dark green apron hung off the hanger. It was all rich fabrics and fine workmanship.

It looked like some kind of fantasy and, although my brain was screaming at me that it was veiled sexism and patriarchy and cultural appropriation, it also looked kind of fun. There was something about the word *bodice* that made me want to capture some of that fantasy.

'You sure you don't want to wear it?'

'I'm sure,' I said. 'But why do you have a dirndl?'

'Because I wear it occasionally.'

'Damn, I forgot how gorgeous you look in a dress! Wear it! Today!'

'Not on the first day,' he said. 'Maybe later in the week.'

'And I'll wear the hemphosen to stay in the Oktoberfest spirit.'

'Hanfhosn,' he corrected me with a grin and his damnably perfect accent. I wasn't sure he ever spoke Dutch any more. 'And we don't call it Oktoberfest here, remember. It's d'Wiesn. And if wearing my shorts gets you into the Wiesn spirit, you're welcome to – as long as I can borrow your shoes.'

I took a quick shower, hurrying because he shared the bathroom with one of his housemates. There was a knock while I was scrubbing the grainy potato feeling off my face. I was safe behind the white shower curtain and I knew Europeans were less weird about nudity, so I called out for the person to come in.

'It's just me,' I heard Max's voice as the door clicked shut again. 'I thought I should shave.'

'Aren't beards an Oktoberfest thing? Oh, not yours.'

'Ha!' he responded and I heard rummaging in the cabinet. 'I was twenty-four that time in Spain and it takes more than two weeks to grow a beard anyway.' He'd had the sweetest wisps of a white goatee on that holiday.

'You're thirty-five, now, but I still don't think you can grow a real beard, even in a month. One day I'll be able to grow a better moustache than you.'

He didn't laugh. I didn't hear anything apart from the dribble of water onto the floor of the shower. I peeked around the curtain – and froze. He was leaning on the basin, staring at the tap, his brow furrowed in deep thought. And he was naked above the waistband of the hosen.

The thick hemp was supple and moulded to his backside like worn leather. The curve of stitching along the waistband accentuated his lean hips and the muscles in his butt. He'd told me about the carbon-neutral bike deliveries he did every day for the brewery and I could totally believe it as I cocked my head and ran my gaze down to his strapping calves, his feet.

They were the same size as mine, but I hadn't remembered the cords of sinew that gave me a sudden foot fetish – or something. Jerking my gaze back up didn't help, because I found his back, smooth and broad and toned, with that new tattoo on his shoulder. It was a stylised snake, fierce and hissing at me, taunting me with everything I'd missed in his life. He'd always been hot – at least, I'd always thought he was, in a kind of aesthetic way. But this…

I had waited far too long to see him, missed him too much

and these were the strange side effects. I hadn't asked for this sudden desire to lick my best friend. I needed to get back to our comfortable old relationship where this weird tension didn't exist and we could count on each other for *anything*.

I stared at his throat, watching him swallow. Yep, I wanted to scrape my tongue up there and make him gasp and— I turned forcibly away, pressing the back of my hand to my forehead. *Shut up, horny Fi!*

Squealing in surprise when I found him looking at me in the mirror, I clutched the shower curtain like it was my first time in the naked sauna. Then he chuckled, his eyes glinting, and I swept aside all the stupid sexual awareness with a long exhale, giving myself a mental shake.

'I forgot how self-conscious Australians are. You've been gone too long. Remember that time in Estonia when the attendant made you take your swimsuit off?'

'I'm not self-conscious!' I insisted, prying my fingers loose from the shower curtain. 'And don't tease me about Estonia. I was only twenty-two and I didn't realise they could have rules enforcing nudity in the sauna!'

'I'm not teasing you,' Max said, his tone so gentle it shivered over my skin. 'You were so nervous you were shaking, but you stripped off and lifted your chin like it was all your idea.'

A choked laugh emerged from my throat. That was a lovely way to remember that day. As soon as the attendant was gone, I'd clutched my towel over my torso like a shield and spent the day hiding behind Max. To be honest, I still wasn't comfortable nude, even though I understood it wasn't always sexual – or it wasn't supposed to be, anyway.

'You've got a new tattoo,' I blurted out.

'So do you,' he said mildly, gesturing in the direction of my ankle, hidden by the curtain. I'd had a little plane inked onto my skin while I was stuck moping in Sydney as the world turned without me.

'You didn't tell me about that one,' I complained.

He glanced over his shoulder, before whipping his gaze back. He picked up the shaving foam and sprayed a little into his hand. 'I didn't realize you wanted to know.'

'Max!' I grumbled. 'I want to know everything!'

He remained silent for long enough that I looked up from the swirl of ink on his back to meet his gaze in the mirror. His mouth was open, as though he was trying to say something, but his expression was… kind of earnest. I swallowed.

'Sorry?' he said eventually. 'Next time I'll take a photo of the festering wound for you.' His smile was back. 'You'd better get dressed if we're going to meet the others on time,' he said, turning away to smear shaving foam onto his cheek.

The others… We hadn't met up all together like this in fifteen years. I hadn't seen Florian or Marco at all. But I was still tempted to blow it all off and hang out in the park with Max, like we had in Freiburg. At least I still had three whole weeks with him.

I tiptoed out of the bathroom wrapped in a towel and pulled on my best jeans and a nice top before Max arrived back in his room, his chin free of fluff and his eyes touched with grey eyeliner. He'd experimented with my subtle eye make-up back in Freiburg, initially to see if it would tone down the striking effect of his white eyelashes and pale skin, but he'd quickly discovered he liked a more dramatic style. I always loved how fabulous he looked in eyeliner, as though he was stretching out his arms and yelling, 'Look out, world! This is me!'

I didn't watch as he pulled on a green-and-white checked

shirt and flipped the suspenders of his hemp lederhosen over his head, buttoning them in front. When he produced a chunky silver chain hung with coins and charms, I gave up pretending I wasn't watching.

'What is that?'

'It's a charivari,' he said with a straight face, even as I wondered if he'd made that up. He attached the chain to the two buttons at his hips, so it hung in an arc over the dick flap. Turning to me with a grin, he settled his thumbs in his waistband and tilted his hips at me. 'Hot?'

I coughed, swallowing a laugh and the truth at the same time. 'Not,' I said drily.

* * *

'Over heeeeeeere! Fi! Fiona! We're here!'

Hearing Isobel's shrill shout brought a grin to my lips and I rushed to the place where my tiny Spanish friend had set up camp. I threw my arms around her – awkwardly, around the tape marking the queue for entry to the Theresienwiese, the holy field of Oktoberfest and the reason for the local name of the festival, d'Wiesn. I wasn't usually so demonstrative, but Isobel was irresistible.

Tanya was with her and I gave her a squeeze, too, although she wasn't as much of a hugger. I'd seen Tanya last year when she and her kids had moved to Australia for school, but it had been a flying visit while I was in Brisbane for a conference and she was busy viewing mansions and it couldn't have been clearer the different courses our lives had taken.

But she'd come. Old times were old times and I was looking forward to rekindling our friendship.

They both wore dirndls, Isobel's in shades of blue and a touch too short and Tanya's in rich black-and-silver tones with a woollen vest.

'Max!' Isobel squealed and threw her arms around him, next. 'I can't believe you look just the same!'

'It's over six years since we visited you in Valencia.'

'I know,' she said with a grin, patting his cheek. 'But I meant you look the same as Freiburg. How do you still look twenty when I look forty?'

'You don't look forty!' I insisted. Perhaps she had a couple of lines at the corners of her eyes and there were a few flourishes of grey in her brown hair, but if she looked forty, then I must as well.

'But I'm so glad you two kept in touch,' she continued. 'It was such a crazy year in Freiburg and I'm excited we're all together again! Have you seen Ryan and Florian? They're in the queue somewhere. The bouncers wouldn't let them join us, but we'll get a table for all of us.'

I tried not to react to Florian's name, but Max bristled at the mention of my Freiburg hook-up. It had taken me a little too long that year to work out that our relationship wasn't supposed to be anything more than just sex – as though I'd needed another reminder that romance was almost always one-sided.

'Here,' said Tanya, reaching into her bag. She solemnly handed both of us a bottle of beer. Lifting her own from the pavement, she held it out, bottom-first.

I blinked at her, my old friend who was now the society wife of a millionaire. Max grabbed both of our bottles and popped the tops with a bottle opener from his charivari, before tapping his with Tanya's. 'Prost,' he said with a wink.

'Prost,' I replied, tapping my beer against his. 'I didn't realise the dick bling had a function,' I muttered.

'Dick bling!' Isobel howled with laughter. I suspected she was a little *too* ready to let her hair down.

'What's the plan, Tanya?' I asked.

'I have eighteen days here,' she said. 'We're going to do it right. Schottenhamel-Festzelt for the first day, Hofbräu tent after that, half a chicken, giant pretzel, stand on the benches and sing, shoot a toy gun – not at an effigy of my husband – personalised gingerbread heart, giant wheel. Did I miss anything?'

'I am determined to end up as a "Bierleiche",' Isobel said, exaggerating the pronunciation as though she was as dreadfully out of practice with German as I was.

Max snorted beer. 'Do you mean determined *not* to end up?' My brain whirred, trying to retrieve the meaning of 'Leiche', but all I was getting was the unexpected mental image of crime scene tape.

'A beer cadaver, right?' Isobel said brightly. '*I* only have eighteen days to *live my life* before I have to go and bleed and sweat and drip milk for the fruits of my womb.'

It was my turn to choke. 'You make it sound like your babies are vampires.'

'You have no idea what it's like to have twins. I'm certain when they're older, they're going to speak at the same time and terrorise me in the mirror. If I'm going to meet my demise anyway, I may as well have fun doing it.' She patted the satin bow of her apron, tied haphazardly under her left rib.

'I really didn't think we were going to be the sensible ones,' I murmured into Max's ear. 'What's she doing with the bow? I hope she's got her emergency contacts in there so her husband can identify the body.'

'That would be more sensible,' he muttered in reply. 'Bow on the left means you're single and looking for…'

'The bratwurst stand?' I suggested. 'I'm mostly sure she's not serious. But why didn't I know about this? Is there a men's equivalent?'

'Nothing similar for lederhosen. That's one way wearing a dirndl could help with your sex plan.'

'You have a sex plan?' Isobel interrupted with delight. 'Tell me! Let me live through you!'

'I don't have a sex plan,' I insisted.

'Fi is looking for an o-fest of a different kind,' Max said with a maddeningly straight face. I gave him a subtle punch in the thigh, wishing I was cruel enough to aim a little higher.

'An o-fest!' Isobel howled again. 'Wait, why?'

'You could suck on my beer any day, gorgeous!'

I blinked, turning slowly to take in a buff dude with no neck, who'd actually said that in real life. He saluted me with his beer, taking a swig and licking his lips afterwards. The action only made me feel vaguely nauseous.

'Not that guy,' Max groaned in my ear. He wrapped an arm around my waist and turned back to Tanya and Isobel. 'We should join the queue.'

'Why not that guy?' I whispered as we headed for the distant end of the throng. 'He doesn't need a neck to be good in bed.'

'I don't think you're taking this seriously,' he muttered.

'Do you want me to take it seriously?' I wasn't even sure what we were talking about any more. The sex plan? That hadn't even been my idea.

There was a catch in his voice that sent a shiver of alarm over my skin, when he said, 'Uh… no, probably, not.' He nodded curtly, biting his lip.

'But I…' I began before I'd thought it through. He glanced at me expectantly and I had to finish. *I want you to stay with me* sounded lame and selfish. 'I'm just glad you're still my wingman.'

He grabbed my hand and squeezed, harder than he realized because it hurt. 'I'll always be your wingman, moppie. *Always*. I'm on your side. If you want the guy with no neck, then… sure. Let's go back. Even he would be an improvement on *Florian*.'

My heart lolloped around in my ribcage, doing somersaults at everything he said. The way he'd said 'always'? That had made my skin prickle. I didn't like these hints that my Peter Pan was growing up, but I *really* didn't like the way he encouraged me back to pick up the buff dude, especially not with that weird tone of voice.

I stared at him for a moment too long. I had to say something to stop him looking at me like that.

'Fi? Max?' I heard dimly from behind me.

Max's expression turned grave and my emotions performed another abrupt U-turn that was in danger of giving me vertigo. Or was that the circulation in my hand cutting off? I turned slowly, clinging to Max.

'Uh, hi Florian.'

Chapter Four

Florian held up a bottle of beer in salute and I was relieved the cordons for the queue removed any obligation to hug or kiss or whatever else you did with the guy you'd wasted large chunks of your study-abroad year stupidly obsessing over.

He looked like a weathered and folded and bent-up version of his twenty-three-year-old self, still with that swish of dark hair and the smile I could never be certain was genuine, but it sure did catch me in the guts. That was interesting. Mr No-Neck had produced no reaction whatsoever, but there was a trickle of something as I looked at Florian and remembered falling into bed with him. Maybe there was hope for the sex plan.

Not that I had a sex plan. I didn't – even though Max was looking at me as though he was worried I'd leap the cordon and get started straight away.

'You guys finally got together! That's great,' Florian said, in a facetious tone that made him sound like a senior manager who didn't actually know what he was talking about. After my recent stint as an acting VP, I'd learned everyone in a position of seniority was pretending to be competent and men just managed to believe their own shit.

I realised a little too late what he meant. 'Oh, we're not—' I dropped Max's hand, annoyed that Florian had made me do it. 'You know, it's just the same – Fi and Max, Max and Fi, best friends forever.'

'BFF,' said Max, making a heart with his fingers. I stifled a snort of laughter that might have been a touch hysterical.

As Florian had been the only German who hung out at the international dorm for the drinking and the parties and the friends who left again within a year, I'd always suspected he had issues with maturity. Now he had a YouTube channel where he performed stupid stunts while inebriated. Did I mention I had bad taste in men? Perhaps I was only capable of reaching orgasm with complete dicks.

'I was always sorry we lost touch,' Florian said, turning to me, his smile growing infuriating because I couldn't tell what he was thinking. 'Are you still in Australia?'

'Yep, still in Sydney. Are you still in Cologne?' I knew he was. I had Google and he was easy to find on the internet.

'Yeah. Funny you never came to visit me.'

'Funny,' I muttered, clearing my throat.

'It'll be good to reconnect.' My mind flew to the various ways to 'reconnect' and I couldn't help thinking bleakly that at least there had been orgasms back then. 'Ryan's just gone to take a piss and Marco's late as always.'

'Oh, good,' I said, before choking on my own inarticulateness.

Thankfully Ryan reappeared – not safely behind the cordon – and I was enveloped in a tight, American hug. I certainly remembered Ryan was a hugger – especially on the rare occasions he'd shared a joint – but that hug was a little… desperate.

'You guys!' he said, slapping Max on the arm so hard he

stumbled. 'We're hanging out like we used to – we're at frickin' Oktoberfest, man!' I glanced at Florian, whose shrug was an indication of just how much Ryan had drunk already.

'Who's taking bets on the first Bierleiche?' Max muttered in my ear.

'Sorry, I don't… drink much these days,' Ryan said. He broke out some pretty mean puppy-dog eyes. 'My wife doesn't do it – drinking, I mean. When's Marco turning up? Is he with you?'

Max and I both shook our heads. 'We'll see you in there,' Max said, grabbing my arm and heading for the back of the queue. He clearly had little patience for Florian which bothered me. Not that I was going to sex-plan Florian. It was just that he seemed like the least complicated prospect here, all of a sudden.

* * *

I'm not too proud to admit to the little thrill that zipped through me as I strode along the floorboards into the Schottenhamel-Festzelt. Calling it a tent was a bit like calling a great white shark a fish. It was more like an enormous temple, where you checked your cynicism and pessimism at the door and lubricated your happiness with beer.

It was at least three stories high, the ceiling draped with pine garlands and strung with ribbons in the blue-and-white colours of the federal state of Bavaria. Decorations shaped like pretzels and gingerbread hearts hovered over hundreds of wooden tables. A platform for the band rose among the tables, like a life raft where your chaotic final hours at sea were accompanied on the euphonium.

The effect was festive and fantastical and far from everyday life – a magical beerland, where anything was possible because you're drunk. I'll admit it wasn't possible for me to check *all* my cynicism at the door, especially since I'd worked in drinks marketing for nearly fifteen years.

No one was drunk yet. No beer was allowed to be sold for another two hours, but it hadn't stopped the punters arriving in throngs. We had to squeeze past large groups of young men in lederhosen, as well as waitresses balancing enormous trays of roasted pork knuckles on their shoulders, as we made our way to the table Isobel and Tanya were guarding with their boobs – I mean lives.

'There must be ten million people here,' I called to Max over the din.

'Six thousand. Not ten million!' he called back.

It was a daunting number – more intimidating than my joking ten million. What kind of chaos could happen in here with so many people under one roof, aside from the guaranteed couple of hundred viral infections? But the main question that distracted me was just how much money was washing around in here. And yet Max's brewery was struggling. It bugged me.

The atmosphere in the tent was kind of weird, with only the hubbub of voices instead of jaunty music blasting from the stage. Tanya had already ordered three half-chickens – to tick off her list – which we were apparently supposed to eat with our fingers. It was probably a good thing we hadn't made it here as students, as we would have spent all our money on liquid meals and it would have been even messier.

I picked at the chicken breast a little, but I always felt strange eating meat in front of Max. He never suggested I should eat vegan, but I didn't want to make him gag.

Our Italian friend Marco had finally arrived, taking up the space of two women at the table and digging into the chicken, which seemed appropriate since the Italian diet consisted almost entirely of tomatoes, wheat and animal products – with a dash of alcohol.

Isobel propped her elbow on the table and leaned over to me. 'See anyone you like for the sex plan?'

'Isobel!' I cried. 'I've only just sat down!'

'You could be sitting down on—'

'Shhh! I've already been hit on by a guy without a neck. You don't need to announce it!'

'You don't need a neck for—' I cut her off with a scowl. 'Fine. Okay. You can be a little picky.' I inwardly groaned.

'Is that the kind of ride you want to go on, Fi?' Florian said with a smug smile. 'Maybe I can take you on the ghost train later.'

'Some rides just make me vomit,' I said breezily. 'Especially the ghost train.'

'Vomiting is on my list,' Tanya announced impassively.

'That should be easier than finding a man for Fi,' Isobel said, so earnestly that I knew she hadn't meant it the way it sounded. Max snickered next to me and I aimed another punch at his thigh, but he caught my fist before it connected. 'You just need beer goggles,' Isobel insisted. 'Everyone looks better with beer goggles.'

I made some kind of noise that implied agreement, but admitted nothing.

'Why aren't *you* married, Florian?' Tanya asked suddenly. 'Aside from the obvious.'

He almost choked on a chicken bone and Isobel walloped

him on the back. 'I'm only thirty-seven,' he said when he'd recovered. 'Not all of us are keen to marry young. Why isn't *Fi* married?'

'I haven't met the right person,' I said facetiously.

'Which is better than meeting the wrong guy,' Tanya muttered.

'I divorced the wrong guy,' Marco piped up, rather cheerfully.

'Oh, I'm sorry,' I said automatically.

'It's okay. We weren't allowed to get married in Italy when we wanted to, but there is no discrimination about divorce these days.'

'We could probably drink to that, if we had a drink,' Max said. He turned to me suddenly. 'Isn't there a song about that? "The Pub with No Beer"! The Australian's nightmare song!'

'How do you even remember that?' I exclaimed. 'I must have talked about that song *once*.'

He gave a wide, innocent shrug. 'I remember a lot of stuff.'

'Sooo many years!' Isobel said and I realised I'd been holding my breath. 'But it's weird that there was a time when you two didn't know each other.'

'And it's the first time we've been to Oktoberfest together,' I pointed out.

'Were the jeans and shirt by choice, by the way, Fi, or you just don't own a dirndl?' Florian asked and my little bubble popped again.

'It's not compulsory.'

'No, but I'd love to see you in one,' he said with a greasy smile.

'Thanks, but I'm not going to tuck my boobs into someone else's traditional dress just for your enjoyment.' He hooted with laughter and that annoyed me, too. What was worse, I still felt that little tingle of possibility. At least someone was chatting me up like old times. I didn't feel like a great person right then.

I *really* needed a beer. This wasn't a reunion of old friends. So far, it was a reunion of crabby millennials. The camaraderie that had made that year abroad so magic appeared to have disappeared with my youth. I glanced at my phone to see how many more minutes I had to endure before we could add beer.

Maybe some things from my life were gone for good and I should go ahead and grieve: looking on the bright side; guilt-free world travel; believing people really liked me… orgasms. But I could always count on beer – and Max. Thank fuck for Max.

I fiddled with my glass of sparkling water, still annoyed that you had to buy water in Germany and weren't allowed to bring your own – and annoyed at myself for such middle-aged anger. Picking it up, I tapped the bottom of my glass against Tanya's and took a sip.

'Fioooooona!' Isobel shrieked, making me jump and spill water down myself. Perhaps if I'd been wearing a dirndl it could have sloshed straight down between my boobs and saved my nice top.

'What?' I snapped.

'You can't say cheers with water! In Spain, that means seven years of bad sex!'

I groaned, pressing the heel of my hand to my forehead. 'That'll bring me up to ten years.'

* * *

'O'zapft is!'

Two hours later, the poor mayor had barely finished declaring the first barrel open when the tent erupted in cheers. The screaming and wolf whistles continued as a TV announcer commentated over the din.

A blonde woman in a black-and-yellow robe stood decoratively on the table next to the barrel and a group of middle-aged men in green felt waistcoats and lederhosen gathered around it, including the mayor with his wooden mallet which he'd used to hammer the tap into the barrel.

I felt as though I'd landed in a low-budget historical drama – except I hadn't got the memo about the costume.

A group of men with waxed beards and felt hats at the next table broke into song. A throng of young folk stood by the bandstand, hands outstretched, eagerly awaiting the first *Maß*, the enormous glass mugs of beer that held a whole litre. Far too cool – or too spiritless – to hustle ourselves, it took the poor waitresses another half an hour to deliver our beers, despite – or because of – Florian's presumptuous finger-snapping.

Max tipped generously, earning him a pat on the cheek from the middle-aged server in a low-cut dirndl. He'd hustled at Oktoberfest before and I was beginning to appreciate how much hard work that would have been.

I grabbed for a mug, lifting it with both hands because I didn't want to break my wrist. The thing weighed a tonne. Not literally a tonne, but it was genuinely a kilo of beer, plus the weight of the mug. But at least I finally had my beer.

With rousing voices, a chorus of 'Ein Prosit' filled the tent. I only remembered a handful of the words, but I raised my beer and sang what I could. The beard men turned and clashed their mugs with ours.

Florian opened his mouth to say something to me, but I held up my hand and took a long, decadent sip. Ah, that German richness, malty and heavy. Sure, a light lager was great for thirty-degree days on Bondi Beach, but for a cool September afternoon in a beer tent, it was perfection.

'I know,' I muttered to Florian after I'd savoured that first glug. 'I forgot to make eye contact when we said cheers. What's another seven years of bad sex to me right now? I've got the bloody message, universe!'

Chapter Five

It was a weird old afternoon in the beer tent. Isobel and Tanya talked kids. I didn't blame them, because they blamed themselves enough and tried to change the subject. I couldn't remember what we'd talked about for hours when we were students. Music? Politics? Maybe we'd talked about plans for the future and since all of those had gone down the toilet in recent years while the world changed and real life landed on us, we struggled with that topic, too.

Florian kept up a flow of conversation about the many stupid things he'd done on camera, like eating a whole jar of gherkins or hanging a string of tampons from his nipple piercing. He'd wink at me after each one and I'd take another long gulp of beer before responding, 'Why didn't you light the vinegar farts?' or, 'How about normalising periods instead of making tampons into a fucking joke?'

He seemed to think I was hitting on him anyway and maybe I was, out of a simple sense of tipsy inevitability.

I was downright gloomy and all the perky music and perky hats and perky… boobs were only making me grumpier. Max was restless too and I didn't know why. I felt like the worst friend for hanging my mood off his gorgeous smile with that little snaggletooth.

Feeling like the worst friend was still better than facing any of the other possible reasons for my grumps. I wasn't unhappy or dissatisfied. I could still enjoy stuff and be a human being and talk about things other than marketing metrics and engagement stats. It was just first-world problems.

Whenever I peered into my mug, there was less beer in it than I expected. I'd just asked myself if I was imagining the brass band playing a song by One Direction when I realised all of the others were staring at Florian with rapt attention. I blinked and tried to focus.

'It's called… the *Wiesn Chellenge*!' He meant challenge of course but his accent rendered the 'a' as an 'e'. Whatever it was, my reaction was an eye-roll. 'You guys will love it. I'll manage the filming and the social media and you guys do the challenges.'

'Uh—' I began.

'Let's do it!' Isobel said, slapping the table with her palm.

'He hasn't explained what it is, yet,' Max pointed out. His ears were pink. I fixated on that for a moment, wondering whether he was just warm or embarrassed about something. I tried to catch his gaze to share the eye-roll, but he was watching Florian intently, nursing his beer.

'There are games and tasks to do in pairs and some kind of mystery challenge to complete as a bigger group. For some of them we meet together with the other teams and others we have to complete in our own time and film them. We post them on social media and get points for the amount of interaction we get, as well as from a judging panel. Then the winning group gets to compete in a final day of challenges to name the winning pair. We'd have an advantage because of my social media following.'

I gagged, imagining the kind of people who followed Florian's douchy channel watching me skull a beer and allocating likes based on how many centimetres of cleavage I showed. Absolutely. Not. No fucking way.

'The best part,' continued Florian, 'is that there is *prize money*. Someone is going to hand over ten thousand euros for this!'

'We're in!' said Tanya.

'Wait a minute,' I said, swallowing when the words didn't quite come out right. 'Who's organising this challenge? It's a marketing thing.'

'Who cares if it's a marketing thing if it's fun?' Tanya asked, although I couldn't tell if she was smiling or not.

'Because some company would be manipulating us into promoting them!'

'Isn't that your entire job?' Isobel asked.

That felt like a slap in the face.

'If you want to do this "chellenge", then *do* it, Florian. You can't force us to make fools of ourselves while you just film it,' I snapped.

'How do you know you'd be making a fool of yourself?' Max piped up and I did a double-take. Wasn't he on my side? Had they all realised I'd become a grumpy hypocrite? 'You could give it a try,' he continued.

'You need to lighten up, Fi,' Ryan said gently. 'We're here to have fun.'

My vision kind of tunnelled and whether it was the jetlag or the beer I didn't know, but something in me snapped.

'It's beer marketing,' I insisted. 'I know about beer marketing. It's an excuse for men to take up too much space as though it's still their right. Unlike the rest of the business world, the beer marketing map still has fucking genders on it and everyone plays along in the name of fun! People drink shit beer in the name of fun because some clever marketer thought of that!'

A voice inside me was yelling, '*Noooooo! Stop!*' but it wasn't enough to counteract the momentum of my freight train of stifled opinions and frustrated attempts to drag my colleagues – and bosses – into the twenty-first century. Even the late twentieth would have been an improvement.

It all came fizzing out, as though I was a beer can and someone had finally given me a shake. 'I just want to enjoy my beer!' I stood, swaying a little admittedly, and my momentum even got me up onto the rickety wooden bench. Lifting my mug, I shouted, 'I *love* beer!'

A surprisingly loud chorus of, 'Bravo!' greeted my statement and echoed around the enormous tent.

'I *love* beer,' I began again, belatedly realising the brass band was taking a break and my words echoed around the tent. 'But do you have any idea what it's like to be a woman who drinks beer? How many people use it as an excuse to comment on my weight or my clothes or my nutrition? I love beer because I'm strong enough not to care what any of you think!' I pointed a wild finger at a man two tables over who blushed fiercely.

Someone wolf-whistled and it was enough for me to return to my senses for a moment. Max curled an arm around my waist, trying to shepherd me back down from my soapbox, but that annoyed me too.

'Beer isn't some test of masculinity – I would take a lot of you down, if it was!' I continued, kind of enjoying myself now. 'Beer advertising gives men a great excuse for toxic drinking culture, but where is the advertising for the strong women who drink beer and don't take your shit?'

'You forgot sexy!' someone yelled out.

'I don't care about being sexy!' I shouted back, but it was enough for my confidence to wobble – along with my legs – and I let Max help me down. I didn't *want to* care about being sexy but why did I keep attracting dicks, or did they attract me?

Oh, shit, the pine wreaths hanging from the ceiling were swirling. The band had started up again, but the music sounded out of tune and I really needed some fresh air.

'Fi, let's—'

I shoved Max away. 'I'm just going to walk around a bit to sober up,' I mumbled. 'Since you guys are having so much fun here, go on without me!'

'Fi—' Max's tone was oddly pleading. I couldn't tell any more if I'd done something wrong or if I should be annoyed with him, I just knew that this 'recapturing my carefree youth' thing had misfired badly and I was still a frustrated thirty-six-year-old with nothing to say except the stuff no one wanted to hear.

'I'll go and make sure she's okay,' I heard Florian say as I stalked away from the table – at least I tried to stalk, but I wasn't stable enough for it.

Things got a bit hazy after that. There were flashing lights and whirling colours and Florian's face up really close. And then I just remembered lying somewhere while everything seemed to move around me and all I could do was call pitifully for Max.

* * *

When I woke up the next morning – if I could call it waking up, when it felt more like 'coming to' – I could still see pine wreaths moving above me in slow circles and a tiny oom-pah band was playing inside my skull.

Jetlag and several litres of beer were a trippy combination.

'Max?' I mumbled, my voice gravelly. As though saying his name brought niggling memories back, a sudden panic gripped me and if I hadn't been half-paralysed I would have sat bolt upright. 'Max?' I repeated, my voice higher this time.

I heard a sleepy mumble that sounded like, 'Mmph, wha? Stooearly, moppie,' and I released a relieved breath.

'I had a weird dream that we argued and got separated,' I said.

'That wasn't a dream,' he grumbled in reply.

My eyes felt like jacket potatoes that had exploded in the microwave when I tried to pry them open. 'What?'

'You were clearly drunk, but I didn't trust what that Arsch mit Ohren would do, so I went after you.'

I tried to rub a few of my brain cells back into existence. 'What arse with ears? You mean Florian?'

He nodded, his mouth pressing into a firm line and I caught myself staring at his mouth again. Oh crap, this weird curiosity about Max hadn't got drowned with my self-respect last night. I'd rather eat my own pride and sleep with Florian than start worrying that I was attracted to Max.

Just. No. He was my safe space.

But I was relieved I hadn't slept with Florian. Without the beer goggles, it was clear it wouldn't even have been worth an orgasm. I had some pretty psychedelic memories of the evening before, making me wonder if I'd kissed him. Erk.

'Are you all right? Do you remember what happened?' Max

asked, sitting up and reaching for his glasses. He was shirtless and shoulder-y and smelled amazing and maybe I wasn't all right if I kept ruining Max this way.

'Most of it,' I rasped. 'I didn't get arrested, did I? I remember flashing colours and something moving all around me.'

'Don't get arrested,' Max pleaded. 'I can't afford bail. But no, that was just the LachFreuHaus. That's where I found you. It's a ride – lights and obstacles and stuff.'

'That explains why the police light was purple instead of blue. What was I doing when you found us?' I asked hesitantly, hoping the answer wasn't 'snogging Florian', although if it was, Max deserved a reward for saving me from myself. But the thought of Max seeing me kissing Florian made my stomach roil – or maybe that was the effects of my liquid dinner.

'You were trying to sleep, poor moppie,' he said with a pained smile, 'on the rolling tube.' His hand brushed my cheek and the ripples of sensation on my face were almost worse than the worry that he'd seen me kissing a douchebag.

He'd seen me kissing douchebags before, but now... I was way too hungover to think about this.

Max's phone rang and he frowned, reaching down to grab it off the floor because Max wasn't quite grown up enough for nightstands. 'Hey, Flo.' He started to say something else, but Florian cut him off, his agitation clear even to me. 'What?' Max turned to me, gesturing wildly. 'Where's your phone?'

I hauled myself out of bed before I realised I had no idea and stared stupidly around the room. It appeared I'd managed to get my jeans off, but my blouse was half unbuttoned and I'd got one arm out of the sleeve.

Max's conversation stalled, but when I turned around to see what was wrong, he started speaking in rapid German, running an agitated hand through his hair.

I eventually found my bag under Max's old corduroy jacket that I'd borrowed yesterday and plugged my phone in. As soon as it connected to the network, I saw I had two voicemail messages. Max kept talking in an increasingly animated tone, groaning and asking questions in disbelief.

The first voicemail was from my boss, Bram Dollersen, Global Director and Senior President of Sexist Bullshit. It was my turn to hiss with disbelief after I listened to it.

'I can't say I'm surprised, Fiona, because I know you're ambitious, but what were you trying to achieve with this? If you were looking to make a splash at our meeting with Servalas on Wednesday, this stunt might end up backfiring because he knows the direction of our next campaign and it's not *this woke bullshit you were spouting. BUT—'* Dollersen chronically overused dramatic 'buts'. *'The video has been shared so many times, it probably doesn't matter any more what the original message was.'*

A shiver of awareness crept up my back. There was only one thing that I'd done last night that might have blown up on the internet: my soapbox rant. Fuck, what had I even said? I remembered rubbishing beer marketing and that was bad enough.

This could cost me my job was one random thought that tip-toed across the back of my mind, but whether I was just hungover or something more serious, I couldn't muster much of a reaction to that.

The second voicemail message was arguably more alarming. *'I've just seen the announcement and I suppose this is an interesting strategy and turned the previous message nicely on its head. It's better to think you'll turn into a beer-maid for this challenge rather than make beer-drinking men into metrosexuals. Although the challenge is run by a competitor, I'd like you to stay in it for now and we'll see if we can work this to our advantage.'*

I gagged, getting distracted by the unsettling fact that he thought 'metrosexual' was still a thing and that he thought I'd ever be a beer-maid. But the words 'announcement' and 'strategy' made me dizzy.

Then I heard Max say, 'She's not going to like this, Florian.'

I was suddenly in the garbage compactor scene from *Star Wars*, with Florian on one side and Bram 'Metrosexual' Dollersen on the other, about to find out what was under all the space junk. I gestured for Max to give me the phone.

'What's going on? What did you film me doing yesterday and how many lawyers do I have to rain down on you?'

'Okay, Fi, stay calm.'

Nothing riled me more than being told to stay calm. Max's hand clamped onto mine.

'Firstly, the video of your beer-tent rant is amazing. It's got more views than *I* usually get. It's trending on a couple of apps, with lots of stitches and the audio is trending too.'

I was going to be sick. Working in marketing, the words 'trending' and 'views' were usually the stuff of bonuses, but it wasn't normally *me* up there – and an uncensored version to boot.

'I didn't give you permission to post anything!' I hissed.

'*I* didn't post it unfortunately. Someone else did. I'm just doing damage control for you.'

'You don't want to know what his idea is,' Max said through gritted teeth.

'I tried calling, but your phone was off and you know how important timing is with these things.'

'What did you do, Florian?' I demanded to know.

'It'll be harmless – you'll see,' he insisted.

'*What did you do?*'

'I just posted a video saying you were in my team for the Beerfest Challenge and that we were sure to win, with Miss 'I Love Beer' on board.'

'I don't want to do the stupid challenge!' I exclaimed. I wanted time with my best friend. Even though yesterday had been weirder than I'd hoped, I wanted to find something of myself outside work, so I could accept the shit situation with Dickwad Dollersen. 'I'm not a beer-maid!'

'How did you know that's one of the challenges?'

Choking on a protest, I heard Dollersen's words in my head. Unless I wanted him to realise that the 'woke bullshit' was my honest and rather sad opinion, which I concealed at all costs in a professional setting, I had no choice. It was Wiesn-Challenge or bust – although the stupid challenge would be bust as well, if I was forced into a dirndl.

'It'll be fun, I promise,' Florian said.

'That does not fill me with confidence,' I muttered.

'Well, perhaps next time you won't get drunk and spill all your secrets,' Florian said in a low tone that sent alarm sizzling up my back.

'What secrets?'

When he spoke, his voice was pitched high, imitating me in a mocking tone. 'Oh Florian, kiss me – *please.*'

'I obviously wasn't thinking straight last night,' I ground out.

But he wasn't finished. 'Kiss me! I'm so confused right now because I want to jump Max and I don't understand why!'

I leaped off the bed and escaped into the hallway before Florian could say anything more. 'Shut up,' I hissed, hoping

Max hadn't heard any of that.

'But maybe he wants to jump you, too,' Florian said in an infuriatingly suggestive tone. 'Oh, right, you also told me he was a relationship disaster area and you couldn't risk going there because he's not "in love" material. Which thing would you *most* like him to *not* hear?'

My head spun, between the question in the negative and the horror at what I'd said. Max and I were *both* relationship disaster areas – together. That was why we were never looking for relationships. At least I was pretty sure we weren't.

'Don't freak out. I won't tell him. I'm not as cruel as you are.'

That insult landed far too close to my nervy switch, the one that was too easily triggered by jerks when they broke up with me. Was I cruel? I could easily have inherited it, given all the stuff I'd heard my mum manipulate my dad with over the years.

'You've never seen me at my cruellest,' I shot back. 'Unless you want to, you'd better make sure you don't film anything too damning for this stupid challenge. If we want to edit something out, you edit it out.'

'Of course,' he said with mock affront. 'I'm on your team.'

'Yeah, right,' I mumbled. 'Fine. We do the challenge. But I'm doing the tasks with Max as my partner.'

'I won't say no to a little extra sexual tension,' Florian responded, his voice smooth.

'Fuck off,' was all I could say in response. I would keep the stupid sexual tension well under control. I needed my best friend on my side. If they were making me do it, at least I was going to win the money for him.

Chapter Six

'I'm sure it won't be too bad,' Isobel pointed out the following day. She sounded almost disappointed. 'The organisers won't want to get sued.'

'But if it's anything like Florian's YouTube channel, it might be in bad taste,' Ryan said warily. 'Did you see the one where he powered a rocket with methane from his own poo?'

'Urgh, that's...' I struggled for the words.

'Actually kind of environmentally friendly,' Max muttered.

I eyed him. 'And completely disgusting.'

We'd gathered on a quiet backstreet in central Munich, huddled under umbrellas. The apartment buildings were grand neoclassical numbers with wrought-iron French balconies and little hats over the windows. It was a far cry from the streets of blocky, rendered apartment buildings where Max lived, with dry cleaners, kebab shops and Romanian supermarkets on every corner.

We were waiting for Florian, who'd received the instructions from the organisers. Several other groups, all in dirndls and lederhosen – 'Tracht', as Max reminded me we were supposed to call the traditional dress – loitered nearby, all awaiting the same fate, sucking from brown bottles of beer. Add in some fat boiled sausages and we'd be enjoying an al fresco Bavarian breakfast.

Max was wearing his non-leather lederhosen with a Snake-tooth beer logo embroidered on his white collared shirt. I was glad he would at least get some free marketing out of this farce. I was the only one in jeans and a jacket, but I was fresh out of fucks.

Given the meeting point and the date, we guessed the first challenge would be something to do with the parade that was due to start in an hour – the 'Trachten' parade. I wanted points for our team – for Max – but not at the cost of my pride on the very first day.

'Everyone ready for the first chellenge?' Florian called as he came around the corner with a flourish, instead of greeting us like a normal person. He had a dorky-looking camera on a stick, waving it around so much the clip would give me motion sickness – not that I wanted to relive this moment on video at any point. 'How are we feeling, Wiesn Champions? I'm going to do a freeze frame and edit in some Queen, there,' he added.

Even Isobel was wary enough of the challenges that she could only muster a mumble in reply. Florian turned off the camera and collapsed the telescope stick.

His eyes zeroed in on me and I gave him my best glare. 'I see some of us are not in the spirit of the Volksfest,' he said, crossing his arms and strutting over to me. That I'd begged this jerk to kiss me was a rather terrible reflection on the state of my love life. 'Jeans, Fiona?' he prompted.

'Jeans, Florian.'

'That could get you disqualified.'

'That would be the simplest solution.'

'It could be the simplest solution for your boss too, right?' I gritted my teeth. Next to me, Max bristled and I gripped his wrist and shook my head.

'I don't own any Tracht,' I said, very calmly, if I say so myself.

Florian grinned then and the roiling unease was back in force. 'I thought that might be the case, so I bought you this.' Reaching into the bag slung over his shoulder, he retrieved a coat hanger and shook out a full outfit, with bodice and skirt, apron and a cropped white blouse. 'Beautiful, isn't it? But you'll have to change quickly in time for the parade.'

The dirndl on the hanger *was* beautiful. The bodice was pale green silk with silver embroidery, edged with ribbons. A silver cord criss-crossed the front. The dark green apron was shiny silk. It was an expensive… joke. Although it was beautiful, the skirt was shorter than usual and the neckline lower and Florian was a first-class dick.

He roared with laughter which suggested I'd spoken that last part aloud. 'I knew you'd be perfect for this, Fi. Tracht is required, as I mentioned in my message. It's all in the competition fine print.'

I balled my fists, but before I could come up with a biting response, Max snatched the hanger and grabbed my elbow, wrapping an arm around my waist when I didn't come. 'I have an idea,' he murmured in my ear and I finally allowed him to pull me sideways out of the fray.

Glancing up and down the street, he led me to a hotel and, ignoring the frown from the starchy receptionist, hurried to the lobby toilets, dragging me into the men's.

When he disappeared into a cubicle with a mumbled, 'Wait there,' leaving me to avert my eyes from the urinals all on my own, I realised what he had in mind – and it flooded me with warmth.

'Max, are you sure about this?'

He gritted his teeth so loudly I could hear it. 'We'll play along, but he can't force you to wear something that makes you uncomfortable.'

The warmth rushed up my chest. 'But what about you?'

'I'm not uncomfortable in a dirndl,' he said simply. And indeed, when he emerged a moment later, the bodice slightly askew, he was… gorgeous. His smooth chest looked comically broad and flat above the plunging neckline and the frilly blouse. His shoulders emerged as though he was a rippled alien from a monster romance who didn't fit properly in the heroine's… world. But he grinned and propped one hand on his hip, giving me a wink.

It was the grin that made the outfit, his soft bottom lip with the crease in it suggesting all kinds of fun and games.

'Do I pass?' he asked, rubbing the back of his neck.

'You look beautiful – way better in it than I would.'

He shoved the lederhosen into my hands with an inarticulate scoff. 'Hurry!' He ushered me into the cubicle.

The leather shorts were still warm. It was impossible not to think about how they'd gripped Max's butt only a moment ago. I tucked the Snaketooth shirt into the waistband, soaking in his body heat from that too, and imagining his friendship was some kind of protective force. It truly was. No one else would swap clothes just to help me make a point.

When we travelled together, it was usually me who haggled with the taxi drivers and argued with the tricky salespeople. But I wondered whether I would have done all that without knowing he was there with me.

'Max?' I called out as I slipped the leather suspenders over my head and wrestled with the buttons.

'Hmm?'

I hesitated, no idea what I wanted to say. 'Thank you,' I said in a small voice.

The gorgeous idiot laughed. 'You don't need to thank me, like I'm your little assistant or something.'

It was probably a good thing that those fluffy feelings dissolved. 'That's not what I meant!' A woolly sock flew over the cubicle door, followed quickly by the other, and I grabbed them both.

'Would you have thanked me when we were twenty-one?' he asked. 'I've got you, moppie. I should never have let you grow doubts about our friendship.'

I flung open the cubicle door with one sock half-on, hopping wildly on one foot. 'I'm *not* doubting you! I'm *appreciating* you!' I said before I'd thought that one through. His chest rose and fell with some emotion and his nostrils flared and there I went appreciating again.

He nodded, once, with a kind of fierceness that made my toes tingle. 'Okay, fine. I could be appreciated.'

His rough tone made me gulp.

'Nearly ready, Fi. Turn around.' I squealed when he grabbed the laces at the back of the leather shorts and tugged them tight.

* * *

I didn't know how the organisers wangled it, but we were in the parade. It was totally not allowed and if we hadn't all been wearing Tracht, we would have ruined the effect of the oldy-worldy costumes everyone else was wearing. At least this way we were funny.

We were tucked in behind a group of women with flowers stuffed down their decolletage and jaunty hats with pink shawls making their outfits look demure and nostalgic, rather than the wardrobe-malfunction-waiting-to-happen that was the neckline of the slutty dirndl.

Behind us was a brass band, as though Florian knew we'd need an audio kick-up-the-bum to keep us marching. They wore tall hats tied under their chins and lots of tassels on their jackets and oom-pahed away despite the light rain.

Max had told me the parade was supposed to be only for historical societies, rifle-shooting clubs and marching bands and really, it looked way too classy for a bunch of rowdies kit up for a beer tent. I hated to think what the stuffy societies would make of Max and me out front – and I suspected that had been Florian's intention when he sent us there.

'Asshat,' I muttered, glancing at him moving through the crowd, recording everything.

'Just think about the look on his face when he saw us coming out of the hotel,' Max murmured into my ear, making me smile. Watching Florian gape at Max in his finery was worth the occasional disapproving look from the crowd.

We garnered a lot of attention – good and bad – between Max and me. I pretended not to hear the cat-calls and graciously acknowledged the cheers that followed me, which were pretty damn touching and went a long way towards making up for my new infamy as the 'I love beer' woman.

One of the ladies in front of us handed Max a hat and some flowers and he made a show of tucking the blooms into his bodice. He threw the hat and tried to catch it on his head, drawing cheers from the crowd. He nabbed the felt shoulder-bag that I was carrying for him and rummaged in it, bumping against me as we hurried along with the parade.

'What are you doing?' I asked.

He held up what he'd been looking for: a little rainbow-coloured hacky sack. He threw it and caught it on the back of his hand, then flipped it over and closed it in his fist. 'Are you trying to help Florian with this farce?' I hissed.

'I'm standing in the Trachtenumzug, the costume parade, wearing a dress. I'm gonna do it with a bit of style.' With a flash of a grin, he threw the hacky sack and caught it on his foot. He hopped and whirled his way towards the Theresienwiese, pausing to catch the sack on his foot or his shoulder – or failing spectacularly to catch it, drawing laughs from the crowd.

Watching Florian recording every moment, I thought of the prize money. Winning would be a way to help Max that didn't involve handing him my money which he wouldn't take. But did we even have a chance, with Florian Fuckface in charge? I had to try.

I skipped out in front of Max and gestured for him to toss the sack, even though it always seemed to bounce off me.

'Remember when we got pickpocketed in Paris?' I called out over the din of the brass band.

'*Pickpocketed in Paris* is the name of my sex tape,' he quipped. 'Of course, I remember. Instead of going to a bank like normal people, we performed in the street until we had enough money for the métro. But no one cared about my juggling. They just wanted to see you catch the hacky sack down your top.'

'That's not how I remember it,' I sniffed. In my memory, Max had juggled and danced and entertained the crowd, while the only things I'd been able to contribute were my boobs which was typical.

On that same trip to Paris, he'd got a room with a guy from the hostel on the second night, but the sex had been so incredibly bad that I'd got a giggling, blow-by-blow account of it the following morning, complete with an octopus-tongue metaphor that had been a running gag for years.

I wondered who was giving him blow-by-blow octopus tongue these days, if it wasn't Ben.

Typically, Max read my mind. 'Are you thinking about the octopus tongue?'

I burst out laughing and he gave me a withering look that didn't last long. '*You* said sex tape!' I poked him and he shoved me in return and before I worked out what was happening, he'd grasped my hand and twirled me around. I squealed as he tugged me to him and we stepped jauntily to the music, hands joined in front of us. 'Shouldn't I lead?' I asked.

'If you know what you're doing.' He spun me around again and managed to wrap me up in my own arm, curling his body around me as we skipped forward.

'You have a point,' I agreed, realising with disbelief that I was grinning. 'Lead on, Fräulein!'

By the time we reached the Theresienwiese, my ears were ringing from the trumpets, my knees were sore from all the slapping and my chest was warm and gloopy from all the feelings. Screw Florian and his stupid challenge. I'd do anything, as long as Max was there with me.

The beerfest was looking up.

Chapter Seven

'The Wiesn-Chellenge has two parts,' a woman announced from her position standing on a bench of a nearby table. She might as well have had 'Junior Marketing Associate' written on her forehead and I couldn't help wondering if I'd looked that eager and clueless straight out of uni.

She worked for one of the competitors of the Beerhemoth and I got hives at the thought of the non-compete clause in my contract, but I had Dollersen's grimy blessing – and very little choice in the matter – so I listened to the poor woman explain the challenge, slurping more beer as I waited to hear our fate, despite knowing that alcohol is a depressant and I certainly didn't need one of those.

'You will receive a list of challenges you must complete before the Wiesn comes to an end in eighteen days, some of which we will organise and others you need to work out yourselves.'

Florian leaned close and whispered, 'Don't worry, you two Sitzpinkler. They won't make you vomit or need your stomachs pumped or spill your darkest secrets while rolling around half-asleep in the LachFreuHaus.'

I sucked in a breath through my nostrils, but didn't let him see a reaction. Sitzpinkler I guessed was some kind of insult about peeing sitting down – the sexist blackmailer.

'To prepare for the second part, we need these pieces of paper,' the organiser continued. 'We will play a little game of Wahrheit-oder-Pflicht over the next two weeks. I believe it's called "truth or dare" in English?'

Tanya rubbed her hands together in something like delight, but Ryan froze in alarm, sloshing his beer.

'How old do they think we are?' I muttered.

Florian's gaze zeroed in on me. 'I see you've noticed our group is at least ten years older than the other contestants.'

I choked, glancing at the other tables in the reserved area to see that Florian was right.

'You did say you wanted to get your mojo back,' Isobel pointed out, adjusting her bodice for the fiftieth time that day. 'We totally would have done this fifteen years ago.'

We would have, which was a disturbing thought. Had we truly been so lame back then? 'Well, maybe some of my mojo – our mojo – deserves to stay in the past,' I suggested with a grimace.

'I think that attitude is exactly why you lost your mojo,' Isobel continued and maybe she had a point. If I couldn't go back, then I had to go forward and I didn't really like what I saw there either.

'And don't you know?' Marco began in a low tone. 'What happens at Oktoberfest, *stays* at Oktoberfest.'

It was a stupid cliché, an excuse to escape the responsibilities and consequences most adults had accepted by now. But I'd be lying if I said I didn't feel a tingle of excitement at his words.

'Write your questions and dares on these papers,' the organiser instructed and I lifted a pen with a troubled frown, not wanting to know what kind of dares the other contestants would set. 'We will collect them and each group will get some of the papers to complete. If you write a dangerous or impossible challenge, there will be consequences, so consider carefully. You're not trying to kill each other.'

Florian snorted at the joke which I hoped meant it was a joke. 'To all of us! Prost!' he said

As the alcohol from the strong beer dribbled into my veins, I racked my brain for ideas for dares that would be fun and flirty – the way I remembered myself being in the past, although I didn't trust my memory so much any more. Max sat across from me, writing furiously already. I wondered what bug he had in his pants to have so many ideas for nasty dares.

He bit his lip in concentration and that was my focus gone. Staring at Max was going to get me into trouble, but it was difficult to stop when that bottom lip looked so springy and inviting and made me think about teeth on skin in other places.

And then some devil made me take up my pen and scribble the words that I should have known would come back to bite me: *Kiss your partner.*

* * *

Our little group was slightly shell-shocked when we emerged from the tent with our list of challenges and a velvet bag of secret dares.

'Turn the camera off for a minute, Florian!' Tanya cried. He was enjoying his role as Chief Schadenfreude Officer far too much.

'We need a plan,' I said, looking down the list of challenges, which was printed onto an actual, no-shit scroll, with a wax seal of one of the competitor's beer brands. 'It looks like we have to do every single ride in this place.'

The tasks were marked with a '1', a '2+' or 'sober', according to how drunk we were supposed to be when completing them.

'I say we just get started,' Tanya said. 'We've had one beer. Pick something.' She ran her finger down the list. 'Hau… den… Lukas,' she read slowly. 'Whoever Lukas is, we have to hit him?'

'Sounds like something for your sex plan, Fi!' Florian quipped.

'Come on,' Max said, grabbing my arm before I whacked someone other than this Lukas.

Max refused to explain what kind of carnival attraction it was. After consulting the Oktoberfest map, we arrived at the spot to find a strongman game, a tall blue-and-white pole with a trigger at the bottom and a bell at the top, set between the legs of a cut-out of a smiling man in lederhosen. Ryan and Marco chuckled and even I managed a shrug. The first task could have been much worse than whamming a hammer as hard as I could to ring a wooden dude's bell.

A group of young guys in lederhosen and white sneakers were trying their luck, gulping beer in between turns. One was distinctly unsteady on his feet, but he slammed the mallet down as though it were Thor's hammer and the puck fled up the pole. But it still didn't quite reach the bell at the top.

'Do you reckon Lukas's smile changes to a grimace if you manage to reach his privates?' I joked to Max.

'It depends on whether he wants you to reach his privates or not,' Max murmured in return and I whacked him with the back of my hand.

'If that big guy didn't get very high, there's no hope for us,'

Tanya declared with a deep sigh.

'Unless I hit the thing with my boobs,' Isobel said, fiddling with them again. 'I should have weaned those babies properly before I came,' she grumbled. 'These things are rock hard.'

'Does that mean,' Marco began, 'you have alcoholic milk right now?'

'You did not ask that!' I said sharply.

'It's just a question,' Marco said. 'I'm not going to drink it – unless she offers.'

'Like the *Grapes of Wrath*,' Ryan said suddenly and we all blinked at him. 'That's what happens at the end of that book. Rosasharn breastfeeds this old dude who's dying of starvation.' We were all still blinking. 'It's like hope and defeat in one image,' he added weakly.

'So, if I found a homeless dude with alcohol addiction and gave him milk. Like that?' Isobel clarified.

'Forget the drunken challenges. I should be filming this conversation,' Florian said, his voice high with disbelief. 'What is wrong with you guys?'

'There's nothing wrong with breastfeeding!' Isobel snapped. 'It's none of your business who or where I feed! You can't tell me not to if someone's hungry! I bet you have no problem with boobs when they're not lactating!'

'Whoa,' Florian said, holding up his hands in that infuriating male pose that's designed to dismiss female emotion as not his problem. It's amazing how many times in my life I'd thought that there should be compulsory empathy training involving wearing fake boobs for a day. Lactating boobs would be even better. I wouldn't even mind if it was equal opportunity and I had to wear a dick.

'This doesn't have anything to do with the challenge,' Tanya pointed out, deep in thought.

'And since Lukas isn't a homeless alcoholic, we should probably try hitting the thing with the hammer,' Max said, 'with all due respect to Isobel's boobs.'

'Oh, no, no, no!' We all looked up at the operator of the carnival game, who was wagging his finger at us. 'You are here for the Wiesn-Chellenge, or? No hammer.' I glanced at my hands with a grimace. 'No hands!' the operator added. He produced a cushion, which he set on the trigger with an inviting pat. 'For the Pobacken – bum cheeks!'

We gave a collective groan, but Florian rubbed his hands in glee. 'I know who's going to win this, Miss Butkus,' he said. *Oh, for fuck's sake.*

'Usually, I say ladies first, but today, the men start and the ladies think strategy,' the operator said. 'You have six tries for the team – three each.'

Marco nodded, holding a hand to Ryan's chest to stop him. 'I go first.' He took several steps back and turned, taking a deep breath as he eyeballed the carnival amusement.

'It's the Oktoberfest Olympics,' I muttered to Max.

'That's a better name than Wiesn-Chellenge,' he quipped.

Marco sprinted the run-up and, at the last minute, spun and shoved his arse onto the cushion with a grunt. The puck gave a pathetic sigh and jumped about three inches. Marco always sounded so elegant when he swore in Italian and Ryan almost grew heart-eyes where he stood.

'Mi dispiace – I'm sorry,' the operator said good-naturedly. 'You try next, Captain America?' I suspected he called all the American visitors that, but Ryan laughed over a blush. He tried the same run-up, with an even more pathetic result.

'This is impossible!' he cried.

They experimented with shorter run-ups and by the third attempt abandoned the run-up entirely, which brought slightly better results. Florian filmed every foul curse from Marco and mild epithet from Ryan with glee.

When they'd finished their turns, I sighed and took a step towards the platform, but Max stopped me with a hand on my arm. 'I have an idea.' He exchanged a few quick words with the operator where all I caught was 'zusammen' meaning 'together'. The operator shrugged and seemed to agree and then Max was beckoning to me from just in front of the trigger.

'Turn around,' he said and I realised what he had planned. My mouth dropped open as I tried to decide if I should protest, but he lifted his eyebrows and dipped his chin at me and I could never say no to my partner in crime. With a laugh, I turned and let him tug me close.

His arms were tight around my waist and I grasped at his hands in alarm until he laced his fingers with mine in reassurance. All of a sudden, I loved this game. His breath gusted on the back of my neck and I suddenly imagined wearing that dirndl with the wide neckline, tilting my head and letting him nibble – as if he would ever do that.

The suspenders of my lederhosen pressed against my heaving boobs and I tried to settle down, conscious that Florian was filming this episode of Horny Fi. Max dropped his hands lower, making a little hitched noise, almost a grunt, and my legs turned to jelly.

'Ready?' he asked, his voice calm, as though we were taking a companionable stroll instead of rubbing up against each other in front of a fairground attraction. My brain was obviously the only one acting out. That litre of beer – and four-year absence – had a lot to answer for.

'Yep,' I said with a swallow.

'One, two – three!' I jumped as he launched us backwards and we landed on the trigger awkwardly. Max grabbed for me as I tumbled and the next thing I knew, the only thing stopping me from faceplanting onto the metal floor were Max's hands splayed on my boobs.

Chapter Eight

I shot my arms out and froze, panting, as I recovered my balance. Max must have been equally shocked because he didn't move his hands – at least, he didn't *re*move them.

As a full-breasted woman, I had a love-hate relationship with those ladies. They were fickle when it came to sexual touch and I just got sick of them taking over the rest of my body as a focal point for others. But Max's accidental touch to the underside of my boobs? Highlight of the past three years.

I heard Florian guffawing behind the camera and Max snatched his hands back. 'You okay?' he asked, a catch in his voice. 'Was that a bad idea?' For a moment, I thought he was talking about him squeezing my boobs. I blessedly realised what he was talking about before I said anything.

'How high did we get it?' Max hauled me to my feet and we turned eagerly to the operator. He indicated a spot on the tower about six inches up. It wasn't great, but it was better than anything Ryan and Marco had achieved. 'It was a brilliant idea,' I said.

'We'll get it higher next time,' Max said, matching my smile. 'And I'll try not to… grope you.' He tilted his head and I could almost believe he was disappointed to make that promise.

'If the result is worse next time, you'll have to grope me again to replicate our success.' I kept my voice light, but he looked as though he'd swallowed his tongue. 'Scientific reasoning,' I added.

'Right,' he said, his lips twitching. 'Come on, moppie. Let's go again.'

I took up my position, my butt squashed against him and we waved to the camera this time. Max gave my hip a swat and I looked around in mock affront. But he winked and closed his arms around me in a hug and suddenly I was grinning back.

'Let's have some fun, Butkus,' he murmured. 'One, two – three!' With a grunt, he hauled me backwards and this time, my shoulder nearly knocked out all his teeth and we barely managed four inches. 'I'm okay,' he croaked, rubbing his jaw.

'Good. I'd hate to be responsible for the death of that snaggletooth.'

He grinned ruefully and ran his tongue along his teeth. 'One more time, Fi. As hard as you can.'

The third time I jumped with more force and he gave a little, 'Oof,' as I landed on him, but the puck barely gained any more height. 'Six inches is all we've got, I think,' I murmured, hauling him to his feet. 'Although size doesn't matter,' I couldn't resist adding.

'With the right… conditions, I could get to eight,' he replied earnestly, but his dimples were deep and I knew him too well to believe he was serious. But that meant… we were both joking about his dick. Crap.

I eyeballed him. 'No more than seven, surely,' I deadpanned. I'd said the puck had jumped six inches, but to be honest, inches didn't mean a lot to me. In my head, I was hurriedly calculating how many centimetres seven inches would be and thinking about Subway subs, my other measure in feet and inches. I'd always wondered why the aubergine emoji had taken off, when there was a perfectly good baguette.

'I'll have to prove it to you, later,' he said with another wink. My mouth was so dry I would need a litre of water before even thinking anything more about baguettes.

Oblivious to the unfortunate overdose of sexual tension, Tanya and Isobel bustled forward, discussing who would be on top, and I took the opportunity to look away from Max and properly oxygenate my brain.

'You might be heavier than me,' Tanya began, 'but my smaller bottom will concentrate the force on the trigger.'

'But I'll squash you!' Isobel cried.

'I'll make that sacrifice. Turn around.' It would take a greater woman than any of us to go against Tanya when she spoke in that tone. And it turned out she was right. They were lighter than Max and me, but better coordinated and perhaps the secret was in Tanya's tiny arse because they shot the puck beyond the ten-inch mark.

It only reminded me of Max's promise to show me his erection later – although that was definitely *not* what he'd meant. He was just goofing around as usual, with no idea that I was silently wondering. He probably thought it would ick me out, which it might have in the past. I licked my lips and tried desperately to clear my head.

Isobel whooped and she and Tanya wrapped their arms around each other and hopped up and down. Isobel snatched Marco's beer bottle and downed it in celebration. I couldn't help but laugh and admit to myself that the challenge had been stupid but fun.

I only hoped the other tasks – and the truth-or-dare challenges – were equally harmless.

'Still don't believe I can reach eight inches?' Max whispered into my ear. My hair stood on end as his breath feathered over my skin. 'With you watching, I might even top that.'

I froze, my lungs empty again as my brain headed for the gutter. I'd heard him once going at it in the shower, in our dodgy hotel room with paper-thin walls in Split. He'd tried to muffle it, but I'd worked out what the noises meant and teased him senseless afterward. I'd never even thought about *watching*.

But I loved that we'd shared so much that nothing embarrassed us any more. Was I screwing that up? My blood rushed in my ears and I couldn't tell if it was terror that I was destroying the foundation of our friendship, or the rollercoaster of feelings.

He stepped away and I gulped for air while I could. He exchanged a few words with the operator again and handed over some money. And I melted into an embarrassed puddle when I realised what he was doing. Of course, he hadn't meant an erection. That was only me.

He shrugged out of his cardigan and took the hammer. Bringing it over his head first, he whacked it onto the trigger and I totally forgot to watch the puck. I was too busy making scientific observations of the muscles in his forearms. My objective opinion: I was going crazy.

Someone draped an arm over my shoulder and I jumped a foot in the air—not literally. That would be twelve inches (or thirty centimetres), which was definitely an exaggeration. I turned to find Florian grinning at me in a disturbing manner.

'Your woman hits the hammer well. He even got above the beginner level.' I followed Florian's gesture to see the markers on the tower.

'He hauls crates of beer these days,' I responded, trying to keep my voice neutral.

* * *

I awoke the following morning in a lethargic fog, my limbs as heavy as a dark beer. I'd been to the toilet about a thousand times during the night, but I'd settled down eventually and now my ear hurt and I felt the hot creases on my face from the pillow. Max's side was empty, but I didn't remember him getting up.

I'd only drunk two mugs of beer yesterday – *only* two litres! – and I remembered everything that had happened, but it all felt so surreal. After hitting Lukas, the scroll had sent us to drink one more beer and then watch the flea circus and I still couldn't quite believe I'd paid to see a bunch of bloodsucking insects play football.

I scratched my neck, agitated at the memory. Even if fleas could pull the equivalent of a freight car for their size, I wished I could un-see it. Even my nose itched now.

After the flea circus, we'd ticked off the ghost train and there my memories got even more trippy. The ride was decorated on the outside with images of scantily-clad women fighting against monsters for some reason and although I could dig that in a steamy romance, it felt gratuitous on a carnival attraction. Max and I were babies when it came to those things which I think Florian remembered, as he took the carriage directly in front of us so he could stick the camera in our faces.

At least we put on a good show. As the headless corpses jumped out at us and blood dripped down the walls, I hugged

71

Max's arm to my chest and refused to let go and he spent a few rooms with his eyes pressed to my shoulder. If I'd been the one in a dirndl, I'm pretty sure Max would have had his face in my boobs... and that might be an argument in favour of the thing.

The dubious horror of the ghost train had been thankfully dulled by the two litres of beer and I mainly remembered, aside from the strobe lights and jerky animatronics, the feeling of Max's hand gripping my knee.

Walking through the turnstiles afterwards on jelly legs, we'd reminisced about the time in Freiburg where we'd stupidly gone to the student cinema showing of the *Day of the Dead*, thinking it might be funny and retro. Max had had to sleep in my bed for two whole weeks afterwards.

'You can sleep with me tonight,' he'd joked last night, curling an arm around my neck in one of his usual gestures of affection. I'd still got the faintest impression that he realised the ambiguity of his statement.

I took a deep breath and flopped back onto the bed. I should pin him down and ask what was going on with him and why things between us seemed off. Or maybe I should leave it alone and just double down my efforts to reconnect with him – with no dick jokes and no... appreciation. So much had changed in the past four years and I couldn't cope if we had too.

The apartment was quiet and I wasn't sure what the plan was for today. We'd ticked off three items from our list, but the little sack of truths and dares hadn't even been opened yet. After waking for the second morning in a row with a brass band between my ears, I wasn't really looking forward to heading back to the Wiesn. Tanya would have some kind of plan.

I fumbled on the floor for my phone. As I suspected, our new 'Wiesn-Chellenge' group chat had a dizzying number of messages. I also had one from Max, which I opened first.

I went to work. Didn't want to wake you.

Was that it? Where was the banter? An emoji at least? I noticed he was online, then typing, and then a kiss emoji appeared and heat flushed up my chest to my face. Another message appeared.

Sorry, I forgot the emoji, so you know I don't hate you.

My nose stung and what the hell was *that*? We must have talked about that some time – we'd talked about pretty much everything over the years. He'd always be my best friend, no matter what. And whatever was the matter with my stinging nose seemed to be affecting my eyes too. Then another message flashed up.

Erm... you don't need to interpret the emoji though. I just... good morning. Mwa.

The somersaults in my stomach suggested it was a little late for the warning – and an unhelpful corner of my brain discovered some reverse psychology in Max's statement. If we weren't the oldest of friends, my head would be spinning, trying to understand what he meant. Okay, my head was spinning anyway.

There was definitely something off between us. I didn't understand why part of me was excited by the prospect while my feeble little heart was in a panic. Stupid sex drive, stealing my best friend.

Another message popped in:

> *Come to the brewery and I'll shout you lunch.*

That was one message I didn't need to agonise over.

> *You don't need to bribe me. I can't wait to see it. I'm up now. I'll come soon.*

My thumb hovered over the keypad for a whole minute before I tapped it one last time to send him his own kiss emoji.

Chapter Nine

It was weird walking into Max's brewery.

I'd seen it all on a video chat, the picture jerky and his voice tense with excitement as he gave me the tour. But it was different being here, smelling the slight tang of yeast from the vats behind glass to one side and running my fingers along the polished wood of the bar.

He'd done this, my best friend who'd taught me how to smoke weed and skull a beer and pick up guys. I was simultaneously unsettled about who he was now and bursting with pride because the place was buzzing and even if I hadn't known Max I'd want to hang here. He was right, it was some kind of destiny for him, Max Brouwer, opening a brewery after years of underpaid hospitality jobs starting with working as a dishpig at a restaurant in Freiburg when he was twenty.

It wasn't fair that they were struggling under the weight of the financials. I wondered if the show Max and I had put on in the ghost train gave us a better chance at winning. I understood there were no guarantees with social media attention. The challenge was all very dubious, but the chance to win the money for Max was enough to awaken my competitive spirit.

'Hi! Welcome.'

I whirled to see a tall, good-looking guy with a swoosh of brown hair on his forehead walking towards me.

'I'm Jan-Philipp, Max's business partner. Call me Jan.' He spoke with an American accent and I remembered Max had told me his business partner had grown up in the States. 'You must be Max's girlfriend. Fiona, right?'

I swallowed my tongue and then choked on it when I tried to set him straight. *Max's girlfriend.* There was a phrase I hadn't heard before. It gave me the weirdest chills. Max *didn't have* a girlfriend or a boyfriend at the moment. If he had, he would have told me. I had to believe that.

I'd met a few of his hook-ups over the years, but he was just as hopeless as me when it came to relationships. Something to do with his distant parents, I suspected. He'd been with Gustav in Freiburg and that had been an unmitigated disaster for his self-esteem. I was pretty sure he hadn't been interested in committing to anyone since.

'Um, Max's friend, yeah,' I managed. Jan smiled, with pleasant little crinkles around his eyes that placed him a couple of years older than Max and me.

A back door banged open and Max appeared, hauling three crates of beer. He glanced up, his hair over his eyes, and saw us.

'Moppie!' The way his face brightened tied me up in knots. *Max's girlfriend…* He set the beers down and approached. His sleeves were rolled up, showing off the bands tattooed on his forearms.

I racked my brain for reminders of how we usually greeted each other. Thankfully, we were such good friends that I had muscle memory for hugging Max. I wrapped an arm around his neck and he gave me a squeeze.

A sigh rippled through my entire body, with relief but not relief at our return to normal. I was just physically relieved to get another hug. Unfortunately, the lust was not relieved in the slightest and I had the weirdest urge to sink my teeth into his ear and lick the little silver stud in the lobe.

'You okay? Still tired?' he asked, making me wonder if I'd held on too long. 'Still pissed at Florian?'

'Need a break from the chellenge, definitely,' I said. 'Do I look that bad?'

'No,' he said, flashing me a quick smile. Someone was perky this morning and it wasn't me. 'Come here.' He took both of my hands and tugged me behind the bar. My skin was sensitive under his fingers and I hated it. I needed my friend back. Where else was I supposed to get honest feelings and cushioning hugs?

With well-practiced hands, he brewed a shot of fresh espresso. I grinned as he reached up to a high shelf and retrieved a half-empty bottle, adding a drop to my coffee. With a shrug, he produced two shot glasses and filled both of them with the clear liquid.

'Day drinking it is,' I murmured. It was probably a good idea, with my weird mood. 'Caffé coretto,' I said more clearly, 'like we had for breakfast in Milan that year.'

'The year you started getting hangovers.'

I made a face at him and swiped the coffee. He leaned against the counter, arms crossed, and watched me expectantly. And even that was hot. Oh crap, how was I supposed to reclaim normal life if I couldn't even handle Max *looking* at me.

His eyes were blue, with a sheen of violet in some lighting conditions. He'd told me once when he was drunk that he wasn't sure which freaked his parents out more: when the doctors had confirmed their baby had albinism or when he introduced a boyfriend to them. Apart from his vision problems, I thought he wore his lack of pigment pretty well, actually. It wasn't the first time I wished I could give his parents the finger.

Bolstered by the more familiar protective feelings towards Max, I lifted the coffee to my mouth and downed it in one with a satisfied sigh. The sting of the grappa and the shock of bitterness should be enough to get rid of the weird flushes of hormones.

Taking the two shots of grappa, he led me to a table and sat across from me, rubbing his glass between his hands. He wasn't wearing the thick knitted cardigan that went with the Tracht. His shoulders were hunched, but it wasn't enough to hide how broad they were.

'Aren't you cold?' I blurted out.

And then he was *looking* at me again, like there was some puzzle here, and I dived for my shot glass as a distraction. There were no more *puzzles* between Max and me. We'd known each other for fifteen years, lived and travelled in each other's pockets. I'd even seen his dick on occasion, although never at its supposed eight-inch – ohhh, *shit*. The tips of my ears burned.

'I'm used to it. Munich winters are even colder than Freiburg and it's a mild September.' I shivered in response, shrinking into my chunky fleece. 'You're just soft, Butkus.'

'You during a heatwave in Australia wasn't a good look.'

'We have different habitats,' he said lightly, but it shot that panic through me again, reminding me that, when the world shut down, our different habitats had kept us apart. He glanced at me curiously again. I grabbed for my glass and knocked back the entire shot in one, gasping and spluttering when I was done. Hopefully it would help.

'I'm out of practice,' I croaked.

Max knocked the rest of his back neatly and winked at me.

'I'm still older than you,' I quipped lamely, but I grimaced when I realized what I'd said. 'That used to work better fifteen years ago.'

'So did most things,' he said with a chuckle.

'Max, do you…?' Oh, dear. *That's* what the grappa gave me courage to do. I inwardly groaned as my big mouth continued without permission. 'Do you have a girlfriend?'

He stared at me with a little bit of panic. What the hell was that? 'Of course not. Why are you suddenly asking that?'

'I don't know about "of course" when you haven't told me much,' I said, trying not to sound peevish. 'Jan seemed to think *I* was your girlfriend.'

'Oh, eh.' He fiddled with his glass. 'Probably because I talk about you so much.' I had to admit that was a good answer. 'And German has the female form of the word 'friend'. Maybe he just meant that.'

'I preferred the first option,' I mumbled.

'What are you thinking about the sex plan?' he asked quietly, changing the subject.

'Argh,' I said with a shrug. 'If we have to spend all day getting tipsy and doing stupid shit for the challenge, then I don't like my chances of meeting someone anyway.'

'Not someone… you've already met?'

I gulped, giving myself some strongly worded advice. He did *not* mean himself. But then, what did he mean?

Chapter Ten

'Are you talking about *Florian?*' I grimaced when I finally realised what Max was hinting at. 'I was kind of hoping I'd stop gravitating towards the same emotionally stunted big guys.' Perhaps I *had* stopped that particular self-destructive behaviour, if I was attracted to Max. I suddenly realised that going after those losers had protected me from all the difficult relationship questions that yawned in front of me when I thought about Max.

He opened his mouth, just a little, but he seemed to reconsider whatever he'd been about to say and licked his lips instead. He tapped the table with his palm. 'Let me give you a tour of the brewery – show you how beer is *supposed* to be brewed.'

We seemed to both breathe a sigh of relief.

'It's not milked from horses?' I joked.

'Only if you believe your own ads.' He grasped my hand and tugged and yeah, I dragged my feet a bit and pretended to be reluctant so he kept hold of my hand all the way through the side door and into the brewery, behind a wall of glass panels.

He slipped an apron over my head and handed me gloves and a plastic cap for my hair. I looped the apron tie around me and secured it neatly in a bow over my left hip, sharing a cheeky smile with Max.

I snapped a selfie of us, determined to shake off this weird sensitivity I'd developed when it came to him. We couldn't get back to normal if I was jealous of his hypothetical girlfriend. One day, maybe he'd— Noooo, I couldn't think about whether he'd find a partner one day and how that would ruin everything. Right now, I was indulging my best friend by showering him with praise and ooh-ing and aah-ing at every piece of equipment he showed me.

Watching Max bouncing between fermentation tanks, speaking animatedly over the drone of the pumps, made me smile. He was self-deprecating about it all, but that would change. What would a confident Max be like? He already had a little more gravitas. Maybe by forty he'd be able to grow a beard.

I met the part-time master brewer, Andreas, an older man who was semi-retired but made sure their operation passed the legal quality requirements. He had a ponytail and arms full of tattoos but also a twinkle in his eye, as though he was everyone's favourite beardy, beer-brewing grandpa.

'He's cute,' I murmured to Max out of the corner of my mouth.

'You're not thinking about the sex plan, are you?' he responded with a snort and I poked him in the stomach, pulling my hand back in dismay. My Max didn't have *abs*, did he? I struggled to remember if he'd had taut abs the last time I'd seen him. Freiburg Max certainly hadn't.

'Stop it. I'm not trying to sex plan *everyone*,' I hissed. 'But you are supposed to be my wingman.'

'I *am* your wingman. And part of that job is teasing you and steering you away from trouble,' he answered with a quick smile. 'Have you forgotten when we used to go out dancing? The secret signals?'

'Not so secret,' I said, laughing as I held my fist to my forehead in our less-than-subtle sign for a dickhead. 'Remember that night in Mallorca when the rugby team turned up!'

'You took one of them back to your hotel room!' he reminded me with a grimace.

'So did you!'

'Yeah, but mine was cute at least.' He turned to me, grasping my hand urgently. 'I know what your problem is!' It would be just like Max to understand me better than I did myself. 'You need to work on your taste.'

I rolled my eyes. 'Watch out. If I say I love your beer, you've got a problem.'

'No worries. You can have great taste in beer and bad taste in men. I wrote the book on it.'

He slung an arm around my neck and steered me to a little bar in the corner where the different beers rested in a well-lit fridge, like the holy relics of a craft beer cult.

'Prepare for a beergasm, moppie,' he whispered into my ear and I shivered, remembering yesterday in technicolour, when we'd essentially humped on the strongman game and he'd felt up my boobs. When he spoke again, his tone was that low, rasping one that seemed to speak to my skin. 'This one's guaranteed.'

I snorted a laugh as I accepted the small glass he poured for me. Lifting it to my nose, I enjoyed his wide, eager eyes, his growing smile, and noticed the exact moment the snaggletooth popped out. 'Hmmm, intense hops and a hint of bitterness. Is this a pils?'

'Yes, it's a pils. Taste it!' He was practically bouncing with his need for my approval.

I lifted the glass to eye level. 'Vivid, golden colour and a nice head. I like a bit of head.'

He made a choking sound. 'Fuck, Fi. Just drink it!'

'You promised me a beergasm.'

'Do you want me to pour it over you?'

'What? And lick it off?' Oops. Shouldn't have said that. I didn't imagine the flare of alarm in his eyes or the frantic blinking. I also couldn't ignore the tightening of my nipples as they went off on a tangent involving trickles of cold beer and a hot mouth.

Why had he said beergasm?

'I'm going to drink it!' I announced, trying to break the tension, but now he was looking at me askance, one eyebrow raised and a cute furrow on his brow.

'Don't choke,' he muttered and I nearly did just that, remembering my stupid joke about head and thinking about Max's tongue and his biceps and his freaking brand-new abs. What was *wrong* with me?

Pull yourself together! I put the glass to my lips and took a long sip.

Pils had never been my favourite style of beer, but it was now. It was a summer evening in a drink – smooth and tender, with a kick of sharpness at the end to keep things interesting. I hummed in appreciation, licking my lips – and caught Max staring at my mouth, just before he dropped his gaze. Or had I imagined it? He was probably just being his eager, beer-brewing, proud self, not staring at my lips as though he'd like to lick beer off them.

I'd definitely imagined that.

'It's perfect, Max,' I murmured earnestly.

* * *

My stomach was full of Bavarian spinach dumplings and vegan cheese and my brain was pleasantly fuzzy after tasting six different types of flavoursome beer when the others arrived at Snaketooth for a strategy meeting. Tanya produced the little velvet bag of dares and set it in the middle of the table, like a sacrifice to the beerfest gods. Florian was under strict instructions not to film until we were ready and I was keeping an eagle eye on him because I didn't trust him.

'We need a plan,' Tanya said.

'I need a beer,' Marco murmured.

'Me, too!' Ryan said emphatically.

'No!' We all rushed to contradict him. After two beers yesterday, he'd been singing Madonna on the ghost train and telling everyone they had nice eyes.

'Plan sober, *do* drunk,' Tanya said grimly, as though it was a quote from Confucius. She unrolled our scroll and, between the wood panelling of our booth, the nostalgic carvings of hops and monks brewing beer and the lame scroll, we could have been in some strange mediaeval re-enactment. 'This says there will be Wiesn-Races on Thursday and some kind of competition on Sunday called Maßkrug…stemmen. Why are German words all so long?'

'Maßkrugstemmen,' Max repeated. 'Who can hold up a beer mug the longest. Why use a whole sentence when a German can use a single word? What else is there?'

'We have to take a shift as a waiter?' Ryan read out.

'How do we organise to be a waiter?' Isobel asked. 'Are the marketing people going to do that or will the tent managers just take us on if we offer to work for free?'

'I think we have to do it ourselves,' Florian said. 'Part of the challenge.'

'I can probably organise it,' Max said. 'I know the Wirt, the manager of the Fuchsbräu tent. I worked for him for a few years.'

'And we know the marketing manager for Fuchsbräu,' Tanya pointed out, gesturing at me.

Max turned to me gravely. 'They won't let you serve unless you're wearing a dirndl.'

Florian snickered in the corner and I felt like throwing something at him.

'Maybe we'll think of a way around it. Perhaps it'll be enough if I do a shift alone,' Max suggested.

I shook my head. 'If it comes to it, I'll put the thing on. You're not going to waiter for both of us.'

'We'll push that to next week then,' Tanya said. 'What are Wiesn-Hits?'

Max grimaced into his beer. 'The pop songs – Schlager, Volksmusik, that stuff with a synthesised backing track that the Germans love. Please don't tell me we have to sing?'

'One song, on a stage, in a tent,' Tanya confirmed, consulting the scroll. 'If we just invade the stage, they're sure to kick us out.'

'It's probably what the organisers want,' I muttered.

Max sighed deeply. 'I can probably call in a favour with my old boss, if we keep it to one song each. Those poor patrons.' He met my gaze. There would be no points for team Snaketooth in the karaoke round.

'I'm very good at karaoke,' Tanya pointed out.

'Are there any country music hits I could sing?' Ryan asked.

'Actually… yes,' Max said with a chuckle. 'That country

roads song is always played at least once.'

'Awesome! You'll have to film me up there for my wife,' Ryan said with a giddy smile.

'What else do we have to do?' I asked, peering at the scroll across the table.

'There's another race of some kind next Tuesday and on Sunday the team with the highest scores has one extra round to decide which of the pairs is the overall winner,' Tanya said in a clipped tone. 'Plus our dares, of course,' she added. All our gazes zeroed in warily on the velvet bag.

'We should look at them,' Isobel suggested.

Tanya snatched the bag and tipped out the little slips of folded paper onto the table unceremoniously. Grabbing the nearest one, she skimmed it. Her brow furrowed. 'Go skinny dipping?' she read aloud.

'What?' Max said, plucking the slip of paper out of her fingers.

I peered over his shoulder. 'That's yours, isn't it,' I accused. 'I recognise your handwriting.' My voice trailed off at the end of the sentence as I realised the implications of that. I grabbed another one and opened it. '"What's the worst thing you've ever done to someone else?"' I read with a frown.

Ryan flushed a deep red. 'That one's mine,' he said in a small voice.

'Joder!' Isobel cursed in Spanish. 'He gave us our own dares?' She reached for a piece of paper, but I snatched it out of her hand. Stretching over the table, I swept up all of the remaining slips of paper and dumped them back into the bag before anyone could find mine.

What *stupidity* had inspired me to write that dare? And what the *joder* would I do when Max saw it? I could only hope he wouldn't recognise my handwriting, or that I came up with a convincing excuse before we read it.

'Let's take them out one-by-one and complete them,' I suggested weakly. 'We need to film it, right?'

Tanya looked ready to contradict me, but I wasn't the only one looking a little green at the prospect of having our own dares read back to us. 'Well then,' she said instead, 'since the swimming will have to wait for another day, I suppose we should drink a beer and film ourselves talking about the worst things we've ever done to other people.'

Lusting after my best friend perhaps? I gulped, glancing at Max. I would need to find another answer – and soon.

Chapter Eleven

'I spanked my wife,' Ryan blurted out as soon as Florian started filming. The little camera clattered to the table and he fumbled to pick it up again.

The rest of us sat, frozen, reflecting on what he'd said – or trying not to. Max hadn't even brought our beers yet. I cleared my throat and opened my mouth to say something, but I had no idea what.

'Good for you!' Isobel saved us all, patting his hand. 'I bet she enjoyed it.'

'W-what? You know what spanking is, right?'

'Ohhh, yeah,' Isobel said with a smile. 'Hot.' As Ryan continued to stare at Isobel, the lump in my throat expanded. Did he mean something non-sexual? Eek.

Max returned with eight mugs of beer in one hand, supported by his other arm. I was totally impressed. 'What did I miss?' he asked. We all blinked at him.

'Ryan spanked his wife. And not in a sexy way,' Tanya said grimly.

'Oh, it was kind of... in a... you know.' Ryan's voice trailed off. 'I've never told a single person this. It's not the sort of thing my friends talk about.'

Max set the beers on the table, his hand wobbling. 'You

didn't need the beer to help you get it off your chest?'

'I need the beer now,' Ryan said and took a long sip, a flush spreading up his neck. 'Isn't that the worst thing you can do to someone? It was disrespectful. Of my own *wife*.'

Tanya laughed darkly. 'There are worse things.'

'You could sleep with other women and suggest it's all in her head when she grows suspicious,' Marco suggested, making Ryan spit his beer across the table. Max sighed and calmly nabbed a serviette to wipe the droplets off the camera, held limply in Florian's hand.

'Turn that off,' I said grimly.

'It's one of our truth or dare tasks,' Tanya pointed out.

'I can't work out if that would get likes or not,' Florian muttered.

I snatched the camera before he realised what I was doing, quickly deleting the footage that had been taken. 'Give him a chance to think of something else.'

'But I'd be ly—'

'Ryan,' I said, cutting him off. 'You'll be forgiven for lying right now. It's just a game that's supposed to lead to entertaining conversation. People don't actually tell the truth.' Especially not now we were all fifteen years older and the whole world appeared in shades of grey, rather than black-and-white.

'They don't? What's yours, then? The worst thing you've done to another person? Or what are you going to pretend is the worst?' Ryan prompted.

'You know what we should do?' Isobel piped up and I didn't trust the glee in her voice. 'Ask Max. Max and Fi are more married than the rest of us. I bet he'd tell a better story about Fi's worst moment than she would.'

I froze, struck with the realisation that Isobel was right. Not that we were 'married' in any way – at least not the fun ones. But Max knew about every selfish thing I'd ever done. It made me wish I'd been a better person when I was younger and not so obsessed with myself.

His hand groped for mine under the table and squeezed and even though I wasn't drunk, my head spun. What did he really think of me?

'If we're really so married,' he began, 'I'm hardly going to pass on my wife's secrets.' The way he said 'my wife' rippled through me. Would he have a wife one day? Perhaps it was one of the worst things I'd ever done, to nurture the hope that he'd always be my Max, too screwed-up for real relationships.

'You guys are *so* married,' Isobel said with a shrill laugh. He flinched which hurt for some reason I wasn't ready to admit – until I realised I was squeezing the life out of his hand. I let up, but his other hand came down on mine and didn't let me go.

I glanced at our mess of hands, nestled on his hemp-clad thigh, and I had the weird sensation of standing on a precipice. The only problem was, I didn't know the way back from the edge.

* * *

I wouldn't have been surprised if Florian ended up releasing footage of me snoring lightly, my face smooshed into my arm, as I napped on the table. I wouldn't even mind, since I was in Max's bar, which was my new favourite place in the world.

When I woke up, it was after eight. The fact that I'd fallen asleep straight after confession time was perhaps not the best indication of how entertaining we'd been on camera, but at least Ryan hadn't humiliated himself.

Max and I had shared one: the time a man at a bus station in Albania had mistaken us for his honoured guests, paid for a meal and shown us to a fancy hotel room before he smoked us out. I'd felt guilty enough airing that one, so I hoped the weirdos who liked this stuff on the internet would be satisfied.

Isobel admitted to stealing her friend's boyfriend when she was nineteen – and he hadn't even been that good. Marco had started a rumour about his own boyfriend and then claimed he didn't know how it started. Ryan had eventually remembered a time he'd eaten his wife's favourite chocolates which we let him get away with, since we knew he would be fixated on spanking for the rest of the evening.

By the time I lifted my head from the table after my nap, the others had disappeared and I wasn't even sure if they'd filmed me snoring or not. Max was behind the bar, but he hurried over as soon as he saw I was awake.

'Moppie?' he said, his thumb smoothing my cheek and making me want to purr. Had he always touched me so divinely? His lips kicked up in that little smile I'd recognise when I was dead. 'Want me to take you home? Or would you rather eat something?'

'You know the answer to that.'

'Jägerschnitzel mit Pommes?' he suggested.

'God, yes.' I groaned in anticipation of the breaded cutlet – made from tofu, chick peas and pea protein, in this joint – with mushroom sauce and chips. It was my German comfort food of choice.

'Careful, or you'll have a foodgasm in front of all these people.'

'I'll come up to the bar,' I offered.

'No need,' Max said, patting the table in front of me. A glance around the cosy brewery revealed several empty tables and more proof of my insensitivity.

I nearly had a foodgasm for real when he presented me with the unnecessarily large plate of breaded, fried non-meat and potatoes, with cranberry chutney and a Coke. 'Maybe your chef is the answer to my sex problem,' I mumbled with my mouth full of mushrooms.

Max slid into the booth beside me. 'She might be into that, if you've changed your mind about women.'

'Unfortunately, I'm still into dicks – not that you need a dick to be a man, but the ones I end up with...'

Max burst out laughing and gave me a playful shove. 'Have all been dicks,' he finished for me.

I wolfed down the food, thinking about the weird afternoon of drunk group therapy. 'I can't decide if we've all changed too much, or if we were this weird back in Freiburg – us and all the others,' I said lightly.

'We were weird back in Freiburg, but it's also been fifteen years. Of course, things have changed.'

'*You* haven't,' I said reflexively, but I regretted it when he chuckled through a grimace and looked away.

'Maybe it would have been better if I had,' he said softly.

'No.' My answer was firm, unequivocal. 'You're not allowed to change.'

His answer was a deep sigh that made his chest heave and reminded me of all the little differences in him that were wreaking havoc in my system. 'You're the only one who's ever thought so.'

Before I could give an indignant reply about the ignorance

of the general population if they couldn't see how amazing he was, he eyeballed me.

'Let's go dancing,' he said suddenly. 'Forget this Wiesn-Challenge nonsense for a few hours. Tonight, when I'm finished here.'

I leaned towards him eagerly. 'Like old times?'

'Like old times.' He shared my grin.

* * *

Tonight became tomorrow as we stepped out of the train station near the dark river and approached the glow of blue light – and the long queue – indicating the entrance to the club, in a historic building that reminded me of the Stalinist stuff in Berlin.

Max had admitted he didn't go out much any more, but he'd been here a lot in the past and we'd agreed that if it sucked, we'd just go. That was a change from years ago when we'd always stay to get our money's worth on the cover charge, even if the place smelled of turpentine and body odour and only played Europop or Schlager.

'Remember when we kissed Karl Marx?' I said, stuffing my cold hands into my pockets. It was only September, but the midnight temperature was midwinter where I came from.

'Was he the guy that tried to pick up both of us that time on Corfu?' Max was incapable of keeping a straight face when he was being silly, so I just chuckled and gave him a shove. 'I still have the photo somewhere,' he continued, answering seriously this time. 'I can't believe we printed a photo of us kissing a statue of Karl Marx and now that's one of the few things I remember about that trip to Berlin with fondness.'

'Yeah, we drank too much and you…'

'I know. I smoked too much.' He chuckled, but there was a tightness to his expression. I could see it in that bottom lip. I shouldn't have brought up Berlin. I had fonder memories than he did.

We'd both been starry-eyed that year, international students with more stamina than sense, seeing the world open up before us for the first time and still capable of falling in love unwisely. Then, the week before we were supposed to go to Berlin, Gustav had told Max their relationship was only about sex.

Max had continued to love unwisely, pining and getting high and drunk until he woke up in the hostel in Berlin disoriented and paranoid and vomiting up everything I could coax him into eating.

A brush of warmth on my cheek distracted me from thoughts of fifteen years ago in Berlin and I belatedly realized Max had pressed a light kiss there. 'We're not reliving *those* old times tonight. Right, moppie?'

'Right. You're a grown-up bar owner these days.' But I cuddled into his side, searching for the old Max, the sensitive, star-crossed lover. He'd been beautiful, too.

'The bank owns the business and our landlord owns the bar. I just brew the beer,' he said dryly.

When we finally got into the club, it wasn't only the pumping music and the proliferation of dark corners and weird lighting that reminded me of old times. As he handed our coats in, the little tinkle of piano at the beginning of Lauryn Hill's 'Doo Wop' made us grab each other and squeal and I pointed frantically at the words in chalk behind the bar.

'Nineties Night!'

Max gripped my hands tight and dragged me into the crush on the dance floor, his smile giddy. The only thing better than Nineties Night would have been Amy Winehouse, Rihanna and some Snow Patrol for my emotional moments, but perhaps 2008, our year in Freiburg, wasn't so far back in history that it got its own club night – yet. The clientele was slightly older than us and we recognised nearly every song.

If I'd had vague thoughts about picking someone up – like old times – I completely forgot about it for the night. I didn't need an orgasm from someone else when I could own the dance floor with my best friend, not caring if we looked like idiots as we twisted and shimmied.

We cared even less than we used to when we were younger, lifting our arms for 'This is how we do it'. I turned and shook my butt to Christina Aguilera, giving him a goofy grin. He swatted one of my cheeks and danced behind me, gripping my hips and giggling into my ear.

We even forgot to drink and, after… some amount of time on the dance floor – my protesting body said sixteen days, while my confused mind insisted it had only been a few minutes – even my little toe was aching. I groped for Max, groaning as I wound my arms around his neck and hung on.

Wow, he smelled real. The hint of brewery on him was delicious and the heady smell of intimacy hit all my starved synapses.

'I missed you way too much,' I mumbled. 'Don't ever change, okay? *Please.* You're beautiful as you are.'

His arms came around me in a heavenly Max-special squeeze. One of his hands lifted to the back of my neck and pressed me into his shoulder. And then I shivered.

I wasn't cold – it was steaming in the crush of Nineties

Night bodies. But something about the brush of his fingertips over the nape of my neck set everything off in me again and I was right back at my sex plan dilemma. Except my wingman wasn't supposed to be helping like *that*. I had to stop this.

He put an end to it, as it turned out, grasping my wrist and unravelling my arms from around his neck. Leaning up, he pressed a light kiss to my temple. 'I know it's three AM when you start calling me "beautiful".'

I glanced over to appreciate the grin I could hear in his voice and something walloped me with sudden self-awareness. That smile, that mouth was the only thing I wanted to see, ever again – except maybe his glinting eyes, as well.

His smile faltered and I doubled down my defences. No rocking the boat or any other questionable euphemisms. This was 'just like old times'. It had to be.

'Come on,' Max said, taking my hand. 'You look like you're finished off.'

I wanted to protest, but I was hobbling like a pirate and when we stepped onto the street, I blinked grainy eyes at the sudden glare of the streetlamps and realized how fusty it had been in there.

'Air is… really delicious, you know,' I muttered. Max steered me in the opposite direction from the way we'd come with an arm around my shoulders. A taxi rumbled past, but there was very little traffic. A group of youngsters gathered on the footpath, laughing and drinking out of cans. Beyond the concrete wall along the bridge was a dark void, radiating cool moisture and producing a soothing murmur of water. 'Is that the river?' I leaned out over the wall and breathed in again. 'You told me about it. The Isar, right? The stream that connects Munich to the mountains.'

'That was very romantic of me.' He gave a little huff. 'Do you want to go down there?'

It was three in the morning and about eight degrees out. But when Max flashed his eyes at me like that, there was no way I'd say no.

Chapter Twelve

The moonlight turned the swift, shallow river to dark amber and the trees to a shadow of green. The bright streetlights of a busy road glimmered in the distance behind us, but the wide riverbank was obscure. Laughter and occasional bursts of music reached us from scattered groups of early morning revellers, but Max and I sat quietly together on the pale stones.

I tugged my hands into the sleeves of my woolly jumper and hugged my knees to my chest. Max gave me a rakish grin and as I watched in horror, he untied his shoelaces, wrenched off his shoes and socks and doused his bare feet in the frigid water with a groan. The clear water somehow made shadows on his pale feet.

I was about to tease him when his groan changed to a sigh and I realized how self-absorbed I'd been for the past few hours – the past few years? 'How many hours were you on your feet today?'

'Same amount as always,' he murmured. He rummaged in his backpack and produced two bottles of Snaketooth Pilsener. He popped the tops and handed one to me, taking a long pull on his own. Rummaging some more, he found a crushed box of cigarettes, fished one out and lit it.

As though the moonlight showed up the truths we'd rather

hide, I noticed the lines at the corners of his lips, the tightness in his mouth.

'I didn't know you'd taken up smoking,' I began lightly.

'Can't afford pot any more,' was all he said in reply. Bitterness. That's what it was. I wanted to yank it out of him and toss it in the river. The hand that lifted the cigarette to his mouth shook slightly and a different kind of fear squeezed in my chest.

'Max,' I said sharply, piercing him with a look. 'What's wrong?'

'Nothing that hasn't always been wrong… with me,' he muttered.

'Is it something about Ben?' I knew his thing with Ben had been up and down for a few years.

'No,' he replied. I stayed still, hoping he'd continue. 'He needed a friend more than anything else. He's going through some shit and it just took us a while to work out that sleeping together wasn't the best thing for our friendship.'

Well, if that wasn't a pertinent reminder to slap myself in the face with, I didn't know what would be.

'I just… wanted the brewery to be a success,' he said, moving his feet restlessly in the water.

'The brewery is *amazing*! I would live there if I could.'

'I don't really trust your opinion,' he said with an indulgent smile.

I gripped his wrist, which had the added bonus of letting the cigarette burn down a little more without him breathing the horrible stuff in. 'Max, I'm a VP at a beer company and I can professionally say your beer is amazing and the bar is great too!'

'Yeah, but you think I'm *beautiful*,' he said with a chuckle that was approaching the laugh I knew and a flash of the snaggletooth. 'Is that your professional opinion?'

I gave his shoulder a shove. I couldn't think of a comeback. He *was* beautiful – in more ways than I'd ever realised. 'Okay, firstly, I'm sorry for all the self-pity and the sex pity when you needed me.'

'Fi, I don't need you.' I gave him another shove, a little harder this time. 'I mean I don't need you to fix my problems!' he insisted, holding his hands up in surrender. He dropped the cigarette by accident and I grabbed it before he could, stealing a drag, like I always did when he had a joint.

'Fuck, that's awful,' I choked. 'I remember you puffing away, trying to get used to these horrible things so you'd look cool and grown-up for Gustav.'

He groaned. 'Sometimes I think you've known me too long.'

'You make that sound like a bad thing!' I said, sharply, so he wouldn't be able to tell how much that comment hurt. His knees crashed into mine and he clutched my shoulders, rubbing his hands up and down as though he could keep me warm.

'I didn't mean it, moppie,' he said roughly. His gaze clashed with mine and that weird feeling swept through me again, as though there was suddenly something else – *everything* else – between us.

But this was Max. I'd known him too long. I needed him too much – and he needed me, even if he was too stubborn to admit it. We were two lonely screw-ups and without each other we were just lonely screw-ups.

'Did you really think I would tell stories about you to the others today?' he asked quietly, dropping his hands.

'No,' I lied, but he convicted me with the tiniest lift of his brow. 'This is what I mean about the four fucking years. Something's different and I can't handle it and I go on about my sex problems because there's nothing else going on in my fucking life and you don't even tell me about that! My friends with kids, I get, because they've literally got no time and they've moved on without me, but I'm lonely, Max, and you're too far away – and I don't just mean the ten thousand kilometres.' Crap, my cheeks were suspiciously hot. 'Fucking pandemic – and growing up,' I muttered, stubbing out the cigarette savagely and leaning my chin on my knees. 'I'm sorry to waste your precious cheap cigarettes, but the last thing I want right now is for you to slowly kill yourself.'

I wanted another hug, a Max special, but I wasn't going to beg for one, not after what I'd just spilled. But instead of holding me, I felt the light stroke of his fingers on my cheek, as he brushed my hair aside. He tipped my face up to the moonlight, rubbing his thumbs in my tears. The look on his face was one I'd never seen before and it terrified me.

He was staring, his eyes hot and his mouth grim, as though I distressed him, as though I wasn't just his moppic. He opened his mouth to say something but lost courage, squeezing his eyes shut and taking a breath.

'Come here,' he muttered instead, and why had I never noticed how deep and smooth his voice was? He wrapped his arms around my waist and dragged me against him, leaning his chin on my shoulder with a sigh. His nose drifted into my hair and, for a moment, I had everything I needed. 'I'm sorry,' he murmured.

'No, Max—'

'I mean it,' he said in this incisive tone I was growing to like. 'Maybe I wanted you to see me differently, this time – not the little screw-up who was tragic over Gustav and always broke, although the second part's still true.'

I turned to get a better look at his profile. 'Max, I love the screw-up.' But I realised the problem as soon as I'd said that. 'And I'll love Maximilian Brouwer, responsible microbrewery owner too, when I get to know him. I'm the one who should apologise.'

'If you loved the screw-up, then you should believe I loved the naïve smart-arse who liked to boss everyone around in Freiburg,' he said drily. 'Although I would *never* describe you as such to anyone else, or tell anyone your worst moments.'

'I'll always be your smart-arse,' I said, responding with relief to the lightness in his tone.

'And maybe I'll always be your screw-up,' he said, taking a sip of beer. I was so close to him, I saw his Adam's apple bob as he drank, and then his throat was looking like the perfect place for my mouth to go exploring and – *shit*. That part hadn't gone away yet, despite the heart-to-heart. 'The Bayern, the Bavarians would call you a Gschaftlhuber,' he continued with a smile.

'Guh-hootle-what-er? I never learned that one. Is that something to do with boobs?'

He grinned and rested his chin on my shoulder again. 'You have lovely tits, you know, Fi.'

Whaaaat? I nearly had a heart attack at that. But he continued before I could work out if I'd really heard Max describe my boobs as 'lovely tits'.

'But no, I meant like a… nosy… parker? That's it, isn't it?'

'Ah, so it's about my nose and not my… tits.' I nearly choked on the word myself, but it was weirdly thrilling. It didn't help that he poked me in the waist and made me squeal.

'Do you really want to know everything about my crappy sex life? Because I'll tell you. I wasn't keeping anything from you on purpose. There just hasn't been much to tell.'

I was a bad friend for enjoying that admission. 'Yep. Every detail.'

He chuckled and I felt it all down my back. 'For the past year, it's been all about masturbation and fantasies about Oscar Isaac and Taylor Swift – occasionally both at once.'

'I approve,' I said warmly.

'Before that, there were a few mistakes where I forgot not to sleep with Ben, but he's been messed up with alcohol and we both wanted something else and it was all pretty awful, hence the Oscar Isaac and—'

'Tay Tay, I get it,' I finished for him. 'I'm sorry it was so shit with Ben.'

'It's okay. It was kind of nice not being the screwed-up one for a change and it wasn't a disaster like Gustav – don't worry. I still meet up with him and he's getting therapy. But yeah, the sex was bad.'

'Bad sex is something I'm also familiar with.'

'I wanted to wash my ears out after you told me about that natural bacteria guy. He probably would have wanted to wash my ears out,' he added thoughtfully and I gave him a shove.

'Don't remind me! It was better than the guy who always wanted the room dark and couldn't keep it up in the light,' I said with a shudder. 'They were worse than octopus tongue, you know. Sometimes I think all the good ones must be taken by now, and then I think how clueless I was – still am – and wonder how anyone manages to form a healthy relationship before thirty-five.'

'Sometimes I think healthy relationships don't exist,' Max

muttered. He hugged me closer. 'Shall we make one of those pacts where, if we're still single at fifty, we have to get married and give each other octopus tongue and natural bacteria?'

I gagged. 'You're horrible.' But at least I wasn't thinking sexy thoughts any more. He was a genius. 'Maybe we should just get married so I can get a visa and live here. Would you do that for me?' I asked lightly.

'I've been waiting years for you to ask,' he said, smoothly and softly and without hesitation. 'You only have to ask, moppie,' he added, more quietly. He cleared his throat. 'But I can only offer you work as a waitress, and you've got New York waiting for you.'

'New York isn't quite confirmed yet, you know,' I felt compelled to point out. If Dollersen suspected I was 'metrosexual', he might change his mind after all. Or I might.

Max shushed me. 'It'll happen. I want to visit you in New York.'

Right, he wanted to visit me and not marry me for immigration purposes. 'I'll have to wait a few years before Snaketooth needs a marketing director. But I could be your waitress in the meantime.' I was joking – at least I told myself that.

'You love your marketing metrics and being in charge of all those minions,' he pointed out. He meant it to sound like a good thing, but I still took it as a dig. 'Capable and bossy' was probably exactly how my team described me on their evaluation forms. That's all anyone saw when they looked at me. 'And you'd be a terrible waitress,' Max added, which didn't buoy my mood.

'Huh! I'll show you at the Wiesn.' I bent my arm and tensed up all the muscles, even though they weren't visible under my thick sweater. 'I reckon I could do eight – ten, even!'

He pinched my bicep and then kissed my cheek, far too fleetingly. He hauled himself to his feet and held out a hand for me. 'If you can do ten, then you'll have no trouble with my eight,' he said with a wink. It took me a second, but then I realised we were back to joking about inches and then I – nope. I wasn't falling into that trap.

'Shut up about your dick.'

He snorted a laugh. 'You started it.'

Wasn't that the problem?

Chapter Thirteen

'I hate you, Max.' Trust Isobel to voice what we were all thinking.

'What? Isn't it beautiful?' Max had the nerve to grin – and then pull his shirt up, sucking all the air out of the entire world as he did so. Bloody hell, my eyes were unprepared. He peeled his arms out of the sleeves, his hunched shoulders drawing my eyes to his pecs.

Max always joked that something had gone wrong with his Dutch genes. Statistically the tallest people in the world, he was only a touch over the female average for his countrymen. But I wouldn't have swapped a couple of extra inches—in height!—for any of that shape. He was taut and compact and… strong.

But that dipshit was making us all go skinny dipping in a river that was fed from the *Alps*.

'I'm sorry,' he said. 'I honestly didn't think you would have to do it. I was picturing those big bearded guys, who would have gone to the English garden and waved their dicks around.' He shoved down his jeans and five pairs of eyes averted themselves. Mine refused.

'Is this legal?' Ryan asked, his voice high.

'Of course. Look around.'

'I've been trying not to,' Ryan mumbled, taking another long glug of beer.

The view was beautiful. Under an endless blue sky, dappled with cheerful clouds, the wide river tumbled gently over smooth stones. The banks rose, green and profuse, on either side, a mixture of dark mountain pines and deciduous trees with the first hints of yellow. It was wild and natural – as were the few other visitors to this stretch of river in the morning.

It was an 'FKK' swimming area, the German 'free body culture'. It wasn't the first time Max and I had found ourselves on a nudist beach, but it was the first time we'd come on purpose.

'This is one of the quieter spots, but during Oktoberfest it will still be packed by this afternoon, so… dive in,' Max said, sliding down his boxers. His butt cheeks flexed with each step and I stared, my mouth hanging open. Florian fumbled for the camera to capture the action, although he'd agreed to edit it very carefully and pixelate where necessary.

Max trotted into the water as though it was a scorching summer afternoon and not a sixteen-degree September morning. Then he plonked that muscly butt into the rippling water, stretching his legs in front of him with a groan of pleasure.

'If you say "come on in the water's lovely" I will hold you under,' I grumbled. I dipped my fingers into the river, intending to cool my hot cheeks, but I gasped at the temperature and snatched my hand back. Naked or not, getting in there was going to be hell.

Marco was already down to his briefs, but he hesitated, his thumbs in the waistband and a grim expression on his face. 'People like to look at cock-and-balls for fun in Germany? The top off, I understand. Equal opportunity for the nipples, but…' He trailed off with a gulp.

'You're keeping that camera up, aren't you, Florian?' Ryan asked, his voice wavering as he pulled off his hoodie.

'That doesn't help *us* much.' Tanya snapped. Florian spun the camera to her as she spoke, but swerved it away again when he noticed Isobel in the background unsnapping her bra.

She sighed deeply as she shrugged out of it. 'That feels good.' I caught a glimpse of some angry-looking blue veins in her boobs and forced my eyes up. 'I want to enjoy a child-free two weeks, but my tetas want the babies. Shit.' She swiped up a towel and wiped herself off. 'Andres is *never* touching me again! He can take his evil twin sperm and eat it.'

Florian turned off the camera with an agitated sigh. 'I don't know how I'm supposed to film this without offending… everyone in the entire world.'

'You should be used to that by now,' I quipped.

'I'm not a complete dickhead, Fi.'

'Could have fooled me,' I muttered, shrugging out of my woolly cardigan and shivering.

He laughed at me, then. 'I'm only a dickhead because you like it.'

I paused, willing myself not to react to his smug tone and the way his words tingled up my back. It wasn't a pleasant tingle – more like the sharp poke of the truth.

'Maybe I've gone off dickheads,' I said gently. I found Max watching me and I gave him a faint smile.

'Older and wiser, huh?' Florian followed my gaze to where Max was sitting, cross-legged now, skipping stones through the water.

'Are you getting in?' I asked, lifting my chin. Florian took a step back in alarm and gestured to the camera.

'I have to supervise. Too much fishing tackle in the shot and I could get fined. Max is the only one with his tackle out so far, I see. Not surprising, since this was his idea.' The glee in Florian's voice made me want to taser him. 'Any fish biting, Max?'

Ryan and Marco went green.

'I see you've got your product-placement organised,' Florian continued, peering at Max's back. 'That's a pretty tattoo. Snaketooth, or? Looks like a nice little business, if you can get it off the ground.'

Max turned to look over his shoulder, his expression sober and I forgot for a moment that I was pissed at Florian. That picture of Max would make an ad I'd like to click on.

'Max, stay right there, exactly like that,' I said urgently, holding my hands up. I rummaged in his messenger bag for his phone, opening the camera app.

'I know what I look like,' he insisted with a groan. 'I don't need a picture.'

'It's not of you. It's advertising. Hit the right groups on social media and a cheap ad campaign could make a big difference.'

'The brewery's social feeds do nothing,' he grumbled.

'Do you have sexy photos like this on them?'

His mouth fell open. The low rays of the sun caught the lenses of his glasses, but I felt him following my movements as I approached the water's edge. 'I'm not so sure a naked photo of me is going to sell any beer, but I'm desperate enough to try, if you think it'll help,' he said with a rueful smile.

'Good,' I said, grinning at him. I crouched and lined up the shot, but it quickly became clear that the framing was wrong from this position. I had to get closer. Putting Max's phone down, I toed off my shoes, tugged off my jeans and socks, whipped off my shirt, and headed for the water in my underwear.

I made it two steps before my feet curled up and died. Every swear word I knew was tumbling from my mouth, finishing with a low and threatening, 'You fucking klootzakje, Max!'

The bastard laughed and splashed me, making me shriek. 'I taught you well. I'm glad you remember how to call me "little ballsack" in Dutch.' He was grinning again and it was almost enough to make me forget my blood was currently abandoning my toes to frostbite.

'It's *freezing*!' I hissed.

'Are you giving up?' Florian called from the bank and I wasn't surprised to see him pointing the camera directly at me.

'Never!' I yelled back.

'Yeee-ah!' screamed Isobel. She whipped down her underwear and took off into the water. Flopping down face-first, she submerged her whole body apart from her head in the shallow water. 'It's n-not quite Marbella, but it's… not much colder than the air, actually.'

'Move your toes,' Max called to me gently. 'Don't stay still for too long.'

'Let me just get this photo,' I mumbled. I was shivering badly by the time I got close enough to frame the shot the way I wanted. 'How you were before,' I said to Max through chattering teeth. I pushed on his shoulder, to indicate he should turn back to look at me, and his skin was impossibly warm from his body heat and the sunlight.

'Ready?' he asked.

I blinked to clear my head and moved away again, lining up the shot. 'Look up and over my shoulder.' He twisted further, the muscles in his torso bunching pleasantly. I licked my lips as I adjusted the focus with the manual settings on his camera, then I snapped a few shots.

'Do you really think posting this kind of thing will help?'

If it had been an ad, I would have bought whatever he was selling. 'It can't hurt. Look.' I unlocked his phone – the code was my birthday, as always – and showed him the photo I'd taken. His tattoo was in focus, looking badass next to the scar on his back from a pre-cancerous keratosis he'd had removed five years ago. His lips were twisted in a thoughtful half-smile and his glasses reflected gold in the slanting sunlight. His hair was mussed. He looked peaceful and comfortable and confident. He looked like adult Max, not my Peter Pan. He was gorgeous.

'It's… me,' he said with a shrug.

'Yeah,' I said quizzically, squeezing his shoulder automatically, before I remembered his skin was bare and snatched my hand back. 'It's you. Your beer. Your pride.' He lifted his gaze to mine with a light in his eyes that made me glow because I'd put it there.

'If it wasn't so genuine, I'd think that was a marketing slogan,' he said.

'It totally is!' I gasped. '"Our beer. Our pride". It's perfect. The fact that it's genuine only makes it better.'

'Okay, okay,' he said. 'I'll schedule a marketing meeting. But not now. Thanks for freezing your feet off to get the shot,' he said with a glint in his eye. 'But now it's time to get naked with me.'

Chapter Fourteen

'Too many clothes, Butkus!' Florian called out behind me. 'You haven't passed the challenge yet!' I cradled my head in my hand and stared at the lazy flow of frigid water swirling around my knees.

'It's like a-all of m-my dick m-mistakes are haunting me. I can't do this in front of him.'

'You can. You're not doing it *for* him anyway,' Max assured me.

'I'm doing it to make up for running my mouth in public – and to hopefully win *you* some money.'

'I'm sorry for my part in this. I wouldn't have chosen to make you do this, but…'

'You think it could be fun?' I prompted caustically. 'To have my naked butt filmed?'

'Florian will edit out the butt. There will be a couple of seconds of you, that's all. I spoke to him yesterday to make sure.'

'You did?' The tight coil of anxiety loosened a little.

The first episode of the 'Wiesn-Chellenge' had gone up on his channel and the footage of Max and I cuddling on the Hau den Lukas had lasted barely ten seconds – nowhere near enough. Quick-fire video editing didn't allow for character development. But I knew the social media audience had zero attention span and the metric was likes and interaction, not the length of the videos. Max was right; it would be okay – and he'd talked to Florian to protect me.

'You sunbathed topless that day at Antibes,' Max reminded me.

'Before we got chased off the beach because we hadn't paid the fee,' I responded drily. 'And you got so sunburnt we had to go to the cinema the next day to keep you cool.'

'I'd forgotten that. It must have been before you started covering me with your hardcore Australian suncream every time we went outside. I mainly remember the sunbathing topless.' His contrite smile was sweet and nearly enough to distract me from that sentence, but my brain backed up and replayed it. Was he suggesting he was attracted to me back then? We were talking… I had to think about it. Thirteen years ago. What? 'This is the same.'

It took me a second to realise he wasn't talking about being attracted to me. 'Getting naked in a freezing alpine river is not the same as sunbathing topless for a few minutes on the French Riviera.'

'No,' he agreed. 'It's so much better.' I groaned and gave him a shove. He grabbed my hands and linked our fingers. 'Come on, moppie. Underwear off and then in the water? Or in the water and then underwear off?'

'And go home commando?' I asked through clenched teeth. 'I'm going to get frostbite before I even decide.'

A high-pitched squeal made us both look up to see Marco tugging Ryan into the water. 'Holy… moly! Hot damn!'

'It's not hot. It's *cold!*' Marco growled as he threw himself into the water.

'Eeeeh!' Ryan screeched as he sank to his knees in the flow. 'That is the weirdest feeling.'

Isobel was out in the middle of the river, rubbing water over her skin as though it had healing properties. Tanya still stood at the water's edge, her hands clutched in the hem of her shirt, her chest heaving with agitated breaths.

'You can do it, Tanya!' Ryan yelled, holding his hands to his mouth. Marco splashed him and they both burst out laughing. 'Nobody's looking!'

'Do you want me to turn around?' Max said, getting my attention again. His smile was far too wide. 'I have seen it all before.' Yeah, but that was before he'd casually called my boobs 'lovely tits'.

'Fuck you,' I replied.

'That's the spirit.'

I shook off his grip on my hands and stalked back to the stony bank. Unclipping my bra, I shrugged out of it, gasping at the whoosh of air on my nipples and the prickle over my skin that felt a lot like a thrill. I shoved my undies down and made a beeline for the water.

I *hated* cold water. Although I lived in Sydney, I didn't go near the waves except in summer and even then I got a shock from the cold. The only time I'd enjoyed swimming in the sea was the time Max and I had bought a crappy Kombi van and driven up the coast of Queensland. The tropical water temperature had been perfect, although we'd transported bed bugs halfway up the coast before we realised what was biting us – and that Max was badly allergic.

He splashed me and I howled, skimming my arm through the water to get him back with a vengeance. 'I was just thinking about those photos from North Queensland when you had a rash all over your face,' I shot at him.

'That was the same trip where you got a tick on your arse.' He tapped his thumb and index finger together, imitating a pair of tweezers, his expression gleeful.

With a Homer Simpson 'why you little—' echoing in my mind, I launched myself at him. We went down, the water sluicing over me.

It was like putting all of my nerve endings on the biggest rollercoaster at Oktoberfest. My skin went into panic mode. My joints seized up. But it was a moment of absolute stillness as the water wiped everything else out of my mind.

Until I realised I was straddling Max. His hands were biting into my thighs.

I reared out of the water and he came up after me, spluttering and shaking out of his hair. His glasses were askew and covered in water droplets, but thankfully still present. I plucked them off his nose, about to wipe them for him and put them back when I realised I wasn't wearing a shirt.

'You're really going to take my glasses right now?' he asked in an oddly pleading tone. His hands shifted on my hips and he squinted at me, his gaze dropping and then jerking back up to my face. He bit his lip and a new thrill zipped through me. He thought I'd taken his glasses so he couldn't see me clearly.

I shook them and shoved them back onto his nose. 'I just wanted to clean them, you idiot. Like you said, you've seen it all before.' But his hands clenched on my skin and I was starting to wonder what would have happened if we hadn't been in ice-cold water. This wasn't anything I'd felt before – not with Max, maybe not with anyone. The frigid water was affecting my lungs. I couldn't seem to get enough air.

'I did the challenge. I'm getting out.' I pushed off him,

ignoring the slide of my fingertips over his wet shoulders, and stomped back to shore.

It felt heavenly to wrap a towel around myself and feel the rays of the morning sun on my skin. The newness of the sensation was like waking up – from a viral fever. Florian passed me a comically small bottle of schnaps and I downed it, gasping at the burn of the herbal liquid through my body.

'I feel like giving you all extra points,' he said casually, sipping his own bottle. He wasn't filming. He sat beside me and we watched the others in silence.

Tanya crouched in the water stoically up to the tips of her bob. Ryan and Marco were splashing each other like it was Brokeback Mountain and Isobel was meditating.

'Not Max or me,' I muttered. 'He thought of this crazy dare and I only lasted a minute.'

With a sudden nod, Tanya stood, curling her arms around herself, and stalked out of the water. I raced to grab a towel for her. The others followed her example soon after, shivering and cursing and groaning as they downed the schnaps.

Max was the last one to haul himself out of the water. He stretched and turned his face up to the sun and I stared rudely. Not at his crotch, although I'll admit to a quick peek. I couldn't work out what the contented expression on his face meant and that scared me.

* * *

We began to forgive Max when he fetched a small charcoal grill from the little wagon he'd schlepped down to the river bank. He set vegan sausages, marinated vegetables and slices of halloumi onto the grill and we gathered around, warming our frozen hands and feet over the coals.

It wasn't a cold day – unless you were from Sydney – so after we'd recovered from the water temperature, the lazy sunlight produced a pleasant lethargy. I leaned my head on Max's shoulder and managed to make myself forget that half an hour before, we'd been rolling around naked in the water and it hadn't quite been harmless.

'This is what we used to do in Freiburg!' Ryan declared, as though he, like me, had kind of forgotten what it was like to be twenty-one.

'We definitely played truth or dare sometimes too,' Isobel said with a snort.

'Without removal of clothing,' Tanya muttered. Perhaps it would take her a little longer to forgive Max. She sighed and produced the little velvet bag from her backpack, placing it in front of her as though it might give her the evil eye. 'We should do another one.'

'I'll pick one!' I volunteered, but Isobel was faster.

Florian fetched the camera grimly, switching it on as Isobel unfolded the slip of paper and tilted her head, reading. Then she burst out laughing. She clutched her sides and howled until Marco looked ready to threaten her with the tongs.

'Okay, the good news is, it's not cold or naked or physically difficult in any way.'

'And the bad news?' Tanya prompted.

Isobel snorted again. 'We might have some explaining to do to our spouses.'

'What?' spluttered Ryan. My stomach flipped. Was this it? My stupid dare?

'It just says, "Kiss your partner".'

Chapter Fifteen

I kept my gaze firmly on the pebbles on front of me, but I
knew Max was staring at me, as though he had laser eyes,
burning my skin. Or maybe it was just his breath gusting
there. Whatever it was, the back of my neck was hot and
tingling and I remembered his fingers right there the other
night at the club and I wished he'd do it again.

'Who wrote this one?' Isobel asked with a grin, but her
question was greeted with silence. 'All right. I'll have to work
it out later. Prepare your lips, Tanya. Have you ever kissed a
girl?'

'I've barely kissed a *man*,' she muttered, taking a deep breath
and lifting her mouth. With Florian gawking into the camera,
they puckered up and shared a quick, smacking kiss. They
froze, peering at each other afterward, until Tanya choked on
a laugh which set Isobel off again. 'You kiss like my daughter,'
Tanya said.

'I know!' Isobel cried. 'Sometimes I kiss my husband like
this and pat his back like he is one of the babies and it puts
him in a bad mood.'

'No matter how I kiss my husband, it puts him in a bad
mood.'

'Really?' said Ryan.

'Don't worry, I don't kiss him often,' Tanya said with a tone that suggested she didn't want to talk about it, but I wondered again about her eighteen days of freedom and hoped we were spending them the way she wanted to. It certainly gave me some perspective about the relative importance of an orgasm deficiency in the face of the real complications of a rocky marriage.

Rocky marriages were something I knew all about and I had the long list of missed calls from my dad to prove it.

'Now you, two,' Tanya said, jerking her chin towards Ryan and Marco. Ryan blanched and Marco was grinding his teeth. I felt terrible.

'It-it doesn't say it has to be on the mouth, right?' I offered weakly.

We all turned to Florian, who shrugged and trained the camera avidly on his friends' discomfort. That would work for me too. I could kiss Max's cheek, although that also sounded weird, after Tanya and Isobel had kissed on the lips.

'Just kiss each other on the cheek.'

'I'm not married any more, but I prefer a kiss on the cheek,' Marco said with a grunt, cupping Ryan's jaw and pressing a kiss just above. A blossoming blush lit up Ryan's face and his eyes glinted with stars. Max stifled a laugh.

'All right, uh, yeah,' Ryan babbled, before leaning over and returning the favour. He gave an enormous sigh of relief.

'Fi and Max are single, so no drama, right?' Isobel said. 'You guys have probably kissed before.'

I tried to resist, but my gaze snapped to his. 'Eh… no, we haven't,' Max admitted, still looking warily at me.

'Never? Not even while drunk?'

'Is it that hard to believe?' I mumbled.

'I mean, I know Max likes guys, but I thought he liked girls, too.'

He coughed and I wasn't sure if he was laughing or choking. 'I like women,' he confirmed. 'There are probably a lot of reasons why we never kissed before, but it won't be a problem now.'

I stared at him, suddenly wondering what all those reasons were, when a moment ago, it had been self-evident to me why we'd never kissed. We'd never been into each other that way. But he'd said it wouldn't be a problem *now*, as though he knew the filthy thoughts I'd been having about his mouth. I gulped.

He leaned towards me and I bent away instinctively. Thoughts flickering dangerously in his eyes, he blinked, and the next thing I knew, his hand was clamped around the back of my neck and he was holding me where I was – and sending shots of adrenaline down my spine.

As he brought his face close, I caught the scent of him, not the cheap deodorant he used to use but something spicy and a little bit older man that did something crazy to my hormones. His breath gusted over my cheek and, after one more pensive glance, his eyes drifted closed. Unable to stand the proximity, my eyes did the same, but it only set off all my other senses, especially the way the tiny hairs on my skin detected his nearness.

My mouth dropped open on a gasp, so when he brushed his lips over mine, the whisper-light kiss was all breath. But the little scrape of his bottom lip sent shivers over my skin and I stifled a moan.

His hand shifted on my neck and the taste of him teased my tongue. Closing my mouth instinctively, I trapped his bottom lip between mine and there was no way I could resist the quick swipe of my tongue over it. I felt and heard his sharp intake of breath and then his other hand came up to cup my jaw and his mouth moved harder on mine.

His tongue swept into my mouth, firm and deep and already three shades too dirty for the Turkish romcoms we watched together while texting each other. I might have whimpered, but my blood was rushing in my ears and I couldn't be certain.

My mouth didn't belong to me any more; he owned it with hot strokes of his tongue and searing pressure on my lips. He held me in place and teased my mouth wide open until I remembered we were in front of the camera and I felt so feverish, I could have ripped my clothes off and thrown myself in the river – again.

He pulled away with an audible smack, heaving in a breath. He stared at me, lifting his chin, but I couldn't maintain eye contact for long enough to work out what that look meant. The only sound was the crackle and spit of the cheese on the grill and our deep, unsteady breaths.

Until Florian gave a low whistle. 'That'll make it worth my rating for mature audiences. I bet you'll get some votes.'

Tingles flooded my skin, up to my hairline, when I thought about the kiss being broadcast. What exactly would the viewers see? The beginning of the end of our friendship? The thought made me panic. Without Max in my life I only had my screwed-up family and the Beerhemoth and neither of those ever made me feel wanted.

Part of my mind was racing ahead imagining the good bits, lots of skin and closeness and blessed relief, but I knew what came afterwards: uncertainty, misunderstandings, power struggle, the emotional abuse most of us never realised we doled out to others.

Not with Max. I couldn't risk him.

'What did you think, Fi?' he asked, his voice still breathy and low. 'You told me how you like kissing back in Freiburg, although you changed your mind by the time we went to the Grand Canyon for your thirtieth. I was better than the lead singer of that band we saw in Slovenia, but not as good as David Sorching in high school, right?'

I was too unsettled to do anything except blush and splutter and completely fail to come up with a rejoinder. The kiss had moved the goalposts of my entire life and he wanted me to rate him?

'Nine out of ten,' I muttered, hauling myself restlessly to my feet. I took a mark off because he ruined it afterward – or had I ruined everything before? I gave myself the excuse of looking for my phone, but I wanted space. Crunching stones behind me suggested I wasn't going to get it.

'Moppie,' he said softly, in that deep tone that shivered under my skin and I couldn't address any of this.

'I'm fine,' I lied. 'Just this stupid… hormones… sex plan,' I muttered, my cheeks burning. Maybe I was making it worse. 'I'll be fine. We'll be fine.' Because we had to be.

'Of course, we'll be fine,' he agreed. 'But… sorry if I pushed you too far.'

'It's *fine.*' I forced my gaze up to his in an attempt to make him believe me. He was watching me so intently, I had to wonder what… intent was behind it. A vein moved in his forehead. I'd never noticed that vein before, along with the little hollow by his jaw and the lines around his mouth. They were marks of maturity that he wore well.

He smiled suddenly and looked away. Giving my elbow a squeeze, he said, 'Fine,' and turned to the others with a chuckle.

He rubbed the back of his head and then shoved his hands into his pockets as he strode back, his shoulders hunched and a funny catch in his gait.

It reminded me of the times he'd chatted someone up and been rejected. I was hurt and so confused that this time it was me who had somehow done it.

Chapter Sixteen

On Wednesday, I had a work junket in the Fuchsbräu tent with Dollersen and the other fusty middle-aged men who ran the Beerhemoth, as well as a group we were courting (read: bribing) for wholesale agreements. I wasn't particularly looking forward to it, but I thought it would probably do me good, forced to spend a few hours without Max.

We hadn't talked about The Kiss, which also freaked me out. He'd been busy at Snaketooth late each night and in the mornings, he'd just poked me and bantered. I was starting to think it really had just been a fun game to him – like old times. I'd worry I was overreacting, except I clearly wasn't. My best friend had owned my mouth with his tongue and got me close to my first non-auto-erotic orgasm in two years. There was no such thing as overreacting. But ignoring, apparently, was a thing.

I'd had a lot of fun mocking up and testing an ad for Snaketooth with the photo I'd taken in the river. With the tiny budget I'd talked Max and Jan-Philipp into investing in social media ads, I'd also got more traffic onto their website. It was Marketing 101-level stuff, the kind of work I hadn't done in years, but I'd got such a thrill out of it that Max had teased me about loving my metrics more than anything else.

It was good to be reminded that I actually enjoyed some parts of my job.

But when I arrived at the VIP table in the tent, instead of a greeting, I got comments about my lack of a dirndl and various mistakes with my name that proved I hadn't quite been welcomed into the senior management fold yet. I'd worn my long, tailored trousers and a nice blouse and I looked like the effortlessly in-charge global marketing VP that I was soon to be, once my promotion was rubber-stamped. If I'd worn a dirndl, they would have commented on… something entirely unrelated to my job. A dirndl was a satiny, beautiful catch-22.

I spent the afternoon worrying about when they'd start deriding me for the 'I love beer' video or the Wiesn-Challenge, but the only one who said anything was Dollersen, with a snicker that turned my stomach. The others, it appeared, weren't keeping up with the latest beer marketing gimmick.

'I hope you're taking notes about this Wiesn-Challenge. We could do something similar next year. We could call it the "I Love Beer Challenge".'

I squeezed my mouth shut. If I wasn't careful, I'd ask him politely to stop rubbing my face in that mistake and remember that I was a private citizen and not just a Beerhemoth employee. The fact that I'd do it politely was frustrating.

'I was concerned after that outburst went viral that… outbursts might happen more often and that would be difficult in your position.'

I gritted my teeth. He hadn't said it, but I understood the implication anyway: difficult women were not welcome at the big table.

As the afternoon progressed into evening, I was goaded into beer after beer and no one was interested in me beyond my apparently inexplicable ability to get people to buy beer – who would have thought that marketing activities actually produced a return on investment? When a logistics bigwig asked if my husband was annoyed he hadn't been invited, I voluntarily glugged the rest of my mug to make sure I kept my mouth shut.

Despite being a tall woman with a lot of beer-drinking under my belt, keeping up with the testosterone around the table was never going to end well. My bladder was ready to mutiny by seven o'clock, while my colleagues – and the cringey pop music that made Germans happy and everyone else want to smash something – were just beginning to get embarrassing.

Giving myself a pep talk so I didn't grouch at the poor toilet attendant, I paid my fee to be a woman and relieved my poor bladder. Sure, it was amazing sometimes being a young woman at the table with the major players, but it was another lonely thing in my life and I was so sick of loneliness.

Those men casually discussing brand acquisitions probably didn't even know I had to pay fifty cents to pee while they could do it for free. That pretty much made my beer more expensive than theirs – except of course it was all free for us today, courtesy of Willi's Blow-Job.

I regretted my heels – if not my life – when one of the operations heads, a slightly patronising dad-type in his mid-fifties, dragged me up onto the bench to bellow 'Hey Baby, ooh, ahh,' into my ear and my head spun like the CD that song had originally been released on. I couldn't quite find the table after I stepped down and then 99 Luftballons started up, the trumpets weirdly muted amid renewed swishing in my bladder, and I was done for the day.

If Max had been there, we would have sung along to that

song together. We'd learned it in German class in Freiburg, crooning into pretend microphones while the rest of the class mutely acted as though they didn't want to do the same. My eyes were all pricky and tingly and I wanted to shove Max and then grab him and make him put everything back the way it used to be.

A shock of cold snapped me out of it for a moment and I noticed with detachment that I was outside, by a nostalgic wooden stand with coloured lights, where a man appeared to be whistling like a bird. *Ahh, I'm quite drunk.*

I turned, determined to put one foot in front of the other, but something was spinning behind my eyes, flashing and whirling and – I realised two things simultaneously: firstly, it wasn't behind my eyes. It was a ride. Secondly, I was about to chuck my guts up.

As I hurled into a bin in a dark corner, I grumbled inwardly to myself that, at thirty-fucking-six, I could have at least learned some lessons to make up for my lower tolerance for alcohol. I was selfish for wishing Max was there to rub my back and hold my hair. Then somehow, he was there, but not.

He was in my ear. Ah, I'd called him.

'Fi? What's up?' *Shit, I'd called him.* Now I was doing nothing but heavy-breathing over the phone while I panicked. I couldn't be responsible for what I might say right now. 'Are you drunk, moppie?' he asked, his voice smooth with amusement.

'Just a little.'

'Where are you? Can I come and take you home?'

Yesssss. I wasn't sure if I said that aloud. 'You're at Snaketooth.'

'Jan can cover for me. Where are you?'

I glanced around in confusion. 'Um… around the corner from a pretzel stand and a safe distance away from a drug deal, I think.'

***

'Remember when we went to that absinthe bar in Prague?' Max said cheerfully as he hauled me out of the taxi near his apartment.

'Do you want me to hurl again?' I replied through gritted teeth. 'I will never forget the colour of our vomit under those UV lights.'

'I still have no idea how we got home. One of us should have stayed sober.'

'Me,' I muttered. 'I'm heavier.' He looked at me askance and the lopsided twist of his brow was ridiculously sexy, like the way he pursed his lips…

'Are you sure you're heavier? I'm not having any trouble getting you up the stairs tonight,' he said evenly. The annoying prick was frustratingly sober.

'You grew *muscles*!' I said accusingly, pinching him on the biceps hard enough to make him flinch. 'And shoulders! You got all fit and—' *Shut your mouth right now, Fiona Jade Butkus.* 'Sexy! You got all sexy!' I never was any good at listening to my voice of reason.

His steps faltered and I couldn't tell if that was an actual grunt of effort or if he was trying to work out what to say. 'I'm… sorry?'

I shoved him. 'You should be. And you should have kept your tongue to yourself.'

'I am sorry for that,' he said. 'I didn't mean to… gross you out.' When I'd taught him that phrase, I'd never expected he'd use it in this context.

'You didn't gross me out!' I said, so loudly he shushed me with a brush of his hand over my lips. 'You basically fucked my mouth!'

He swallowed and I was staring at his throat again. 'That was *not* fucking your mouth,' he said, his voice almost a purr.

His words registered with a burst of embarrassment and a whole slideshow of X-rated fantasies. Had his hand been so tight on my hip a moment ago? 'With your tongue! I meant with your tongue! God, what is wrong with you – us – me? You're not supposed to be in the sex plan,' I insisted, waggling my finger at him. 'I just need to rediscover how to have an orgasm with someone else. I'm not going to fuzzy any lines with you just for that. I don't really want to sleep with Florian again, but since he's the only dick for miles…'

I must have been really wasted because it sounded like he growled, deep in his throat. 'Good luck with that, Fi. You're right. I'm not one of the dicks you usually choose.' His fingers let up and I missed that pressure.

My head tumbled onto his shoulder and I felt like crying. I just needed to get over this weird mid-thirties hormonal thing. I needed to get laid and see how I felt then, rather than cannibalising the best thing in my life because I was horny and lonely.

'Can you imagine if we screwed up, how bad we'd hurt each other?' I asked in a small voice, as we shuffled along the hall to his apartment. 'I couldn't do that to you. I couldn't do *without* you. I already want to kill Gustav and punch your parents. What I've seen of relationships…' An image of my mum belittling my dad when he came around to collect my sisters and me was enough to kill off the stupid hormones. I'd cling to that, if it hadn't made me want to vomit again.

But Max was there, his hand smoothing my hair this time. 'I know, moppie.' But he kept talking and, despite the comfort of the familiar touch, my unease didn't entirely recede. 'But Gustav was fifteen years ago. I'm not messed up about that any more. There are some good things about growing older.' He pressed a kiss to the top of my head.

I leaned too heavily on him as we stumbled into his apartment, but he supported me admirably. He held my hair and rubbed my back as I slumped over the toilet bowl like a teenager at a party who'd had too many bottles of Smirnoff Ice. Then he tucked me into bed with a glass of water and a little box of painkillers and I wondered how I would ever deserve him.

* * *

At lunchtime on Friday, the sight of a mug of beer still made my stomach roil, but this was serious. I had ten thousand big ones to win for Max and my pride to uphold. So, I downed my first beer as if I was an Aussie fan at the cricket ground on a hot Sunday afternoon.

The other Wiesn-Challenge hostages cheered and I was shocked when Florian smacked a kiss to my cheek. Next to me, Max bristled and I loved him for his protective instincts. I settled a hand on his shoulder in a wordless order to stand down, as Florian took a seat next to me with a grin.

'You two are getting a lot of votes,' he said, clinking his mug against mine. 'You look hot in lederhosen, but it's funny that you'll show off your arse and lick your friend on camera, but not wear a dirndl.'

'Funny,' I agreed with a false smile, tugging self-consciously on the suspenders of Max's lederhosen, which I'd borrowed again. 'But if we're getting votes, perhaps you shouldn't complain about what I'm *not* wearing.'

'I'm not complaining!' he insisted. 'Max looks nice, today.' When Florian flashed Max a leering grin, I had to curl my hands into fists to stop them going for his face, fingernails first. It was Max's turn to place a hand on my arm to settle me down.

He was wearing his own dirndl, today, the pretty, embroidered, green number with a silver chain hooked along the front of the bodice. He'd tied the apron with the bow at the back this morning, but I'd stubbornly retied it on his left hip. His sceptical look, with the creases on his forehead, was still keeping me warm.

On the schedule of juvenile torment today were a series of competitions for the whole group. The first was Maßkrugstemmen, which Max translated for me as lifting weights, except the weight is a Maßkrug, a beer mug. At least we were competing at holding our beer literally and not figuratively.

The women went first. We had ten seconds to drink as much off the top as we could and then, at the poor Junior Marketing Associate's whistle, we held our arms straight and waited for our muscles to give out. It was all fiercely eye-roll worthy, but my competitive spirit reared up like a bear spotting flannel in the woods.

Tanya crashed out early with a groan, but Isobel remained, grinning and mouthy, into the last three with me and a pretty German woman in a fierce, buttoned-up dirndl. The men slapped the table and cat-called and if I got any more comments about my boobs, I was going to pour the beer down their butt-cleavage. What had I said about women's clothes and a catch-22?

When my arm was not only shaking, but also hot and burny, only thoughts about Max and Snaketooth kept me going. Isobel's eyes were glazed and her chest was heaving. If Max hadn't leaped to his feet and caught her mug when her knees gave out, she would have poured it all down her gorgeous bodice.

Feeding off my competitor's grimaces and my righteous indignation, I held out until she slammed down her Maß with an infernal howl. I had to admit she had more style. I cracked, with a string of foul language, and cradled my poor arm as I set the beer down with a whimper. But the cheers from my friends and Max's arms wrapping around me buoyed my mood.

I shuddered, stumbling and glad of the extra support. Max's arm tightened over my torso and I felt his breath on my ear. 'You are so hot right now,' he said.

With a huff, I decided he was joking. 'Yeah, I've lost all feeling in my fingers,' I rasped. It was the perfect thing to say because he took my hand and gently stroked from the middle of my palm all the way to my fingertips, his chin resting on my shoulder. When it was his turn for the stupid competition, I almost believed I hadn't imagined his lips ghosting over my neck as he pulled away.

Despite all of the muscles we'd now extensively discussed, Max bombed out in the middle of the pack among the men. I tried to give him a friendly punch in the shoulder, but my arm crumpled.

When we were instructed to finish our beers in preparation

for the next challenge, I had to leave the heavy glass on the table and tip it into my mouth until I was able to lift it with my left hand, but at least I had a great dirty scowl prepared when Florian stuck his camera in my face.

'Ready for the next chellenge, Butkus?' he asked.

'That's 'Butt-Kiss' to you,' I growled. I was, after all, allowed to make those jokes myself.

'You'll have an advantage – Max, too, I imagine.' He paused dramatically, with a lift of his eyebrows that made me want to punch him. 'Up next is… the high-heel races!'

Chapter Seventeen

I was certain the statue of Bavaria, holding a wreath and a sword and staring disdainfully over the Theresienwiese, would not have approved of holding drunken races in high-heels around her plinth. I gazed up at the enormous figure, feeling a certain solidarity from her – or I was just tipsy, which was also true. She was a symbol made to look like a woman and I was a woman who was sick of being just a symbol. Plus, she was wearing a bearskin and I imagined she got shit for that.

A crowd had gathered, even more than the usual flock of tipsy visitors trying, and sometimes failing, to remain steady on the grassy hill below the statue. The blokes were laughing nervously, but Max and I just squeezed each other's hands.

The challenge was a relay race in four-inch heels, up the concrete steps, around the long-suffering statue, and back down the steps. After hastily applying lipstick to our partners, we would swap places – and swap shoes, in this case.

'This one's in the bag,' I whispered and Max agreed with a firm nod that dissolved into a grin. 'I'll go first.'

We accepted a pair of black peep-toe pumps and a stick of fire-engine red lipstick and Max took his place in one of the chairs lined up at the finish line, slipping off his sneakers and socks. *Let the games begin.*

The novelty horn sounded and I lurched for the stairs. They were those annoying granny steps that are lower than you expect and it took me half of the first flight to work out that I could safely take three at a time, with my long legs. Racing around the plinth, I twisted my ankle as I hobbled back, but it wasn't bad. Balancing on the balls of my feet, I hurtled down and whipped out the lipstick.

Ignore the suppleness. It is a blank canvas and not Max's mouth. I nearly lost it on the first swipe, as I smeared red over the little indent and remembered my tongue there.

'It doesn't have to be neat,' he muttered and I let him think that was why I'd hesitated. With a quick brush to his bowed upper lip, I pressed the stick into his hand and urged him up. He slipped his feet into the heels and swaggered off.

I had seen Max in a frock and heels numerous times. He liked to dress up, but heels were no one's friend, so he looked like Ace Ventura in a tutu as he made a dash up the steps.

My beer-holding nemesis from the Maßkrugstemmen was a few steps ahead, leaping gracefully up to the statue, and Isobel wasn't far behind, but my race had set Max and me up well, despite my wobble about Max's mouth. At least I was fairly certain *he* wouldn't have the same distraction.

Leaping down the stairs four at a time and risking a broken ankle propelled Max to the front. Heart pounding, I puckered up and lifted my chin as he hurtled back to me, flipping the cap off the lipstick so hard it flew into the crowd. He grasped the back of my head and pressed the stick of lippie against my bottom lip. Then he just… stayed there, holding my mouth open and staring in something like alarm.

'Max!' I said sharply and he shook himself out of it, licking his lips and finishing the task. Relay accomplished, I tugged him up onto the chair with me and shot up my hand to claim victory. A glance along the line of chairs showed three groups all finished, but I was ninety-five percent sure we'd got there first and I would never admit that five percent doubt. I wiggled my hand to get the organiser's attention and nearly tipped over the chair.

'Yes, all right, Fi. You two won, despite the sexual tension,' Florian said, lowering his camera with a smug grin. 'How's that working out for you two?'

'Ha!' I shouted back, tamping down my panic. Max's arms tightened around me and I realised he was holding us both steady on the rickety chair. I hated that Florian knew what was going on inside me, but I was getting worried Max would work it out even without that jerk saying anything.

Half an hour later, the adrenaline crash and residual blood-alcohol had me in its grips and I was quietly flatlining as we sat in a shell-shocked group on the grass by the Bavaria statue. Ryan and Marco had been so slow that only Ryan had lipstick on and he seemed to have forgotten about it as he blinked at the flashing lights of the Volksfest against the dimming evening sky. Tanya pulled out a makeup mirror and removed her lipstick with a tight sigh. Isobel groaned, nursing her arm and her ankles in turn.

'I am too old for the beerfest,' she muttered, tugging at her bodice. 'My boobs itch.'

'They're trying to get us to quit,' I said. 'But we won't,' I added on a murmur.

'Of course, we won't,' Tanya snapped.

'At least Florian's not here to enjoy our misfortune,' I grumbled.

'He's not enjoying your misfortune,' Tanya said with a huff. 'He's trying to get you to sleep with him.'

I snorted. 'Strange way to go about that.'

'She's right,' Max said casually – too casually.

'Guys know when other guys want to sleep with their women,' Isobel added, nodding enthusiastically. My hair stood on end when the part of that sentence that landed most heavily was the part where she referred to me as Max's *woman*. But he only chuckled.

'Are you suggesting I should sleep with Florian to stop him teasing me?'

'We forgot all about your sex plan, Fi!' Isobel said suddenly. 'But you can do better than filthy Florian.'

Ouch, I hoped so.

'Do you want to sleep with him?' Max's blurted question quieted everyone else and my skin crawled with too much subtext, too many suspicions, hopes and fears. Was he asking as my wingman or… something else? 'It's a simple question, Fi.'

I shivered at his tone and almost wasn't brave enough to meet his gaze, but when I did, the heat in his eyes made the truth tumble out before I'd acknowledged what it was. 'No.'

Max turned away, releasing a deep breath and the others all breathed again, as well, as though a pivotal moment had passed and we were through to the other side of… something. When had my sweetheart Max become so broody? And why did I feel it under my skin?

'I still don't think that's what he wants,' I insisted. 'He's making fun of me.'

'Querida,' Isobel said, placing a hand on my arm, 'that is what boys do when they like you.'

'It's not what *men* do,' Max muttered. He hauled himself to his feet. 'I have to get back to Snaketooth for the Friday night crowd.'

I snatched his hand and used him to pull myself to standing. 'I'm coming with you.'

* * *

We headed straight for the toilets when we arrived at Snake-tooth to make sure the last of the lipstick was gone. I handed Max a makeup remover wipe, but he left the eyeliner, giving me a wink in the mirror. He'd just pushed open the door to precede me into the bar area when Jan appeared, his hands opening and closing restlessly.

'Hausner ist hier,' he muttered, speaking in German, but it was easy enough to understand.

'Who's Hausner?' I whispered.

'A guy who might invest,' Max explained, his gaze never leaving Jan's. 'Does he want to discuss it, or is he just here to check things out?'

'Who knows,' Jan answered in agitation. 'I hate this stuff.'

Max squeezed his arm. 'I know. I'll handle him.' I blinked, staring at Max's shoulders as he squared them, realising that it wasn't just their physical breadth that had developed over the years.

'Max, you're… wearing a dirndl,' Jan pointed out with a wince. 'Not that it doesn't look great on you.'

I clamped a hand around Max's wrist and dragged him back into the toilets. 'Give us a minute,' I called to Jan over my shoulder. Hustling him into the farthest cubicle, I squeezed in behind. With hurried hands, I undid the buttons at the front of my – Max's – lederhosen and flipped the suspenders over my head.

'Fi, what are you doing?'

'That's a stupid question,' I said, popping open the buttons on the dick flap at the front. The tight shorts caught on my hips and I fumbled for the tie at the back. The cubicle was so small, I clocked Max's chin with my shoulder. 'Sorry.'

'Okay, *why* are you doing this? Do you have spare clothes somewhere?'

'You are wearing my spare clothes. Strip.' The spots of pink on his cheeks were sweet and I wanted to order him to strip again, just to see what he'd do. But he reached around me to still my hands and eyeballed me.

'I'm not going to make you wear a dirndl.'

'You're not making me. *I'm* making *you* give me your dirndl.' I shook off his hands and continued the fight with the tie at my back. I couldn't bend without grating my head along Max's new abs, so I gave up and had the discussion instead.

'But you have a… position on dirndls. No,' he insisted.

'I don't have to wear a dirndl for the challenge or my asshole boss and I don't have to wear a dirndl for you. But I want to. Give me the dress, Max.'

His nostrils flared once, then he took my face in his hands and my heart was looping all over the place as he closed the short distance. His jaw tense and his expression tight with emotion, he pressed a single, hard kiss to my lips and pulled away again. 'Thank you, Fi.'

Ah, it was a thank-you kiss. Okay. Perhaps that wasn't a big deal between friends. It hadn't felt weird. A kiss on the mouth was what the moment had called for. Except that now my nipples were tight and tender and I was staring at his hands as they fumbled with the silver chain on the front of his bodice.

'Don't thank me like I'm your little assistant,' I protested faintly, repeating his words from the first day of the challenge. His gaze rose slowly to mine. 'Although I'm not sure assistants are supposed to get thank-you kisses.' I cut myself off. The crinkles deepened at the corners of his eyes. He tipped his head up to me and my breath caught. But he stopped and swung pointedly away.

I wondered if we'd been a breath away from a hot make-out session in a bathroom. I couldn't help thinking that, if we ever had sex, a toilet cubicle would totally be our MO. That should have been a weird thought and somehow it wasn't.

He got back to work on the chain holding his bodice closed. 'I'm sure I… knew how to do this properly, last time I wore this,' he said, his voice high.

'Here, you've got it…' With halting hands, I unwound the chain from his finger and worked it through the hook on one side. 'You're a bit… tangled.'

Abandoning my attempt to escape my own faux-leather wardrobe malfunction, I helped him untie his bonds, gradually loosening the bodice as each hook came free. The ribbon was next and, when I'd unwound that from all of the fastenings, I peered at the hook-and-eye closing the top of the bodice.

My fingers brushed the skin of his chest, just above the blouse. The scent of him tickled my nostrils – and my belly, somehow. I made the mistake of glancing up and noticed how close he was, his gaze fixed on me.

I cleared my thick throat. 'Do you still use *Dark Temptation?*' I teased, giving him a sniff for show. I knew he didn't. The scent of the cheap deodorant would probably allow me to literally travel back in time, I'd used it myself on so many occasions after a night out.

'No,' he said with an inarticulate cough. 'Are you finished?'

'Nearly,' I said with a nod. Back to the task at hand. I managed the hook-and-eye and dragged the zip down, trying not to stare at his bare stomach, but wow, the ridges and hollows and that flat bit that made me think about what came next.

He shrugged out of the bodice with some difficulty because… those shoulders. The band tattooed on his forearm caught my eye and I stared at the little clench of muscle there, even though I'd sat with him when he got that first tattoo, screaming like a baby, and seen it a million times since.

It was an out-of-body experience, like he wasn't Max, but he clearly *was* Max, even though I was so turned on, I was probably wasting electricity.

He whipped the cropped blouse over his head, flashing me armpits and a belly button and a normal person would have been completely turned off by that. I was obviously not normal.

'Turn around,' he said and I whirled without questioning him.

Chapter Eighteen

Only when I was staring at the wall a few inches from my nose did I wonder why he suddenly wanted privacy when he'd already shimmied out of the dirndl. Then I felt his hands in the middle of my back, working the tie free, and I was asking myself whether someone had let all the air out of this cubicle.

The shorts sagged on my waist and he dropped down to loosen the ties at my calves. I made the mistake of looking down and caught sight of him crouched next to me, naked except for his boxers and a pair of my shiny court shoes.

I tore my eyes back up and leaned my hands against the chipboard, trying not to analyse all the innuendo that had gone on in my head over the past few minutes. He stood and I shoved the shorts down my legs, handing them over without looking at him. My skin was sensitive as I unbuttoned the white shirt and slipped it off my shoulders. I could feel him behind me and my stupid brain imagined his eyes grazing my back, following the straps of my bra and then down to… my really unattractive cotton knickers. There had been no sex plan today and I'd grown to value comfort in my underwear.

I half-turned so we could swap shirts and pretended my nipples weren't standing to attention as I tugged the cropped blouse over them. Stepping into the dress, I pulled the bodice up over my shoulders.

Trying not to look at Max as he tucked in his shirt, it was impossible not to notice how much better he looked in the lederhosen than I did. The shirt was a touch tight over his shoulders. Urgh, since when was I such a shoulder woman?

I fumbled with the hook-and-eye and averted my gaze from his. As the moments ticked by, I slowly accepted what I should have known from the beginning.

'It's too tight,' I groaned.

He nodded firmly and swallowed. 'Hold still.' And then he shoved his fingers in between my boobs and manhandled me into stupid thing.

'Don't break it,' I gasped.

'Don't worry,' he said with a grunt of effort. 'Your boobs are soft.'

And fuck if my bones didn't all melt right then and there. Boobs being soft probably wasn't supposed to be a compliment. He was stating a fact. Perky, firm breasts were where it was at in the steamy historical romances I used to devour, the sexy pages all rumpled and dog-eared. I was a full-breasted woman who had been living in standard gravity for thirty-six years. I didn't do 'perky' any more.

But the word 'soft' in Max's voice had me picturing him tearing off his glasses and burying his face in there. Perhaps that also had something to do with the heat of his breath on my collarbone as he worked on the zip.

He got it closed by some miracle and started on the ribbon and the hooks. I worked to get my breath under control so I didn't pop the zip from raw sexual tension. The hem scraped along the top of my nipples like some kind of S&M device, while the backs of Max's fingers brushed the underboob bit and I was trying not to pant.

'Are you sure you're okay?'

Aside from the fact that I was so turned on I was crossing my legs under the satin skirt? 'Yeah, I'm fine,' I assured no one. He glanced up at me and I suspected we were both thinking about the last time we'd overused the word 'fine' in a conversation. 'It's not the dirndl,' I snapped. 'It's you touching my boobs.'

'Sorry, I know you don't always like… touching, on your tits.'

He had to stop calling them that, or I'd grab his hands and shove them there and make him fix what he'd done to me. I couldn't believe he'd remembered everything I'd told him about my fickle body that liked some touches one day and not the next.

'It's okay,' I said, my bosom heaving ridiculously in the tight bodice. 'Apparently, it's a boob day.'

Max's mouth twitched with a smile and he licked his lips slowly. 'That's… good?' He tied off the bodice and dropped his hands. I hoped he wouldn't notice that I was leaning on the door for support, since my legs had turned to custard. 'Are you sure this is okay? I can just meet him in the dirndl. If he has a problem with that, he can… go shove it. That's the expression, isn't it?'

I managed a wobbly smile. 'I taught you well.' I smoothed a hand over his shoulder, aiming for friendly affection. 'It's okay, Max. It's kind of fun, playing a role or something.' Eek, I had to stop thinking sexy thoughts. 'Do you think my German is good enough to waitress for the evening?'

'You don't have to—'

'I want to. Did you see that crowd in there? Since my little marketing campaign obviously got you into this situation, it's only fair that I help you out.'

'Thanks, moppie,' he said with an indulgent smile. I preferred his earlier way of thanking me. 'And you look hot in my dirndl.'

* * *

I did not feel hot later that night after hours on my feet, my hair tangled and limp and sweat patches in my armpits, but I did feel immeasurably good.

Jan closed the door behind the last patrons, raised both arms above his head and shook his fists with a silent yell. He hopped to Max, grabbed his shoulders and shook him. 'Alter! Wir haben's geschafft! Verdammte Scheiße, wie viele Leute waren heut' da?!'

After spending the evening practising my rusty German, I caught the gist of what he said: 'We did it. Holy shit, there were a lot of people here,' something like that. I sank into a chair with a grin, watching them slap each other and then hug and then slap each other again. Men could be strange creatures.

They talked over each other, Jan just barely letting Max explain about Hausner, but my tired brain stopped listening after the initial confirmation that the quick, informal discussion with the investor had gone well. He'd stayed most of the night soaking up the vibes which had to be a good sign.

My hands were sticky from beer and sweat and I stared at my palms curiously. I was accustomed to giving orders to others, analysing and computing facts and developing strategies, but there was nothing quite like getting your hands dirty and performing a simple task.

I didn't mean simple as in easy. I'd been run off my feet, hopping between tables, keeping the orders coming and bragging about Snaketooth to every customer. I'd worked for a semester waiting tables in Sydney and I'd hated every minute of it, but I'd been damn lazy as a student.

That night, every ounce of my waning mid-thirties energy had been expended for a good cause: amazing beer, good food and my best friend. It was so much better than the Oktoberfest junket I'd endured two days ago. Watching the money in my belt add up throughout the night had been more thrilling than a board meeting where my strategy was approved.

But I was exhausted. I was nearly asleep when Max sidled up and hauled me to my feet. 'Poor moppie, you're done.' He brushed his hand over my cheek and drew me in for a hug that was like a full-body sigh. 'You get employee of the month.'

'I stink,' I protested weakly. But instead of pulling away, his nose dropped to my neck and he breathed deeply. Goose bumps raced up my chest.

'You're amazing,' he whispered against my neck. I could feel the tiredness in him too, the satisfaction. My hands rose of their own accord to run through his hair and he shuddered.

'Get a room!' Jan called out with a laugh as he emerged from the staff room with his jacket.

'Let's go home,' Max said, pressing a kiss to my cheek.

My head spun, wondering if anything had changed between us or not, trying to remember that the kissing and the closeness would only hurt us both in the end, but everything felt so good, so bright, like the lights coming on again after the power cut of the past few years. He held my hand, slipping his fingers between mine, and I couldn't remember any more if we'd always done that or not.

I dropped his hand self-consciously when we arrived home and greeted his housemates, who were watching TV on the sofa. Max was acting normally, while my mind raced and my body was on alert somehow.

Trying to calm down under the warm spray of the shower, I thought of all the sweat and grime washing away and ignored the sensation of the water on my nipples. It didn't work. I'd just let out a frustrated grumble when the door opened and Max came in.

'You okay?' he asked conversationally. I heard the sounds of him loading up his toothbrush.

'Yeah,' I managed to answer, hoping he'd attribute my breathy voice to tiredness. I turned off the shower, then froze, no idea what to do next. I wasn't strong enough right now to just step out of the shower in front of him, naked. Besides, I was pretty sure we didn't use to do that.

'Can I hand you a towel?'

'Yes, please.' The towel appeared at the side of the curtain and I grabbed at it with relief. Then I remembered it was one of those ridiculously small European towels. I wrapped it around myself anyway and squared my shoulders before whipping the curtain to the side, grabbing my pyjamas from the shelf and quickly shimmying into my undies and pyjamas under the towel. Phew, done.

Max's eyes were on me in the mirror as I snatched my toothbrush from the basin. I ignored him and focussed on breathing through this weird moment – and scrubbing my teeth clean after the long day. But my gaze kept accidentally clashing with his before we both hurriedly looked away. He brushed and spat, his brow lifting and lowering as he stared at his own reflection. Then he caught me staring again and I rushed to spit.

He finished first, lifting a hand to the back of his head which made his open shirt gape. 'I'll just… eh… shower.' He fiddled with the hem of his shirt.

I threw my toothbrushing into overdrive and rinsed with the devil on my tail. 'I'll… see you in bed.' I legged it out of there before my illicit fantasies rushed back.

I pretended I was asleep when he came back, although my eyes were open a slit to catch the image of him rubbing his towel absently over his bare chest. When he slipped into bed beside me, the smell of soap and warm skin assailed my nose. I froze, trying to stop myself from gulping in huge breaths of pure Max.

He shifted behind me, then paused. I felt his glance in my direction at the same time I heard the soft rasp of his head on the pillow. 'Fi,' he began in that low voice that made everything worse. 'Do you want me to give you an orgasm?'

Chapter Nineteen

'Fuck off, Max!' I slid off the pillow and tugged the blanket up over my head, staying firmly turned away. 'You did not just suggest that,' I mumbled through a mouthful of sheets.

I felt him shifting behind me. 'I'm serious.' His hand landed on my head, through the blanket. He probably thought it was my shoulder. 'If it's worrying you, then let's try it.'

What was worrying me was how much I wanted to lick my best friend. Allowing him to touch me would not solve that.

'You could take the orgasm thing out of the equation, gain some perspective,' he said lightly. I pulled the blanket down and peeked over my shoulder. 'Prove there's nothing wrong with you after all.'

'Like... getting it out of my system?' Ohhh, yeah. That had appeal, even though Max couldn't know that I'd actually meant getting my sudden attraction to *him* out of my system.

'There's no reason I can't help you with that.'

Fifteen years of friendship was no reason? 'Max, how can you—'

'You want an orgasm from another person, right? *I'm* a person, Fi. I'm even a man, since you prefer those.'

'But we're—'

'It'll be okay,' he purred. His fingers skimmed down my

back under the blanket and my eyes crossed at the shivers over my skin.

'You'll just give me a pity orgasm and then we go back to being old friends who love each other at our worst?'

'Not a pity orgasm.' His voice was so low and smooth. His mouth was at my ear now. His breath wasn't quite steady and I asked myself for the first time what *he* wanted out of this. 'A friendly fuck.'

Flames whooshed over my skin at those words, prickling and searing and I couldn't think straight. 'A friendly… What the hell, Max?' I panted.

'It doesn't have to be a fuck. Just let me get you off. I promise we'll be okay afterward.'

I was crawling out of my skin. At this rate, he could probably press my buttons like a light switch and I'd blow a fuse. All those guys who'd rubbed and licked and poked with no success, and all Max had to do was breathe on me and I was almost gone. It couldn't be that easy. But then, Max did have a big advantage over every other man in the world when it came to me.

'Are you sure you can?' I didn't know if I was doubting him or taunting him.

He chuckled, making the air between us heat and vibrate. 'Yes, Fi. I'll get you off. Can I?' The eagerness in his voice curled up inside me, next to my old memories of Max, somewhere deep and necessary to my existence.

'I-I suppose you could try.' I rolled onto my back in a less-than-sexy invitation. He propped himself up on an elbow and regarded me with unexpected warmth. His lips twitched. Lowering his head slowly, he pressed a kiss to my temple and while I appreciated the nod to friendship first, the kiss also shot straight into my veins, rushing for my heart with some fizzing, fragile essence.

'Just do me, Max,' he said in a high-pitched voice.

I whacked him on the shoulder. 'I can still change my mind.'

'You won't, though.'

He came closer, his breath feathering along my jaw, and my body evaporated in a puff of steam. It explained the hiss that emerged from my mouth when his tongue scraped up my throat. Lifting my chin, I swallowed the torrent of swearing that rose to my lips. I needed so much more, but I could barely stand the teasing tingle of his tongue flicking my skin. He was only touching my neck and I was a mess.

'Still boob day?' he asked as his hands slipped under the clothes at my waist.

All I could do was nod and pant and let him lift my shirt up and off. He fumbled for his glasses and shoved them on and it was almost painful how he looked at me, full of heat and wanting.

'Holy fucking hell, Fi,' he breathed, scraping my nipple with his thumb and then soothing it with his palm.

I tossed my head to the side, barely able to breathe. I couldn't understand why he wasn't getting on with it, why he was driving me crazy with the lightest of touches, but I was so wound up, I was a little afraid of what would happen if he went to town on me.

He groaned, low and tight, as he filled his hands with my boobs. 'I want to fuck these.'

I nearly swallowed my tongue. 'You did not just say that,' I managed through the haze of sensation he was strumming over me.

'Sorry,' he murmured. 'Maybe I shouldn't have.' He gave me

a quick grin and it hit me again that this was Max panting for me. 'I don't want you to think I'm the same as those losers who only see your tits,' he said through his teeth. 'But *damn* they are beautiful tits.'

I shook my head vigorously. 'I think you're the only one—' I swallowed, afraid of the words that were tumbling out, but it was too late to stop. 'The only one who can say that and… make me want it.' Oh, no, it was as though I was drunk and spilling everything.

'Not now,' he murmured with a soft smile, dropping his head to flick his tongue over one nipple. I made an embarrassing wheezing noise and grabbed his head. 'You're too sensitive right now.' Another light rasp of his tongue.

'Don't tell me I'm— Ohhhhh.' I gasped and whined and jerked my legs up when he sucked my nipple into his mouth, letting go again almost straight away.

'Too sensitive,' he repeated on a murmur. 'Just like I said,' he continued, skimming his mouth along my belly and drawing my pyjama bottoms down a little. 'It's a shame. I could have played for longer.'

I tried to scoff a response, but his fingers dug into my butt and pulled down my underwear and then the rude bastard was blowing on me between my legs as he flung my clothes away, as though he knew how little he had to do to make me squirm.

He paused to look at me and lick his lips. 'You even smell good,' he groaned. Swiping off his glasses, he dipped his head and then I was grappling for the headboard and holding on as his mouth devoured me. He scraped his tongue up, deep and slow and firm. Turning his attention to my clit, he sucked and flicked and knew exactly how much pressure to apply to stir me up to panting.

The only sound I could make was a deep gurgle of choked need as he worked me over. The orgasm *loomed*, growing and tugging at its bonds and longing to soar. Instead of me grasping after the elusive pleasure, Max was forcing it on me.

With a slight change in pressure, he teased me with two fingers and I shuddered with the first splinters. 'That's it, Fi,' he rasped. 'Come for me. Now.'

After winding me up so tight I was almost sobbing, finely, carefully, with a flick of his tongue over my clit and a hint of shallow pressure with his fingers, he broke me. I thrashed and moaned and had finger cramps from gripping the sheets and I might have clocked him in the head with my knee if he hadn't caught my legs and held them, pressing soft kisses to my clit as I slowly came down.

My lungs ached. I was so hot and swollen between my legs that I'd swagger like a cowboy if I tried to walk right now. Although it had felt like an hour, I'd only held out for a minute or two before that explosive orgasm. I obviously didn't have any trouble climaxing with someone else.

At least, I didn't have any trouble with *Max*. The reality of what he'd done to me burst like confetti, but I wasn't shocked or confused. I was afraid. He'd promised we'd be okay, but how could I be okay, after he'd effortlessly broken me to pieces?

He flopped onto the bed beside me, leaning his head on his forearm in a cocky pose that reminded me of his confidence with my body. I hadn't expected Max to ever look me in the eye and promise to get me off. I stared at him, soaking in this new facet of my best friend that I'd never suspected was there.

'I hate to think what all the dicks were doing wrong with

you, moppie,' he muttered. 'You were beautiful.'

Beautiful, sensitive, you smell good... I want to fuck these. Was that really how Max saw me? Or was he helping me get this – us – out of my system? He glanced at me and vaulted up. I didn't want to know what he saw on my face.

'It's okay,' he whispered, smoothing my hair back from my face. His thumb brushed my cheek and I realised with a distant kind of alarm that he'd wiped away a tear.

'M-Max?'

'I'm here. I'm always here.'

But would he be, if we followed where this led – and then destroyed each other, when feelings changed? I was leaving soon. Maybe this could be a short and very enjoyable blip in our friendship, something we might reminisce about with a chuckle in years to come: *'Remember that time you were so horny I had to eat you out and you came in, like, thirty seconds?'*

I couldn't picture that happening for real.

He slipped on his glasses – he was far-sighted, I knew, so he needed them to see my face up close – and studied me. I was scared and mixed-up and still tender from a mind-blowing orgasm, but I was certain he was too far away and slipped an arm around him and tugged. His response was to roll on top of me, framing my face with his hands.

The press of his erection was obvious and there was only one direction I could go – forwards. I tipped up my chin. He stilled, his eyes hot, then he dipped his head. The gusts of my laboured breaths mingled with his as we hesitated. His eyelids lowered. And he feathered his lips over mine, so light, so sweet; that kiss had no business being so incredibly tender.

I lifted my lips again and with a deep breath, he kissed me, harder this time. I darted my tongue out, needing to taste him, and when he opened his mouth on mine, it felt strangely as though this wasn't the first time we'd kissed in private, for the pure joy of it.

It felt like a riddle that, after fifteen years, I finally understood.

Chapter Twenty

One graze of his lips became another, which became several quick nips to my jaw and then another scorching kiss. His mouth was firm on mine, his tongue insistent – magic kisses with a life of their own. He'd nudged my thighs apart with his knees and settled heavily over me with the occasional abortive thrust, as though he didn't quite trust how on-board I was with this.

He was holding back and the look on his face was the hottest thing I'd ever seen.

He adjusted his glasses and sat back on his knees, his gaze raking thoroughly over me, before he took them off and tossed them on the floor. I went straight for the waistband of his boxers and pulled and I think I said, 'Fuck. Me,' aloud when I finally had him in my hands. Because he was really, fully erect, long and hot and hard and while now was definitely not the time to get out the ruler, I suspected he hadn't been exaggerating about the eight inches. He grabbed for the top of the headboard and hissed as I scraped my palm over the plump head, curling the fingers of my other hand around the base.

'Was that an... invitation?' he asked between breaths. 'Please tell me that was an invitation.' His tone, a little playful, coaxing, was so typical of Max when he was leading me astray.

It was the tone he'd used to drag me into the Cristiania commune in Copenhagen and a sex club in London, which we'd fled right back out of again because… apparently we'd been waiting for this moment to cross that line.

My mouth watered as I played a little longer. 'A friendly fuck?' I asked lightly. 'Is it your turn now?'

He grabbed my thigh, more tightly than I would have expected. 'Yes,' he said, his tone dropping. 'My turn to make you come again – with my cock.' The words sizzled up my spine. The speculative look in his eyes suggested he'd worked out that I liked hearing him talk like that. 'You don't need an orgasm any more, but it's my turn to make you have another one anyway. I want to make you feel how hard I am for you, how I'm flipping out because you are so beautiful when you're aroused and I can't believe you'd let me do all the stuff I'm thinking about doing to you.'

Holy shit, I had not been prepared for that.

'I'll tell you everything later,' he added with a hint of a smile, as though he could read my thoughts. He dropped his hands to the bed and leaned down to press a quick, hard kiss to my mouth. 'Don't worry. I won't push you too far.'

He hopped off me and I lay there, wondering what was happening, why I hadn't seen this joyful lustiness in Max all along, and how my skin could be so achy again already. And how I could be missing him, when he was only across the room… rummaging in my suitcase. I propped myself up on my elbows.

He straightened, holding up the foil packet he'd been looking for in the zip pocket along the side of my suitcase. 'You still keep them in the same place.'

'You don't have any of your own?'

He laughed, striding back to me with a spring in his step. Collapsing on top of me again, he buried his face in my neck and nuzzled my ear. His hand urged my thigh up and it all made such complete sense, even though my brain should have been exploding with the combination of familiar affection and brand-new dirty talk.

'I'm pretty sure mine are out of date,' he murmured against my shoulder, then he sank his teeth into my neck, making me squeal.

'You should ask a woman before you bite her,' I panted, clawing at the sheets as he kept nibbling, more gently, now. I had never realised my neck was such a wild erogenous zone, but maybe it was just Max's mouth. He'd leave a mark and I would revel in it tomorrow.

'Sorry,' he panted. 'Your neck makes me crazy. Can I do it again?'

I could barely answer, my throat was so tight. 'Y-yes,' I choked out.

With a heavy exhale, he slid his palms down my arms and linked his fingers with mine and the action pinched so deeply, I might have called everything off if I hadn't been completely out of my mind with wanting. Then he raised my arms slowly above my head and gripped both of my wrists in one hand and a new shiver of anticipation started up, along with a throb that echoed through my whole body.

'Look at you, moppie,' he mumbled, his jaw slack. 'Are you really here for me?'

An alarming crack opened up somewhere deep inside me. The bite? Sure, yes please. But the gentleness in his voice, the nickname that reminded me that this was my best friend, *that* was what I was worried I couldn't take.

When he skimmed his hand over me, settling on my thigh, the flirty lightness warped and deepened and I scrambled to prepare my emotions for everything I could sense was coming. Slipping his hands around the back of my knees, he urged my legs up.

'You'll have to take it deep,' he murmured into my ear. 'I don't think I can manage anything else tonight.'

My hair stood on end. 'Yes,' I muttered, the anticipation making me claw at him.

He lifted himself far enough to grasp his cock, press the condom down the length, and then guide the head to where we both wanted it, all without breaking eye contact. I wasn't sure how clearly he could see me, so I murmured reassuringly, but the hitched moan as he pushed in the first inch wasn't on purpose.

'Okay?' he asked through gritted teeth, panting over me.

'Yes!' I assured him, the word emerging from my mouth like a sob. 'Please, yes!'

With a tight grip on my knee, he pressed further in with a hiss and a guttural curse that could only have been in Dutch. He seemed to trip all sorts of little alarms in me until I was going off like a police light, panting as he eased all the way in.

He stayed pressed tight for a moment which we both seemed to need, if his gaping mouth and haggard breaths were an indication. The pressure rode up, from a pounding throb where the base of his cock surged against me, to a less-defined sensation winding up inside.

Pressing my knee back, he propped himself up with his other arm and he hadn't been kidding about deep. I whined and shifted, my hands groping for his butt cheeks for some way to relieve the pressure, and then he lost it with a drawn-out groan, jerking against me so hard, I gasped.

Thrusting again, he lost grip on my knee and fumbled for my butt with an inarticulate grunt. My vision blurred, but not so much that I couldn't make out his expression – tight and just as overcome with sensation as I felt.

He blurted something out, but I had no idea what. All I was aware of was his cock riding me hard, a fierce rhythm, the pound of his body against mine, over and over. I pulled his hair. His fingers gouged my thigh.

Then his mouth was at my neck again, nipping in a frenzy that made my eyes roll back in my head. 'Max!' I cried.

'Yes,' he groaned. 'You know who's fucking you.'

'Max,' I repeated on a whimper, wrapping my arms around his neck as the pressure inside me rose up, ready to break. His teeth sank into my shoulder and everything went white as the climax ripped through me. I clung to awareness, needing to see him too, but he was already with me, the bite digging in as he drove hard, coming with a cry and a jolt of relief.

He settled his forehead against my shoulder, gasping for breath, and it felt strange that I hadn't previously known I could feel like this – that *he* would feel like this – with me.

'You...' I wasn't even sure how to finish that.

He lifted his head, his white hair falling over his forehead, his expression dazed and rueful and utterly gorgeous. 'Me,' he said with a twitch of a smile. I pressed a light kiss to his lips and he nuzzled my chin. With a sigh, he pulled out and collapsed next to me, scraping off the condom and holding it off the bed until he caught his breath. He reached for his glasses and shoved them on.

'You... bite,' I said softly, rolling onto my side. It was the strangest sensation. As he smiled at me, I was looking forward to whatever this moment would be with more anticipation than anything in recent memory – even more than the two orgasms that had felt as necessary as breathing.

'I bite,' he repeated with a chuckle. 'Does that surprise you?'

'I… yes.' Our gazes met for a hesitant moment. 'I suppose I assumed… if I'd thought about it…' I reconsidered this topic of conversation before I'd even finished the sentence, but Max cocked his head and prompted me.

'You assumed?'

'From everything you've said about your partners in the past, I thought *I'd* be the… one on top. Oh, shit, is that awful to say?'

His smile dimmed and I felt suddenly cold, worried I'd ruined the moment, but he pressed a kiss to my forehead and shook his head. 'I get it. Just give me a second.'

He hauled himself off the bed and disposed of the condom. When he returned, he slipped under the blanket and faced me – the weirdest sleepover we'd ever had.

'I know you're worried about sex and power dynamics, but this is *us* we're talking about. Sex doesn't change us that way. I didn't bite you to try to dominate you.'

'I didn't mean that,' I assured him, even as his words made my thoughts spin. 'You know I liked it. I was just surprised. Are you like that with everyone in bed? Guys too?'

'This is really what you want to talk about right now? Whether I bite other people and how it works if I'm with a guy?' Actually, yes. I was dying to know. With anyone else, I wouldn't even dare wonder, but this was Max. He was too important to me not to understand, especially now I was realising I'd projected my own weird experiences of sex onto him. 'The answer is… it depends,' he said. 'Sorry if that's disappointing.'

'It's not disappointing,' I said peevishly. 'It's just… I never thought there was so much I didn't know about you.'

'Now you know,' he said softly. 'I don't always bite, but… I wanted to bite you.' The words seared onto my brain somehow, adding a layer of twisting emotion to everything Max and I had ever done together. 'It's… new – with us. Sex is different with everyone, right?'

I felt the truth of his words under my skin. *Everything* was new with us which is why I had no idea what to do or think – how afraid I should be of all the changes.

I was making a big deal out of this. I concentrated on dragging air into my tight lungs. No matter what happened in the present, it wouldn't colour the past. I couldn't let it change how I thought about Max and every wonderful memory we'd made together.

'And with guys,' he continued, 'sometimes I give it, sometimes I take it, sometimes it's different entirely. Sex doesn't have to be just penetration and you don't have to have one dominant person.' He eyed me, sensing he was blowing my mind a little bit. 'Poor moppie, you've never slept with anyone with an imagination before?'

'Obviously not an imagination like yours,' I muttered. 'I wouldn't have asked except… it's us,' I explained with a gulp.

'You already know too much.'

I kind of felt as though I didn't know enough.

'But…' The lines of his face were starker somehow, as he considered his words. 'I'm more careful these days – with myself. Don't worry.'

I knew he was talking about Gustav, his boyfriend in

Freiburg, where he'd had no guidance and only deep insecurity from ambivalent and disapproving parents. Max had idolised Gustav, who'd never pictured their relationship as anything more than physical. Max had learned the hard way that sex could be good and hurtful at the same time.

It had certainly felt as though he'd managed to move past it. That joy in the act just then… I would remember that for the rest of my life and that was all him.

He brushed the hair back from my forehead and pressed a kiss there and I felt keenly the privilege of being his closest friend. 'If we'd done this a few years ago…' he began, but trailed off.

'You wouldn't have told me you wanted to fuck my boobs?'

He had the nerve to smirk at me, but there was enough puppy-dog-eagerness in his expression as well that I was almost ready to ask him to tell me everything he had in mind. 'That just kind of came out.'

'You're making me wonder what else might come out next time.' As soon as I said it, I realised how much we had to talk about. 'If— you don't have to— I don't know what…'

'Moppie,' he said gently, plucking off his glasses and rubbing his eyes, 'can we just roll with it for a little while? We can talk it through if you want, but I'm not sure right now is the best time.'

I certainly wasn't thinking straight, so he had a point. 'When did you get so wise?'

'It's called "learning from your mistakes",' he said wryly.

'Yeah, I'm not very good at that,' I admitted softly.

He pulled me to him and settled my head on his shoulder, taking the time beforehand to fluff up his pillow so I could nestle comfortably against him. The sensation of his skin on mine was consuming and my thoughts scattered as tiredness thickened in my limbs.

The last thing I heard before I went to sleep was a murmured sentence that showed exactly how well he knew me. 'No, Fi. You're just no good at *making* mistakes.'

Chapter Twenty-One

Saturday dawned brilliantly, with September sunshine peeking around Max's curtains like a larking voyeur as he pressed me into the mattress and we went another round of our new joint hobby. Then he made coffee and slices of heavy German rye bread with pepper paste and chives and we fought over the local newspaper.

Nothing had changed and yet everything had. Max had been right last night. I was very not ready to talk about it.

'Morning!' Max's housemate Miska said as she breezed through the kitchen to the fridge. 'So much for the "just friends" thing, hey?' I sucked my coffee through my nose and spent the next few moments spluttering. Miska glanced back from the fridge with a chuckle. 'I haven't heard noises like that through the wall for a long time.'

'Maybe I should get a hotel room,' I mumbled through gritted teeth after she'd swept out of the kitchen again.

Max studied me seriously for a moment before giving me a quick smile. 'Or I could just get a gag.' I decided he was joking, although I wondered.

I'd decided it was time to take my destiny into my own hands and buy a dirndl for that day's challenge – waitering in a beer tent. Although we might have earned good tips by cross-dressing, I would never expose Max to the obnoxiousness of drunk people and this way I could choose my own outfit.

Max had a fit of laughter when I met him and the others at the Theresienwiese after my morning shopping. I had perhaps overcompensated. The blouse of my dirndl buttoned right up to my neck and the bodice was less S&M nipple device and more Nanny McPhee, although it was a pretty sky-blue colour that reminded me of Max's eyes.

I should have known the day would go downhill after the beautiful start. The first thing that went wrong was that Max reached for my hand and I pretended I hadn't noticed. But I noticed everything about his reaction to my panicked rebuff, from the bob of his Adam's apple as he swallowed to the tightness in his jaw. The remorse pulled me in too many different directions.

I felt as though I'd become someone else. The old me would never in a million years have slept with Max. It unnerved me and I didn't know what to do next and I hated the feeling.

Did he seriously want to hold my hand in public? Why, when we'd go back to being friends when I went home next week? It wasn't like I'd call him every week, chatting manically about everything, like always, but flash him my bits at the end. Actually, that idea had its appeal, but I still couldn't go public about the development in our relationship until I understood what was going on.

'Are you okay, Fi?' Ryan asked suddenly and I realised I'd missed a strategy talk and probably had a strange grimace on my face.

'Yes,' I snapped. 'This is for team points. We pool our tips at the end and whichever team gets the most tips wins.'

'And Max is going to train us on how to carry beer mugs.'

I immediately pictured this 'training' with Max's arms around me, my back to his chest, as he demonstrated hefting a bazillion beers while brushing his forearm along my nipples and it didn't matter that I was buttoned up like someone out of Downton and had had three orgasms in the past twenty-four hours, the Max-lust was back.

'It can't be that hard,' I blurted out. I was acting strangely. Any minute now, Isobel would grab my shoulders and declare that she just *knew* that Max and I had had sex and I would panic. 'Er, I was employee of the month last night,' I insisted, nearly choking on my words when Max's lips quirked and I picked up on the double meaning. 'At Snaketooth,' I added.

'You were serving half-litres at Snaketooth,' Max explained, frustratingly unruffled. 'Here, there is only the Maß, a full litre. And everything we drop comes out of our tips.'

'Shiiiiit,' Isobel muttered.

'Can I order one already?' Florian asked, holding up the camera.

'If you want it over your head,' Tanya retorted.

'If you want to drink it through your asshole, asshole,' Isobel added.

I shared a glance with Max. Our chances of winning this challenge weren't good.

* * *

'Then you put them against your chest and hold your arm around them like this.'

I wasn't sure whether to laugh or faint. Max's arm was curled around me as he demonstrated how to support the weight of six enormous glass mugs of golden, frothy beer.

The gust of his breath at my ear and the shudder of his chest against my back suggested he was laughing. The temptation to poke him was overwhelming, but my hands were currently clutching mug handles for dear life.

'I can't do that,' Tanya said with a sharp shake of her head.

'You can,' Max said gently, dropping his arm. 'Try five. Hold them closer to you and you'll spread the weight.'

We stood in the tiny staff area of the Fuchsbräu tent while outside the chaotic babble of the punters droned ominously. It wasn't even lunchtime, but the band was already drowned out by the high spirits of the crowd.

'It's hard work,' Max continued, 'but we only have to do it for five hours. The Bedienung here, the wait staff, usually work twelve-hour shifts.'

A woman in a green dirndl swept into the staff room and her face lit up when she saw Max. This had already happened several times. This woman was young and pretty and looked beautifully proportionate in her dirndl and as much as I understood how it felt to be happy to see Max, she didn't have to squeeze him quite so tight, did she? They exchanged a few words in German and just as each time before, she expressed her disappointment that he wasn't staying for the rest of the Volksfest.

As we stepped out to survey the enormous tent, with its ribbons and nostalgic agrarian decorations and thousands of bobbing heads, I muttered, 'You're popular, here.' Urk, I was such a bad friend.

'You're cute when you're jealous,' he quipped. 'Not so cute when you're pretending we didn't spend last night fucking.'

I blushed to the roots of my hair and hoped no one was watching. Who even was he? 'It's not any of their business!'

CHAPTER TWENTY-ONE

'Are you ashamed that you slept with me?'

'Can we not have this conversation here?' I hissed. 'You promised we'd be okay.'

'We are okay, even if you're ashamed. *I* don't regret anything and I knew I never would.'

The funny thing was, I believed him. He was challenging me and prompting me, but I didn't doubt he still valued our friendship and apparently he was completely okay with everything that had happened last night.

'I'm not ashamed,' I insisted. 'I'm…' *Terrified of losing you* sounded lame, especially since he was acting like our friendship wasn't affected. But last night had already proven that I hadn't known him as well as I'd thought. 'I'm processing,' I finished, gritting my teeth. 'And I'm not cute, even when I'm jealous.'

'But you are jealous.' It wasn't a question. 'I want to kiss you right now.'

Gulp. 'If by "kiss" you mean another make-out session, then that's not a good idea for a variety of reasons.'

'Maybe I could control myself,' he said, his voice high. I only had to give him a hard look and he ceded with a shrug. If he kissed me now, I wasn't sure *I* trusted myself to stop and I was supposed to be the responsible one. 'You can make it up to me, later,' he purred as he brushed past me.

He led us to the manager of the tent, the 'Wirt', a man called Stefan, who shook our hands hurriedly. Stefan smoothed his slicked-back hair and eyeballed Max. 'Und du übernimmst die *persönliche* Verantwortung, gell?' he said in a concerning tone.

I understood enough to work out it was a veiled threat that Max would pay if anything went wrong. Max had apparently called in a favour to allow us to work in the tent at all – that and the promise of passing on all of our tips, after we'd counted them. I was much less willing to work for Stefan for free than I had been for Max, but there was more riding on us today.

Our patch was an awkwardly-placed set of ten tables in the furthest corner. They were packed with punters and very thirsty. Max suggested we remain in pairs at the beginning until we'd worked out the gig and we lucked out with a table full of visitors from Spain and another from England, so at least our wobbly German wasn't a problem. Isobel adjusted her boobs and tossed her head, dragging Tanya into the fray while Ryan tried frantically to introduce Marco to the concept of a customer-service attitude.

Max quickly left me on my own when it was clear that my German was functional and he would be more efficient by himself. I think he single-handedly earned half of our team's tips. He was a flirt, a clown, a tour guide or a confidant, depending on what worked best. I was itching to photograph him for another marketing shot. He could sell beer to a teetotaller and it struck me as absurd that his skill was underpaid and disregarded. Max was irreplaceable.

He stole the table of Australians off me, charming them with his convincing accent. After their third drink, they dragged him up onto the bench with them, threw their arms around him and sang 'Ein Prosit' into his ears, although it sounded more like, 'Ein Prosit, ein Prosit, day Google flight,' because they couldn't pronounce 'der Gemütlichkeit'.

I was left with a bunch of day-trippers from a river cruise with about seven hundred years between them who requested 'seniors' portions' of everything, which I was most definitely not allowed to give them. They managed half a chicken and a beer each, with many awkward trips to the toilets. The oldest lady, stooped and Swedish, enjoyed the Blaskapelle, the traditional brass band, so much that I couldn't resist helping her up onto the bench for half a song, until I started to wonder how comprehensive her travel insurance was and how many times her family would kill me if something happened to her.

The tips weren't astronomical from my oldies, but I'd weirdly had fun. I also wished I'd paid higher tips in the past. The people who did this job twelve hours a day for eighteen days and somehow kept their sense of humour were my new heroes.

Isobel convinced me to unbutton my blouse so I showed a tiny hint of cleavage. I told myself it would help me stay cool while I walked my beer marathon between the kegs and the tables.

The afternoon had its share of leering drunks and clicky, demanding fingers, but I passed the hours with a smile on my face – until the smile was wiped off by a hand on my butt. I was holding six beers to my chest and I stopped so suddenly they sloshed down my boob crack.

'Is one of them for me, love?' Another pat on my butt. What was it with dudes and butts?

It wasn't someone from our patch. No tips needed to be sacrificed. I took a moment to gather my fucks and then swung to face him.

I nearly dropped the beers when I recognised another face at the table – thankfully *not* the person who'd groped me. 'Dollersen!' I cried, before I'd considered that it might have been better to hope my new boss, the guy responsible for confirming my promotion, didn't recognise me. A chorus of swear words rang in my head.

He peered at me, suddenly appearing sober enough that this encounter really didn't bode well. 'Fiona Butkus? What are you—?' He laughed, slapping his thigh. 'This is the next part of your challenge? Wow, you are going above and beyond.'

'Bring the beer, darling!' the first man called out. 'Come and lean over me while you put them down.' I froze, hesitating over a cutting retort. I'd never had panicky thoughts about getting fired before. I'd always been too good at my job. For the first time, I asked myself if I was in serious trouble here. And I still considered dumping the beers over their heads, paying Max back for the lost revenue and giving Dollersen the finger. What had come over me?

I searched out Max in indecision and he met my gaze in alarm. I could handle this on my own, hopefully without losing my job, but I just wanted to reassure myself that he was still as wonderful as he always had been.

Chapter Twenty-Two

An arm snaked over my shoulder. 'Bram Dollersen, big guy in beer, right?' I froze as Florian extended his hand to Dollersen without letting me go. Okay, now I rather wanted Max to come – quickly. 'Florian Weber, local celebrity, and current manager of this darling.'

'Manager?' Dollersen repeated.

'The Wiesn-Chellenge. Have you heard of it?' He was such a dick. What was he up to?

'I've heard of it, but I haven't heard of you.'

Hopefully Dollersen was sufficiently tranquilised by lashings of beer to forget this had ever happened.

'What's holding up those beers, darling?' called Dollersen's obnoxious friend.

'She's not your darling and those beers are for someone else,' came Max's voice from behind me. I would have grabbed him in a giant squeeze where I stood if I wasn't currently holding six mugs of Munich's finest Oktoberfest beer.

'Who are *you*?' Dollersen spluttered.

'This is Max Brouwer, my… old friend, who I'm spending my vacation time with. Look, I have to deliver these beers, Mr Dollersen.'

Urgh, 'Mr Dollersen' sounded so lame after he'd laughed at

me and his obnoxious friend had pinched my butt.

'Interesting vacation, Miss Butkus.' I gritted my teeth. Being called 'miss' in this situation felt super patronising. 'But it's good to see you've got an outfit for Monday evening with Hardcastle and Sons, even if it is… that one.'

As though he could tell how close I was to dumping them onto my boss's head, Max guided me by the beers in the direction of our patch and nodded sagely in response to all of my mutterings. 'Bram fucking Dollar-sign! Tell *him* to get his fucking boobs out.'

'Sorry for the delay, guys,' Max said, smiling for the blokes at my table. 'Some asshole tried to hijack your beers, but Fi protected them with all her…'

I rolled my eyes. 'My boobs. I protected them with my boobs, all right. Here, have your beers. Give the money to this klootzak. I have to go wash my cleavage. And pay a fucking tip!'

* * *

Grabbing a wad of hand towels, I leaned heavily on the cracked basin in the staff toilets and stared at my reflection in the mirror, suffering an overdose of cliché. My makeup had worn off, but I had no desire to freshen it up. The boobs that had redeemed themselves so thoroughly last night were in my bad books again.

You've been depressed.

I'd disputed that statement ten days ago, but it still sneaked into my brain at odd times, like now. Max knew about depression. He'd only managed to finish his degree with the help of mild sedatives and the university counsellor. He wouldn't have used the word lightly, as he'd claimed. Had he meant to suggest that I was *depressed* depressed, like when you took away the travel and the cutting jokes, I was a gaping hole of nothing?

I let dicks like Florian and Dollersen get to me, but the stuff Max said worried me more.

The door swung open and there he was, neglecting our tables for me. 'I'm all right,' I insisted, pushing off from the basin and tugging on the hem of my blouse to inspect my sticky beer-bosom. 'Although do you know an emergency dry-cleaner?'

He tugged my hands away and wrapped them in his and my stupid eyes stung. Pulling me into a cubicle, he curled his arms around my neck and pulled my head to his shoulder.

'They're idiots,' I said sharply, but the taste of salt on my tongue brought reality rudely into focus. 'I don't know what's wrong with me.'

Max's arms tightened. 'There's nothing wrong with you. They insulted you and treated you badly. You're allowed to feel hurt.'

'No, I'm not! That's my *boss*, my work. You have no idea how much I put into this job – how hard I've tried to prove to jerks like him that I'm good enough to deserve to be where I am. I'm the only woman at that table – well, not that table, right now.' That was a worry for another day.

'You talk to me every week,' he said gently. 'I know how hard you work.'

'Like I have nothing else to talk about?' I snapped. 'Shit, Max, this isn't your fault,' I wheezed. 'Maybe you should just go and let me hate myself alone for a moment.'

'I'm staying right here,' he said gently, his palm smoothing down my spine.

'What about the tips,' I tried weakly, but his other hand was in my hair, his thumb brushing my ear, and I couldn't have moved if I'd wanted to.

'A table of Italians arrived and the others are doing fine. Besides, those guys you told off handed over an impressive amount.'

I chuckled, although it still sounded dark, even to my own ears. 'I don't... want to do this,' I ground out.

'Do what? Cuddle?'

He said 'cuddle', like innocent and inhibited Fiona, who'd spoken like that when she was twenty-one and still a virgin. It was so sweet it hurt. 'I don't want to think about this... Or lean on you,' I murmured.

'I understand that,' he began. I was already worried about the 'but'. 'But I'm sick of watching you believe it's your fault. Dollersen is the dick. *You* are...'

'A shit friend?'

'So honest and capable and beautiful, you intimidate most people.'

I poked him. 'I intimidate *you*. Are you sucking up?'

'I don't need to suck up,' he said. 'Maybe you used to intimidate me sometimes, but not any more.' His hand sneaked lower. My back hit the chipboard wall of the toilet cubicle, although I hadn't realised Max had pressed me into it. Goose bumps rushed up my skin.

'I could still intimidate you if I wanted to,' I insisted.

'I might even let you,' he murmured, his lips close to mine, and I blinked, wondering what we were talking about now because his tone was making me think of Bedroom Max. 'You deserve a lot better than the way they treated you.'

'I'm probably overreacting,' I muttered, making one last attempt.

His hand tightened on my butt. 'Then I'm overreacting too, because I couldn't stand seeing his hand on your arse or his eyes on your tits.' Goose bumps progressed to tingles and I lost the will to protest in about a second. 'That got your attention,' he mused. Giving a brief nod, he continued, 'If this is what I have to do to convince you… So be it.' His smile sent my feelings scattering. Lifting one slow hand, he tweaked the hem of my blouse so it gaped a little more. 'Let me help you clean up.' I flushed at his suggestion, then froze when the twinkle in his eye hinted at what he meant. He dipped his head, pausing to gust his warm breath over the swell of my breasts, and then his tongue dived between them, making me whimper.

He sucked and licked and poured so much attention onto my boobs that I fumbled for the wall for balance. I barely noticed him dragging down the zip of my bodice and opening the remaining buttons of my blouse, but I couldn't miss the whoosh of cool air when he tugged down the cup of my bra and one popped out. Max hissed and bit me.

'Holy shit, Max, you and your tee—' I couldn't finish the word because he'd sucked the tip so far into his mouth, my nipple rubbed his palate as he scraped his tongue along the bottom. He propped his knee on the closed toilet lid and grabbed for the hem of my skirt. 'What are you—?' I couldn't finish any of my sentences with his hands and mouth on me. Nudging aside my undies, he shoved two fingers up, making me gasp and grab for his shoulders.

His voice was low and urgent in my ear. 'You are beautiful—' *Thrust.* 'And desirable.' Another one, so hard I saw stars.

'You're worth anything – *everything*.' The heel of his hand ground against my clit and I bucked so hard the cubicle shook. A quick, dirty orgasm swelled in my veins and bore down on me. He groaned against my neck, gentling to shallow thrusts. 'I want to make you come a hundred times a day. The way you're shaking with it, so wet, you want this so much.'

I want you *so much,* I silently corrected.

'You and your dirty m—' I cried out as he gave it to me hard again, clamping a hand over my mouth when I made too much noise.

'Come all over my hand, Fi.' With his fingers shoved high, I was glad to obey, biting down on the flesh of his palm as I sobbed with it.

I was wobblier than I wanted to admit to myself when he dislodged his fingers, gently, as though he knew I was so sensitive the touch was almost painful. The towels I'd grabbed a lifetime ago to clean myself found a different use as he mopped both of us up.

'You're so much better than all the dicks,' he said, not meeting my gaze. He just gently fixed my bra and got to work on the buttons of my blouse. 'You're scared and soft and you put others before yourself. I know it's hard, but you're real in a world of fakers; you're glass, in a world of plastic. Not everyone appreciates your beauty, but that doesn't mean you're not beautiful. It means they're wrong. You have so much passion and you're capable of so many things and all I want to do is stand next to you and watch you discover what you really want – then go and get it.'

I would have cut him off halfway through with a sceptical snort, except he'd just detonated me with an orgasm and my nerves were still recovering. He forced me to listen, while his gentle hands took care of me.

It was pure temptation, an easy road to hell, to lean on him and use him to make me feel better about myself.

He sighed and I looked up to find him studying me. 'And fuck you,' he said.

'What?'

'The only things I want to do are to stand next to you and… also fuck you.' A smile twitched on his lips and relief coursed through me that he was letting that moment of truth fade again – for now.

'Erm, you'd probably need to stand behind me for that,' I quipped.

'Good point,' he said sagely. 'We get off work at five.'

'I already got off, thank you very much.'

Touching his fingers to his forehead in a lazy salute, he drawled, 'Happy to be of service.'

He positively skipped back among the vast rows of tables to our patch, even though he had to be suffering a fairly epic case of blue balls.

'Thank God you're back,' Ryan said, swiping the back of his hand along his sweaty forehead.

'What took you so long?' Tanya asked.

'You look like you've been having sex in the toilets,' Isobel said, 'messing the hair. And that spot on your neck is a chupetón, a… love bite!' She broke into a peal of laughter. 'Oh, I can only dream,' she said, wiping her eyes.

I helplessly shared her laughter, avoiding Max's gaze. The way Tanya looked at me, though, made me wonder how long we'd be able to hide from the others that we now apparently couldn't keep our hands off each other.

Chapter Twenty-Three

'Lean over a little more. Yes! Just like that.' I snapped two photos in quick succession, the second catching Max's raised eyebrow at the innuendo in my words.

The Sunday lunch rush at Snaketooth wasn't exactly rushing, so I'd talked him into a few marketing shots behind the bar. I'd forgotten how much I enjoyed taking my own photos and Max was the perfect model. I could spend all day experimenting with the play of light over his arms as he pulled a beer. The movement of each muscle and tendon fascinated me.

'When are you going to take photos of me like that?' Jan asked as he dumped a handful of empty mugs into the sink.

'I'm sorry, but out of the two of you, Max is the hot one,' I said with a straight face. Poor Max snorted beer.

Jan guffawed. 'I thought something was different. You two finally popped!' He gave Max a friendly shove. Max blushed furiously. 'I knew he was into you, Fi.' He draped an arm around my shoulders and squeezed and I belatedly realised what he'd meant by 'popped'. My colloquial German was more than rusty. But what did he mean, he'd known Max was into me? I was still in shock about that little revelation. 'He's never been with a woman since I've known him, but when he talks about you, everything's different.'

Max cleared his throat and gave Jan a subtle shake of his head.

'Um… we're not… talking about it,' I said through my teeth, not wanting Jan to feel awkward.

'Okay, good luck with that,' Jan said after a moment's hesitation.

'But I could… get a shot of both of you. It would be great for the website. The professional photos you got of the food and drink are great, but you want the history, the people, too.'

Max leaned on the bar and crossed his arms. 'We don't have any history. We opened nine months ago.' Jan dropped his arm around Max's shoulders and I snapped the shot of them looking like Jerry and George from Seinfeld, except those two probably would have made a joke about the awkwardness of showing male affection – not that there's anything wrong with that – whereas these two touchy-feelies were comfortable.

'That's crap, Max. You made me taste your first vat of homebrew ten years ago. Then you spat a mouthful all over my shirt when I pointed out that the lactose sugar additive in the recipe came from milk.'

'Urgh, I was an idiot,' he mumbled.

'But some people don't know beer isn't necessarily vegan,' I said. 'It's a great story, really on-brand.'

'Because I am so "on-brand",' Max grumbled.

'All German beer that meets the purity laws is vegan,' Jan said. 'I can't believe you brewed something with lactose!'

'Even in Germany, craft beers with additives are a growth segment,' I pointed out defensively. They both turned to me with identical expressions of disgust. 'I'm aware you're not allowed to call that beer in Germany, but the rest of the world moves with the times.'

'Unfortunately, our business is in Munich, and a little vegan history is no match for centuries of traditional brewing – as the Wiesn makes bloody clear every year.' I hated hearing him so down about Snaketooth's prospects, but that 'bloody', said in a perfect Australian accent, was all our lovely history rolled into one word.

'You'd be surprised, you know,' I began. He didn't want me mixing in his business, but that restriction pinched the longer I spent at Snaketooth. 'The big drinks companies fight with aggressive pricing and enormous volumes which is an advantage, but the market is changing. Low-margin sales volumes are dropping, but in the premium category, demand is there.'

Jan blinked at her. 'I have no idea what you just said. Premium category growth segment sounds like an expensive male prostitute.'

'We're not a premium category,' Max snorted. '*And* we can't fight on price or we'll make even more of a loss! I know you want to help, Fi, but this is not how to do it. *I'm* not the way to advertise this place – and thank fuck for that.' He stalked off, leaving everything unfinished and churning, the immature deadbeat.

'Thanks for trying to help,' Jan said. 'He's… sensitive.'

'I know,' I said emphatically. 'Has he even told his parents about this place?'

'Are you joking? Of course not.' He eyed me. 'Tell me, what are the chances of you two winning this money from the Wiesn-Challenge? It doesn't solve our problems, but it would take the pressure off for a few months.'

'Realistically? I'm not sure. A week ago, I would have said

no chance, but… our team has the most points at the moment, depending on how much we made in tips yesterday, so we'd have a good chance of getting to do the final day challenges.' Which would pit Max and I against the others. Ouch.

'I'm… worried about him,' Jan admitted. I glanced at him in surprise. 'He's putting too much pressure on this, on himself.'

'I know. Look, if things get really bad, then I'll find a way to become a silent investor. I have savings and I want to do it, just not… hopefully not at the cost of…' Max. The thought of something serious coming between us made me nauseous.

'He wants to prove something to you.'

'He doesn't have to,' I insisted. But for some reason, his quiet three AM admissions on the riverbank wafted through my thoughts. He wanted me to see him differently, but I loved the old Max. Now we'd muddied things further with scorching sex. 'I'd better go talk to him.'

* * *

I wasn't surprised to find him out the back with a cigarette which he immediately extinguished, clearing the smoke with his hand.

'Max,' I began, my tone pleading. But I wasn't sure where to go from there. *I don't want to fight* would probably have been the best approach, but instead I blurted out, 'Don't kill yourself with those.'

His gaze rose sharply to mine and I realised my choice of words was even poorer than I'd thought. I knew what he was going to bring up and it hurt already.

'I don't think like that any more, you know,' he said, an edge to his voice. 'Is that why you… you call me to check on me? To make sure my reasons to live are hanging in there?' I wanted to shake him. 'Thanks for adding "sex with you" to that list. It's right on top.' His voice trailed off into a huff.

'I don't call you to check on you,' I retorted. 'I call you because I miss you and I'm lonely when I don't talk to you.' I sat pointedly on the step outside the door and he stretched out next to me.

We'd been sitting like this, one night at the beginning of summer, by the funny little castle on a hill in Freiburg that was actually an old water tower. We'd been sober for once and he'd told me he felt certain he wasn't meant to live to old age. I'd been too upset to contradict him and all I'd managed to do was rough him up and make him promise to come on trips with me when I visited Europe in the years to come.

Even afterwards, it had hurt so much when I thought of how he saw himself in the future: going blind, with skin cancer, and all alone.

'I tried to forget when you told me that, you know,' I added. I'd tried to forget the panic at the thought that he might be right, that his suspicion that he'd die young could be correct.

'I shouldn't have said it. I was being dramatic.'

'No, it was honest, Max, and that's all I ever needed from you. I prefer to know you're mixed-up and struggling, than to worry about what you're not telling me.' Like his feelings right now, whether he was struggling to believe we'd now had sex four times.

'Well, I'm not mixed up any more – at least not like that. It's a better way to give my parents the finger to live a long time and enjoy it, rather than vindicating their impression that there is something fundamentally wrong with their child. Even if I have to work my whole life as a waiter, doing Oktoberfest every year for the extra cash, piling the beers up on my walker. I'm even getting my skin checked twice a year. And I'll do my fucking prostate when the time comes.'

'Good,' I said emphatically.

'That someone will give me a prostate exam?'

I punched him on the arm, but he caught my fist as I withdrew it, pried open my fingers and slipped his in between. The touch flooded my synapses. It made no sense. There were much hotter things he'd done to me that didn't have the power of that finger-tangle.

'I used to have nightmares where you died,' I said, the words tumbling out of me. Ouch, I probably shouldn't have told him that. I hadn't thought about it in years. 'After I got home from Freiburg. I had really weird reverse culture shock. Not from Germany, of course, because our experience wasn't real Germany, but from… that student thing and… you. When you weren't there any more… One time, in my dream, you got hit by a car and I couldn't sleep for a week. It was like I was mourning you and you weren't even gone. It was horrible.'

'Fi,' he ground out, his fingers digging painfully into mine. 'No. You shouldn't have—'

'I started making plans after the time I dreamed you got sawn in half by a falling lift. There were some weird movies mixed in with my real terror that I'd never see you again.'

'Oh, God,' he spluttered, gagging. 'You… started making all your travel plans because you were afraid I'd die?'

I stared past the dumpster into the lush, green canopy in the park behind Snaketooth. September in Munich was like one last hurrah of summer before the trees gave up their leaves and… I went home again.

'I suppose I did. It became the best thing in my life.' *Until I realised* you're *the best thing in my life,* which might have been at that very moment.

'That makes it a little better that I gave you nightmares. I can't believe you— Actually I can. You even… love fiercely.'

The way he said that word seemed to hang between us in a way he hadn't expected and he glanced away. I adored that description of me. It made me want to be the person he saw when he looked at me, the woman of glass.

But he continued, and the illusion cracked. 'It's why I can't let you get too involved at Snaketooth. This is my mess and I will sink or swim with it. You…'

'Me,' I prompted, catching his gaze. He didn't smile at the reference to the first time we'd had sex. His eyes were deep with every year of memories, every moment we'd been there for each other.

'I won't let my messes bring you down again.'

'What do you mean "again"?'

'I don't want you to be afraid for me like that. Don't you think…' He squeezed his eyes shut. 'That year in Freiburg would have been a lot better for you if I had got my shit together sooner.'

'Maximilian Gerard Brouwer, shut your mouth. Don't you dare touch my memories of Freiburg. We were all basket-cases back then and that's what made it so magical. For the first time in my life, I didn't have to have all the answers – I didn't even have to ask any questions – and you wanted to hang out with me. It's not like you cried on my shoulder the whole time.'

'Only sometimes,' he said drily.

'And the rest of the time, you were teaching me to let go and have fun!' I turned to face him fully and we gazed at each other, that year still so alive between us. I'd scratched 'Fi loves Max' somewhere into my brain that year, entirely innocent and naïve and… safe. I'd stubbornly traced the letters every time we'd seen each other since, even as they weathered, but those words were a lot less innocent now. And safe? I didn't want to think about it.

He moved quickly, grasping my head with both hands before drawing me to him with a groan. A kiss was some kind of answer for now. He tilted his head and clashed his lips with mine, pushing and tugging and owning the kiss, even without tongue.

God, his mouth. I needed more, closer. How did he know exactly the right amount of pressure to make me crack? It wasn't quite teasing, it was… aching – firm, raw kisses, like he was holding back so he didn't overpower me.

I knew the taste of him now, the press of his downy lips and the heat of his breath, but the simple, stirred-up kiss blew everything over inside me. I slammed my lips into his with a whimper and he caught me, his hand slipping around the back of my head and cradling me to him. He'd just given me his tongue in a sweeping, burning kiss, when the door behind us banged open and we jumped apart.

'Ah, shit, I'm sorry, you two,' Jan muttered.

'It's okay,' I mumbled, swiping at my mouth to distract myself from the pounding in my veins.

'What's the matter?' Max asked.

'Your friend Florian is here and he's brought a camera crew.'

Chapter Twenty-Four

'I thought you'd be happy.'

I couldn't get my head around Florian. The idiot manipulated me, but then he went and acted like he'd brought me
flowers by bringing his crew to film Snaketooth for publicity
on his channel. Isobel had been winking wildly at me ever
since she turned up half an hour ago when I'd put out the call
for help.

'This place will be overflowing with bookings now.' What
was the problem with all the people in my life? They either
thought far too much of themselves, or far too little.

'It's a great place,' I commented, swallowing my annoyance
at his attitude. 'Do you want to film a tour of the microbrewery too? I could try to convince Max.'

'No, I thought we'd do the next round of truths while I'm
here. I'm in the mood for more nudity, swearing and sexual
tension – or have you found a way to blow that last one?'

'No comment,' I said through gritted teeth.

Florian dipped his head to whisper in my ear, 'I knew he'd
be shit in bed. I ruined you for everyone else, didn't I?'

'You certainly ruined something,' I said with a false smile. I
left Florian to hop up on a bar stool for the palate-cleansing
view of Max making up cocktails, his sleeves rolled up. Gosh,

if anyone could ruin me…

'Why is Florian really here, do you think?' Max asked with a grimace.

'Who knows. He wants us to play a round of truth of dare. Marco will be here in a minute.' I paused. 'A bit of exposure like this should be a good thing, even if it is from him.'

'I need help from Florian even less than I need it from you.'

'Gee, thanks. But you'll take the money from the Wiesn-Challenge, from a competitor?'

'I'll win that money legitimately and I don't think we can call ourselves competitors of a big manufacturer.' He sighed. 'You know I have to make it on my own. This place is… like an extension of me.'

I inwardly screamed at him. That was the problem. He projected too much onto his business and then he didn't believe it could succeed.

When Marco arrived, we gathered around the corner booth that I'd come to think of as 'our table' with trepidation. The velvet bag sat in the middle.

Max had silently slipped a hot cast-iron pan of Kaiser-schmarrn in front of me, a fluffy, broken-up pancake-thing with sour cherries and icing sugar. As far as peace offerings went, it wasn't as good as that kiss, but it was melt-in-my-mouth delicious. There must have been a secret to getting it so creamy without using butter.

'What's the matter with you guys?' Florian asked. 'You look like characters in a movie before the murdering rapist neighbour appears with his spoons. Which one of you is first to go, hmm?'

'His… spoons?' Ryan repeated with a grimace.

'Isobel,' Marco said. 'She's the first to die.'

'What? I have kids at home!'

'Your skirt is the shortest,' Marco explained. 'It could be a compliment. The attractive woman is always the first to die.'

'Short skirts don't mean a thing,' I said, waving my fork at him. 'But Tanya is the one who hangs in there until the end and then calmly shoots the murderer in the face.'

'Yeah, even though she's missing six fingers, a foot and a kidney!' Florian added with glee. My stomach lurched, turning over all the Kaiserschmarrn.

'I can picture that,' Tanya agreed. 'Except if this murdering rapist neighbour had killed all of you and maimed me, I'd probably want to kill him slowly with his own spoons, even though I'm bleeding to death beside him.' Even Florian gulped at that.

He rubbed his hands together. 'Lucky it's daytime and the neighbour is a sex shop, not a murdering rapist.'

'Really?' Ryan asked. 'There's a sex shop next door? Like, toys and stuff, or… services?'

'There's no sex shop next door!' Max called out from behind the bar, making a few heads turn.

Florian shrugged. 'There could have been, in this part of town. Who's taking out the next paper? Max, you'd better join us.'

Max reluctantly came, flinging a tea towel over his shoulder in a move I wished I could have videoed for my sexy marketing campaign with him as the star. He leaned on my chair and nodded at the bag. 'Go on. I have drinks to serve.'

Tanya snatched the bag and pulled one out. We all drew in a breath. When her eyes scanned the slip of paper for several long moments, her brows migrating slowly up her forehead, dread thickened in the air.

CHAPTER TWENTY-FOUR

'What?' Ryan blurted out.

Tanya huffed and set the paper down carefully in front of her. Florian snatched it and read it, a grin stretching. '"What is something you know about someone else, that you shouldn't know?" This is going to be good! Who's first?'

I heard a groan in the back of Max's throat and he pushed off my chair to slip behind the bar, returning a moment later with a bottle and six shot glasses. The herbal tang of Jägermeister reached my nose as he popped the lid and poured the dark liquid. Florian reached for one.

'None for you,' Max grumbled.

'I'll join in!' he insisted. 'I know Fi reads erotic romance novels. I found her stash in Freiburg one day, with all the sexy pages crumpled.' Isobel whacked him on the arm and he shrank back. 'What?'

She snorted. 'I don't think she cares that you know that. She used to lend them to me. Remember that one where they get married for… whatever reasons, and they're not sleeping together, but she makes him promise no sex with anyone else for three months and it drives him crazy. I should try that with my husband!'

'I think I read that one, too,' Max said with a chuckle.

'You liked the description of the hot hero as a "tuning fork",' I reminded him and he burst out laughing.

'It wasn't the tuning fork, it was the fact that he *vibrated*. It just made me think of… other things that vibrate and it sounded weird.'

'Yes, but you can't write in a book that the character vibrated like a vibrator,' I quipped. 'To say nothing of the fact that the toy was definitely not called that back in… historical romance times.'

'There's a bit about handprints on her butt too, I think!' Isobel remembered, giving Ryan a nudge. 'You'll have to do better than that, Florian!'

Florian opened his mouth, but I grabbed his arm and shook my head vigorously. 'He's not playing. And he can buy his own Jägermeister.'

'Afraid of what else I remember?' he asked with a wink and I let go of his arm with flick. Max bristled like mad and I suddenly remembered how hot it was in that book when the tuning fork hero had experienced a fit of jealousy over the wallflower heroine.

Stuck between the desire to keep the conversation kind and the knowledge that an internet audience would award us points, our confessions varied from tame to titillating, getting rowdier after we ordered cocktails and shots and anything that *didn't* contain beer.

Marco knew that Isobel called her husband 'Tarzan' which made her gape and smack him.

'You said it when you were talking to him on the phone in public,' he pointed out. 'I understood a bit because Spanish isn't too far from Italian.'

'It's normally only during sex, but he was lonely,' she said defensively, her words petering out when she realised she'd made it worse.

'Thanks, Jane,' said Max, with a snort of laughter, pulling up a chair next to me.

Ryan knew that Marco had lied on a job application back in Freiburg and forged a certificate. Isobel knew that I'd got wildly drunk at my work do the other night because apparently I'd texted her some gibberish. Her statement alarmed me enough to check my phone, to make sure I hadn't written something about how hot Max was, but I'd just sent: *Google funny shit. Max is coming.*

I tried not to think about all the stuff I knew about Max. Most of it, he'd told me himself, so it didn't count for the question. I knew he'd lost his virginity with a girl at school when he was eighteen, and that Gustav had been his first boyfriend. I knew where he kept his pin numbers and that his usual text password was CatCradle99? after the Kurt Vonnegut book. I knew shoulder massages made him purr like a cat.

My thoughts went a little off-course after that, reminding myself that I now knew which way his cock pointed when it was erect and the filthy words that tumbled out of his mouth during sex. I shifted in my chair.

It took everything I had in me not to blurt out, 'Max is vegan, but he eats pussy,' when it was my turn. The vegan thing was always a cheap shot. 'Umm, Max has a teddy bear in the back of his cupboard called Potato-Face,' I said instead.

'How do you know that?' he spluttered.

'You told me the story when you were drunk in the cabin on the fjord in 2015, and I saw he's still in there. It's sweet,' I insisted. 'You were dating a guy with a kid and he gave you a farewell present when you two broke up.'

'It's not *sweet*. It was a disaster. I should have introduced the "don't meet kids" rule earlier. I would have thrown the bear out if it didn't feel disrespectful.' The word 'disaster' rang in my head, hitting a little too close to home, since I'd said it myself just over a week ago.

Florian had the nerve to meet my gaze. He'd probably made a transcript of that conversation and studied it before each of our encounters in case he needed some fresh blackmail.

'Wait, your ex-boyfriend gave you the teddy bear? That is weird,' Ryan said.

'No! The kid gave me the teddy bear. And I meant it would be disrespectful to the kid, not the teddy bear! She farts in bed,' he said emphatically, nudging my shoulder.

I crossed my arms and gave him a dry look. '*Everyone* farts in bed.' All of the faces around the table were frozen in various stages of cringe. 'Oh, don't give me that. You've all farted in bed at least once!'

'But no one else I know has farted during s—' I shoved a hand over his mouth.

'I suppose the question is how you know that,' Tanya said, sending me a slow, pointed glance.

'They sleep together all the time!' Isobel said with a wave of her hand. 'Even when they stayed with me in Valencia six years ago, I made up two beds and they were together the next morning, like little puppies.'

'I don't think *anyone* has ever compared me to a puppy before,' I muttered. 'Max, I can totally see.' I turned to him. 'A dead puppy,' I whispered.

'When we visited you in Valencia, Fi had just broken up with... which dick was it? Matty or Benno or some other one-syllable nickname that you Australians shorten and then make long again for no reason.'

'You've had your turn,' I grumbled.

'Everyone's had their turn,' he replied, looking around the table. 'Except... Tanya.'

Eek. I could already see her casually telling everyone that Max and I were sleeping together, except that wouldn't be clear enough, as our previous conversation had proven. She'd have to say 'having sex' and then I'd die on the spot.

She glanced at me briefly before calmly tearing the piece of paper to shreds. Then she surprised us all. 'My husband is impotent.'

Well, now my fart confession felt trivial.

'You mean like premature ejaculation? Because that's pretty normal at our age with kids and life and stuff,' Ryan said. He belatedly choked. 'So I hear.'

'No, I mean he's impotent. He can't get it up. At all.'

'But you have kids!' Ryan said.

'I *really* wanted those kids,' was all she said in response.

'Wait,' Florian said, 'you'd be expected to know that about your own husband, so it isn't a secret you shouldn't know. It doesn't count.'

'I shouldn't have said it anyway,' Tanya muttered. Colour had risen on her cheeks, but I wasn't sure whether she regretted saying it in front of the camera or regretted telling us anything at all.

'He'll edit it out!' I said sharply, giving Florian side-eye. Tanya was the strongest of all of us. I didn't like thinking her marriage could bring her down.

She huffed and crossed her arms over her chest. 'He wishes I didn't know. But fine. Edit it out.' She paused, her expression grim, and then announced, 'The secret I know is that Fi and Max are having sex.'

Chapter Twenty-Five

I was certain they'd all hear my blood rushing in the silence. Where had all the other patrons gone? Were they all staring at me, judging me for ruining fifteen years of friendship for a few wild orgasms? Breathing felt like wrestling reluctant air into my lungs.

'With who?' Isobel asked with a quizzical smile.

Tanya groaned. 'Each other!'

'Like…' She made a jerky hand gesture involving an outstretched finger.

'Do you need me to explain it to you, Isobel?' Florian asked with a snort.

'But…' Her confusion dug deep into me. Florian could fuck off, but what could I say to Isobel? I knew what question was coming and it landed, cold, in my stomach. 'Are you… together then?'

'Fi and Max were probably more together *before* they started having sex,' Tanya said. I wished I didn't understand what she meant. 'I'm quite annoyed. If I choose sides, it has to be Fi, but I will feel sad for you, Max.'

'I… appreciate it?' he mumbled.

Florian leaned into the table and looked into the camera, which, mortifyingly, was still running. 'Und das war's! Wette verloren, Alter! Der Bums-o-meter schlägt wieder zu. It's official! They're doing it. I win again!' He reached around and switched off the camera.

'What was that about a bet?' Max asked as I pressed a hand to my forehead and took a big gulp of my Hugo.

'One of my followers thought you were hot and I let them down gently,' Florian explained to Max. 'They didn't believe you were into Fi, so we had a little bet. I won, but the odds weren't great. Most of my followers thought you were already fucking last week.'

I choked on my drink, elderflower and prosecco shooting up my nose.

'I would have to choose Fi, too,' Isobel said, her expression tormented. 'But it would break my heart.'

Max leaned heavily on the table and covered his eyes with his hand. 'Can we skip the break-up plans and any further bets? Yes, we started sleeping together… really…'

'Fucking,' I said with a roll of my eyes. When he glared at me, I leaned close and said, 'What? You have no trouble saying the word in bed.' It was Ryan's turn to choke on his margarita.

'It's not Armageddon,' Max continued. 'We're not twenty any more. Give us some credit for being adults about this.'

'We were *not* adults at Freiburg, were we?' Isobel exclaimed. 'Remember that vomit-basin in the toilets at the student residence? We used to take bets who could get it in there from furthest away!'

'I think I blocked that out,' Ryan said, his face green-tinged.

And just like that, the group seemed to move on from the fact that I'd crossed a forbidden line with my best friend. If only I could let it go so easily. Max grabbed my hand under the table. It felt like 'I told you so', but, when I glanced at him, his expression was still grim and that was worse.

Being the pessimist was my job. Max was supposed to tell me everything would be okay and then describe in explicit detail what he wanted to do to me in bed. He wasn't supposed to acknowledge the gaping uncertainty of what would happen when I left after Oktoberfest.

I told myself firmly that *nothing* would happen. Our friendship would definitely survive this. The sex was so good that even I would become an optimist.

* * *

Tanya followed me into the bathrooms later in the afternoon, when Florian had thankfully left us alone again to do more of his influencing. 'I'm sorry, Fi,' she said bluntly. 'I couldn't think of anything else.'

I shrugged and squeezed some soap onto my hands. I was so mixed up, I wasn't sure whether to grumble at her or absolve her. Max didn't seem to mind everyone knowing.

'It's just,' she continued, 'I would like to win. I know the chances aren't good, but if there was a way...'

I blinked at her in the mirror. 'The Wiesn-Chellenge is that important to you?'

'No, the money is,' she retorted. 'For *me*.'

I turned the tap off slowly as concern crept up my spine. 'You want to leave Carson,' I whispered. She nodded curtly. 'Oh, shit, Tanya. He hasn't hurt you, has he?'

'Not anything that truly does damage. I'm not worth the effort. He's too busy hurting the people who tell stories on him in the media.' I clutched her arm. 'Don't say you're sorry. I'm strong enough for this. But money always helps.'

'If you don't win, I can—'

'It hasn't come to that, yet.'

'Your move to Australia,' I said suddenly. 'You're getting the kids out. The courts should protect you.'

She nodded, giving a small sigh that was all the weakness Tanya would ever show.

'If I can help—'

'I shared this with you as an apology, so you understand I didn't betray your secret willingly, but I don't expect anything. I know Max needs the money badly too. Back in Freiburg, we could borrow five euros for lunch, or even fifty euros to see us through until our stipend was paid. Now we have thousands, but we need thousands more, and we're in more trouble than ever,' she said bitterly.

'And then I'm standing here, with none of the responsibilities and all the money and no one will take it from me!'

She chuckled, with kind condescension that reminded me how much more of life she'd experienced than I had. 'Max can't take your money because it's not your money he wants.'

'Well, that's abstruse.'

'He wants *you* – committed, loving, *everything* with you.'

I couldn't help laughing, but it was tight and uncomfortable. 'Max doesn't do committed, loving *anything*. I was more likely to keep him when we were just friends. He gave up on relationships a long time ago and I'm not convinced I'd be good for him anyway.'

Tanya regarded me sagely. 'But you want him.'

Panic gripped me, as I imagined having a conversation very similar to this one, except it was Max and I, standing under the harsh lights of the Munich airport. I might suggest we try long-distance and he'd say, 'Long-distance *what*?' and I wouldn't have an answer.

'Fi, are you sure *he's* the one who doesn't do relationships?'

You'd better believe I wiped up my hands and got out of there *fast*.

* * *

Max and I had listened to a lot of Arcade Fire in the dorm in Freiburg and we'd seen them live twice over the years. It was a surprisingly not-weird sex soundtrack. Sex and Max had quickly become a not-weird combination, even when memories were involved.

He could be sunk in deep, all his tendons standing out and his face contorted with the intensity of us together, and I'd still dreamily think of the time we got stranded in Dresden after a freak snowfall and had to sleep curled up in the train station.

The way he felt – the way *I* felt – was so unexpected. In the past, sex had been about touching the right places, giving and taking pleasure. But I didn't even have space to think about that with Max. He didn't touch me with the intent to arouse me – not since we got that first public-service orgasm out of the way. He touched me because he had to, sometimes hard, greedy clutches and sometimes tense, aching strokes.

As the orchestral opening of 'No Cars Go' sounded from the little Bluetooth speaker in the corner of Max's room, he kneeled over me, all panting breaths and hot eyes. Grasping the headboard, he leaned down until the tip of his cock landed on my sternum. We both watched as he traced a slippery path up between my breasts. My mouth watered. My breath was so tight I couldn't even groan.

'Keep going,' I murmured, meeting his gaze with a new shared understanding, one we'd built only a few days ago, the first time he'd held my naked breasts in his hands. It was so similar to the years of in-jokes and knowing looks and yet… entirely different.

Watching his own actions with an expression somewhere between wonder and pain, he grasped my breasts and pressed them over his cock. With a choked groan, he thrust hard, rocking the bed. He was on edge already and it was the hottest thing I'd ever seen, Max trying desperately to hold off, while his body went wild for me, grinding and pumping, his grip growing painful.

I arched up, lifting my arms to the headboard to offer him everything, and relishing the feeling of him taking what I offered, rough and raw and frantic. The sheen of sweat on his body shimmered in the slanting morning light and I wanted to hold onto that image for all of my fantasies in the years to come.

'Your tits,' he ground out, too far gone for anything more. 'I'm going to come and it's going to make a mess.' Even that sounded hot.

'Then make a mess,' I dared him, dropping my hands to hold his where they were.

He grimaced. 'When did my fantasy Fi take over the real one? Ohhh, yeah.' His voice was tight and rough, his words tumbling out from deep inside. 'These tits. I'm going to make a mess all over you.'

Then he stiffened and jerked, as his cock pulsed between my boobs, and I could only whimper with relief along with him as hot liquid burst onto my skin, spilling up my chest and down my shoulders. It was sticky and spicy and he was the only person I would ever allow to do that to me. Seeing how much he wanted it, how he bowed with the force of his climax, made me feel like the hottest person in the world – maybe the *only* person in the world.

He took a few breaths to recover and then, brimming with energy, he sank between my legs and latched hard onto my clit, making me squeal. He spread his come all over my nipples as he played there, working me with his mouth and his other hand, and I came so hard I could have sung the organ parts on that Arcade Fire album.

After soothing me through the come-down with kisses and laps of his tongue, he collapsed onto the bed beside me, looking decidedly sheepish. The album had finished, but I couldn't have said whether it was while he was fucking my boobs or getting me off. 'I'll clean you up,' he murmured, grabbing his glasses and hauling himself up to dash to the bathroom.

He was thorough with the warm washcloth, biting his lip as he watched the strokes of the cloth over my skin. He met my gaze, my eager, cheerful best friend Max. 'I've never done that before,' he admitted quietly, as he smoothed the cloth along my chest one last time.

'Neither have I.' I paused, watching him drop the cloth to the floor and flop down beside me. 'I'm glad we did it.'

His smile softened and I turned to mush. 'Me, too, moppie.' He pressed a dewy kiss to my cheek and I floated and lifted and expanded, somehow. How had I done without him for four whole years?

Even if we managed to end this fling without hurting each other, how could I go back to just seeing him on video calls, in person only twice a year, if I was lucky? Sure, New York was closer, once the promotion went through, but it was still five time zones and an ocean away.

Give us some credit for being adults about this, Max had said, which was code for keeping our feelings in check. I didn't feel much like an adult about this. I felt like a twenty-one-year-old exchange student ready to get her heart broken.

It didn't bode well.

Chapter Twenty-Six

It was apparently true that everyone loved a romance. When our truth session aired on Monday night, while I was stuck 'entertaining' for work and pointedly not wearing my dirndl, Florian's stats jumped again. The hashtag #FilovesMax trended briefly in Germany. Our team was clearly out in front of all the others, although that could definitely change because the singing round was still to come.

On the Tuesday of the second week of Oktoberfest, the sun burst out, bathing the Munich main square, the Marienplatz, and its ornate, neogothic town hall with warmth. That day's challenge, another race, was due to start on the square at eleven. I wasn't a runner at the best of times and after the work bloodbath (beerbath?) the night before, I was less than enthusiastic. Max was pumped, as usual. I hoped he would carry us.

There was still no sign of Florian or the organisers when the clock chimed, four times for the hour and then eleven deep gongs. Isobel grabbed my arm and pointed. 'Look! The glockenspiel!' Similar murmurs rippled through the large crowd of tourists on the square.

Ryan fumbled for his camera and we all stood side-by-side, watching the jaunty figures judder past on their rails as the carillon played its creepy, slightly out-of-tune song. I could see how the figures might look realistic at this distance, although up close they were probably the stuff of nightmares. There were bearded men with flags and musicians behind them. At the back, an aristocratic couple in funny hats watched the clockwork display with empty eyes.

The figures on the lower level shuddered to life as the next song began, looking distinctly drunk as they whirled past in front of a guy in an even more ridiculous hat.

'They're dancing away the plague,' Max explained with a grin.

'I think the plague might have been less scary than those guys.'

He cocked his head and studied me for longer than was entirely comfortable. I was about to nudge him pointedly with my shoulder, when he said, 'Is that a defensive thing, being cynical?'

'Are you psychoanalysing me, Brouwer? This is definitely defensive, but that means you should watch out!'

He had the strangest glint in his eye, like he was seeing me for the first time, and it *terrified* me. Max was the last bastion of safety for the real me, the flawed, insecure… cynical me. He was supposed to love me no matter what I did, because that was Max. I hadn't thought it was possible to let him too close, but perhaps I'd done it. I hated feeling afraid that he wouldn't like me any more.

I inwardly cringed, waiting for his judgement to land, but instead, he brought his face close to mine, his eyes wide and warm and full of affection. Only a second before he kissed me did his eyelids drop closed.

I could only describe the kiss as 'chaste'. It was the kind of kiss he used to give me on the cheek all the time, but on my lips: a light, cushiony buss, playful and giving and it should not have been enough for my knees to wobble, but my heart was beating strangely and I felt loopy when he pulled back again.

Then I noticed everyone staring at us and gulped.

'Did you just kiss her like you kiss your mom?' Ryan asked, his voice high.

'You kiss your mum?' Max asked with a grimace.

'Not any more. But as a kid, you know. Up until twelve or something, sure. It's normal.'

I was such a mixed-up emotional mess that Ryan's statement made me want to cry. Perhaps it was the weird mid-thirties hormones striking again. I didn't know if it was normal or not to kiss your mum. I was starting to think that 'normal' didn't exist. But I couldn't even remember a time my mum had kissed me *at all*.

The first time Max had hugged me, we'd known each other about two weeks. I'd just found out my oldest sister was getting married and it had freaked me out. I'd made a dash to the kitchen for chocolate (because I'd still naively thought that everyone kept their chocolate in the fridge) and he'd happened upon me while I was all blotchy and standoffish. But then he'd approached and opened his arms wide.

I still don't know why I'd gone into them. My family weren't huggers. They didn't do affection at all. But something made me shuffle towards the stringy boy who liked the same music as I did and let him wrap his arms around me. I could still feel that moment in my soul.

I'd learned in the intervening years that my mother was not the most normal parent, but nobody could hug like Max.

'I think it was a sweet kiss,' Isobel said. 'We don't want to be eaten every time we kiss. I hope you don't stick your tongue in every time you kiss your wife. If my husband did that, he would be out.' Her voice lacked its usual edge and I wondered if she wasn't secretly missing her husband. Her curly hair was a mess today, which was also unusual.

'No! I, uh,' Ryan's sentence petered out. 'I kiss my wife just like they kissed, actually. Maybe you were right when you said they were just as married as the rest of us.'

I felt Max bristle and wished I could grab Ryan and clock him with one of the wooden plague dancers in feathered hats. The last thing I wanted was Max worrying about falling into a committed relationship when he wasn't ready – possibly would never *be* ready. I respected that.

His parents were these creepy twin parts of the same distant and disapproving person and perhaps neither of us should have blamed our upbringing for so much, but it was better than drinking and substance abuse.

The wooden figures were still twirling when Florian swept into the square on an electric scooter. 'Super! You can all tick the glockenspiel off your list of tourist sights now!'

'Shh,' I hissed. 'I'm watching the show.'

'You know I love it when you bite, Fi,' Florian said, his voice low. Max's bristle this time was almost a full raise of the hackles.

'I'm never going to bite *you*,' I assured Florian, but my words were for Max.

When the bells finally fell silent, all of the poor unfortunate souls taking part in the Wiesn-Challenge gathered to hear our fate in front of the giant pole with a golden Mary on top. The monument was a weird, phallic juxtaposition that made me think of revering mothers and chaste kisses.

It was a man explaining the challenge, just as young and covered in branding as the woman who'd hosted the other challenges so far.

'Today's chellenge,' he began, 'is a biergarten race! I have prepared all of you a map.' He handed around a wiggly, hand-drawn diagram, where the only discernible markings were three Biergärten, beer gardens, indicated with mugs of beer. The last one was also marked with an 'X'. 'The first ones to drink a beer at each one will be the winner, with points for second and third place, as well.'

That sounded fairly tame. If the biergartens had half-litres on offer, it would be a rather nice day out, even for someone in their mid-thirties.

'But there's a catch!' Ah. Of course there was a catch. 'You have to move under your own steam, so no taxis between the beer gardens. And… only one of you can move.' I blinked. Had he mistranslated something? 'Take a moment to decide which of you will carry the other one. Decide carefully, because this line—' He gestured to a path marked on the map. 'Is more than six kilometres. One of you must move the other all of this distance. You can stop and rest, but that will make you slower. Choose wisely, my friends!'

'All right, Indiana Jones,' mumbled Ryan. All Max had to do was look at me to communicate that *we* both knew it wasn't Indiana Jones who said that, but the undead knight.

'One partner has to carry the other one for a pub crawl. Do I understand right?' Marco asked.

'You two have a difficult decision to make,' Florian said, gesturing to Max and me and shoving his camera in our faces.

Max tugged on my hand. 'It's not a difficult decision. I'm

transporting you.' He made to grab me around the waist.

'Max! You can't carry me for six kilometres! I weigh more than you!'

'That's an assumption. Muscle weighs more than fat, you know. Come here.'

I took a step back. 'Gee, thanks for the fat comment. Someone's grown an ego just from a few trifling muscles.'

'On your marks!' the organiser called out over the kerfuffle.

'It's not *you*, it's female physiology,' Max continued in an urgent tone. 'I think you understand how much I like your body, so stop arguing and let's go! I have an idea.' He closed his arms around me and hauled me up, slipping his forearms under my butt. I squealed and clung to him as he staggered.

'Get set!' came the shout from behind me.

Over Max's shoulder, I caught sight of Ryan hopping deftly up onto Marco's back and Isobel wrestling Tanya up. Poor Tanya – and poor Isobel. This challenge was stacked firmly against them, as Isobel wasn't much bigger than Tanya and she looked peaked today. Perhaps the first beer would help, before the next two hindered again.

'Go!'

Max bore me out of the square with hurried steps and much grunting. But instead of heading for the park, like everyone else, he took off in the opposite direction. Although my mind swirled with questions, I just hung on to him, remembering his assurance that he had an idea.

'Nothing but your own power!' Florian reminded us. 'Or you'll be disqualified!' I hoped Max's idea was a good one.

Florian followed us, swishing on his scooter, even though it was entirely unnecessary given our current pace. Beads of sweat popped out on Max's forehead and I gripped him more tightly with my legs. 'Put me down and have a rest.'

'Not yet,' he groaned, shifting me. 'We'll be there soon.'

'I can only imagine you're cheating, Brouwer,' Florian taunted us.

'I'm only using my own power,' he ground out. 'A bit of brainpower and some physics, but it will all originate from me.'

'It's so hot when you say "brainpower" and "physics",' I whispered in his ear, making him laugh.

'Are you enjoying this?' he asked, shifting me again until his hands were on my butt.

'Yes. Sorry.'

His smile widened. 'Don't apologise. Making you feel good is one of my goals in life.'

My heartbeat stuttered again, until I told myself it was just sexual innuendo, well within the rules. 'It would be better if you were feeling good at the same time.'

He pressed a kiss to my cheek. 'I will soon. Trust me.'

Even that simple, throwaway line landed on me like a tonne of bricks. *Trust...* What a terrifying thing that was. I trusted him as a friend, without a doubt. But these warping, expanding, out-of-control feelings that kept jumping out at me?

'Thank fuck. Here we are,' he said with a groan, staggering to a cobbled square with a rippling water feature and a row of lime trees. He put me down unsteadily outside a little row of shops with arched windows.

'What now?' I asked.

'Now for the physics.'

Chapter Twenty-Seven

Ten minutes later, I was flying through the park with the wind in my hair, laughing from deep in my stomach. We'd sailed past Isobel and Tanya near the entrance to the park, calling out encouragement while they watched us speed past in dismay.

A beefy guy in lederhosen from one of the other teams was jogging along the creek in front of us, carrying his partner on his back as though he weighed nothing. Max rang the bell and slipped ahead of them while I couldn't help yelling, 'So long, suckers!' and waggling my middle fingers at them as we went past.

Max guffawed behind me, or he tried to, but he was breathing hard from exertion.

I stretched out my arms and stared up at the blue, wispy sky, the crowns of the trees sweeping past at the edges of my vision. The stream pattered past on my left, the Englischer Garten, the giant green lung of Munich, spread out before us, and it felt a bit like life.

'You're brilliant, Max.'

'That's what I like to hear,' he said with a grunt, 'almost as much as, "Yes, Max! Please, more, just like that!"' he said in a teasing falsetto.

'Just when I was having a moment of non-sexual enjoyment!'

I grumbled, but I was smiling too broadly to be convincing.

'You've had far too many moments of sexual non-enjoyment, so you deserve it,' he quipped.

'Speaking of non-sexual, is that a nudist spot?' I asked, peering across the creek.

'Mmhmm, but no stopping today to indulge your new joy in free body culture.' I didn't really want to join them, but there *was* a strange joy in knowing there were places you could go where you could put your saggy belly-button on show and give your cellulite some fresh air. I felt very generous towards my body for the first time in months – perhaps years.

I felt much more generous towards Max's body. He pedalled up a little rise, struggling with the weight of the enormous cargo bicycle he'd rented and me, squashed into the box on the front. But those muscles in his thighs were a bit more than trifling and we made it over the hill.

He manoeuvred us over a narrow bridge that had me clutching the sides of the box in nervousness and a moment later, we pulled to a stop, crunching gravel, near the green lacquered tables of the first biergarten, by the Chinese Tower. Putting a tiered fake East Asian monument in the middle of a public park felt a bit like racist cultural appropriation from two hundred years ago, but the English Garden wasn't exactly English either, so the Chinese Tower would have to be overlooked that day in the pursuit of beer – and victory.

'Sit. I'll get the beer,' I ordered Max as he helped me climb out of the box.

He shook his head. 'You're not allowed to move, remember.' I cursed at how close I'd come to getting us disqualified. He hoisted me up onto his back and hobbled to the nearest table before racing for the counter to order the beer.

A small beer turned out to be half a litre, which would be lethal if it was the only thing offered at the Sydney Cricket Ground during a test match, but Max assured me the legal blood alcohol limit for riding a bicycle was higher than for driving a car in Bavaria. He also grabbed me a pretzel, packed in serviettes, to enjoy on the next leg and if that wasn't true… friendship, I wasn't sure what was.

We filmed each other downing our beers (I was definitely not staring at Max's Adam's apple) and he hauled me back to the cargo bike, leaping onto the saddle and taking off again.

I slowly gained an appreciation for the scale of the park, as Max pedalled furiously along the gravel path, passing playgrounds and kiosks and happy groups sunning themselves on picnic blankets. Babbling creeks of clear water criss-crossed the space. After we zoomed over a wider bridge with wrought-iron railings, Max turned left to avoid a pedestrian-only path and a moment later, a lake opened out beside us.

The still water reflected the lush trees and bushes on all sides and the tufts of cloud. Red and blue paddleboats meandered across to the island in the middle.

'Have we ever rented a paddleboat?' I asked Max.

'We considered it on that lake in Slovenia, but you thought it would be tacky, so we got drunk instead.'

'Wow, because that wasn't tacky at all. I can't believe I didn't remember that.'

'You can't remember everything,' he mused.

'We've done so much over the years, sometimes I look at the old photos and I have more memories of the photo than the actual experience. Like Oslo.'

'You've forgotten a whole city?'

I broke a curve off the pretzel, brushed most of the salt off out of habit, and bit into it. The enormous ones were always so good: fluffy inside, with just the right hint of sweet-sour-salty on the coating and giant cracks along the thick edge.

'I remember that park where I got frostbite and you had to keep swapping gloves with me,' I added.

'I'd forgotten that,' he said with another chuckle that got lost in a grunt of effort as his legs pumped. 'Lucky you'll be gone in the winter, so you can't use my back to warm up your hands.'

'Yeah,' I huffed. 'Lucky you.'

He slammed the brakes on so hard the pretzel nearly flew out of my hand. Engaging the park brake, he leaped off the saddle, leaned over the side of the box and kissed me – hard and rough and with a little nip of his teeth that made me squeak.

Just as quickly, he jerked away and returned to the seat, heaving us into motion with a grunt. I could only turn and stare at him, frozen. When our momentum carried us forward more comfortably, he released a long breath. 'For someone so experienced at making sarcastic jokes, you're terrible at recognising them. Winter or summer, I'd always rather you touch me than not. Do you understand?'

I nodded dumbly, the pretzel swinging from my limp fingers.

Less than a minute later, he braked again, pushing the bike the last few metres into the next biergarten. It was right on the lake, in the shadow of enormous maples and horse chestnuts, the latter already browning with the approach of autumn.

He hauled me out and carried me to a table before taking off for the bar. I stared across the lake, glittering in the midday sun. The air was fresh and cool and I could have sat at that table all afternoon, remembering Max's eyes as he'd scolded me and told me he wanted my hands on him. There were more than a few reasons I wished we could blow off the challenge, but at least we were together.

I was so content, I had to psych myself up when Max returned with the tall half-litre beers and resist the temptation to sip slowly and savour the rich, golden brew.

But when Florian zipped up on his scooter, my idyll splintered and I was ready to go again. Max trundled me back to the bike and set off before Florian could make even one snide remark.

Following a road for a short stretch, we turned off across the meadows, which felt endless and lonely on this side of the park. The creeks flowed fast and clear and there were even some sheep grazing. We swung past another, smaller group of naturists, who waved – thankfully only their hands.

'We're not lost, are we?' I asked, after we'd been crunching over gravel for longer than the other two legs.

'Nope,' he rasped. He was panting, now. 'Give me some credit.'

'I'll give you a lot more than credit when we get home.' I peered over my shoulder to catch his wide grin.

Finally, we pulled up by the entrance to the final biergarten, a little arch with striped poles supporting a sign bearing the name in gothic script. Florian and the woman from the organising team were waiting for us.

'All right, you two cheaters!' Florian said instead of a greeting.

I stood, wobbling a bit in the bike. 'We did not cheat! Max got us here under his own steam and they can't penalise us for finding a creative solution!' I looked wildly to the junior marketing associate for backup.

Max curled his arms around my waist. 'Quick, let's drink our beer. He's just messing with you.'

'As long as that's not an ebike, it counts,' the woman confirmed, peering at the vehicle to confirm it didn't have a motor.

I gave a cheer as Max hauled me out of the bike. He shook with effort as he stumbled into the biergarten. I guessed his knees were wobbly and his thighs burning, but he had a little smile on his face as he bore me to a table and I clutched him tight.

He'd grown up so well. The thought struck me with goose bumps up my neck. He was proud and confident and going after what he wanted and… happy. I had always thought I was all of those things too, but now I'd apparently arrived at a pinnacle in my career, my pride and confidence felt even more fragile and happiness only a fuzzy, ephemeral concept. Twenty minutes ago, the thing I'd wanted most in the world was to go on a paddleboat with Max. Who even was I?

He stumbled and plopped me onto the bench with zero grace, but with one final deep breath, he took off at a jog for the bar. He returned in record time, his forehead shiny with sweat, and plonked the beers onto the table. My hero – or was that 'my beer-o'. Yep, I had not been giving Max enough credit – maybe for years, maybe ever.

'We're not finished, yet. Drink!' Max said urgently.

As we clinked the heavy bottoms of our glasses and I stared at him, his hair mussed and his expression slightly worse-for-wear, everything I wanted in life shifted.

We downed our beer while Florian filmed with his phone. I glugged as fast as I could to keep up with Max, holding his gaze. He finished half a minute before me and when I'd swilled the last drop, he tipped the glass upside down over his head. I copied him, whooping and grinning and enjoying the cool drops of beer down the side of my face.

'Congratulations!' the organiser called out. 'You've won the biergarten race!'

'Ha,' I said, turning to Florian and waggling the finger of my spare hand at him. 'We won!'

Florian nodded slowly, his expression dry. 'You won.'

Max came around the table to enfold me in a hug that lifted me a few centimetres off the ground.

'Oof. How are you even still standing?' I asked.

He studied me with a warm, soft expression that made a puddle of my insides. His lips looked more inviting than a drip on an ice cream cone. Then his smile turned cheeky. Slowly, purposefully, he came close and, with a nuzzle to my jaw, licked the trail of beer up the side of my face.

My hair stood on end and my legs were wobbly, as though I'd cycled a grown adult across an epic city park with only the straining muscles of my thighs.

Max wrapped an arm around my neck in one of those 'I want to rough you up' hugs that he'd always given me and although it was silly and comforting and everything I loved about him, it also made me want him to rough me up a bit more, in a naughtier way.

'All right, no need to get my content reported to the censors,' Florian grumbled.

'You could edit that bit out,' I suggested, but Max looked disappointed at that idea, the weirdo.

'It's a fine line, Butkus,' Florian said. 'And the viewers shipping you two is working for me.'

'Wait, is it still called shipping if we're already together?' I asked. They both blinked at me.

'You're really together?' Florian asked, incredulous. His eyes narrowed and I knew exactly what he was thinking about. *Shit.*

I hated that he'd *heard me* say all that crap a week ago. I hated that I'd said it – that I'd meant it – because I was discovering I'd been entirely *wrong*. Max was not a disaster – *I* was.

There were a few things I regretted in my life: letting my mum help me pick out my formal dress for the end of high school; taking a shot called a 'Kim Jong Un Nuclear Bomb' at a dive bar in Mexico; not discovering Radiohead before they were cool. Up until that point, few of them had had anything to do with Max.

The worst part was that I feared I'd always taken him for granted that way. What kind of friend did that make me? Maybe I was just using him to make me feel better, like my mum had always done to my dad. Why was he letting me use him when he should have known by now what a difficult person I could be?

For a second, I let myself wonder what it would be like if we stayed together, really together. But the dark jungle of my inadequacies was so overgrown that a tender little shoot like that had no hope of thriving. I was too afraid to nurture it.

Chapter Twenty-Eight

'Ouch! Keep it together, Max!'

'Ah, shit. Sorry, moppie. Let me start again. Stay still for a minute and let me just get it… in there.' He was nervous, I could tell. It was Thursday and considering what we had planned for this afternoon, I shouldn't have been surprised.

'Owwww!' I yelled, grabbing at my hair. 'Why did I even let you braid it?'

'You're welcome to do it yourself.'

He knew very well I didn't know how to braid and we wanted to look especially good that day because Stefan from Fuchsbräu was letting us get up on stage and sing – at least until he hauled us back down with the hook of a walking stick amid a shower of tomatoes from all the hecklers. Max and I had always loved music, but that didn't mean anyone should let us loose with a microphone.

'Why do you know how to braid?'

Shoving the comb between his teeth, he finessed the first strands into the beginning of a braid and breathed out in relief when it didn't unravel. He tugged the comb out of his mouth again to sweep up the next strands. 'You remember when I had long hair?'

'Yes! You looked like Daði from the Icelandic Eurovision

entry, but before he made it cool.'

'Albino Daði,' he quipped. I tried to laugh, but 'albino' was a word he used so infrequently that I sometimes imagined he liked the fact that he stuck out in a crowd. 'For the two years I had long hair, I worked at Oktoberfest, sometimes in a dirndl with my hair braided,' he said with a small smile.

'I want photos!'

'No!' he said defensively, catching the comb conveniently in a knot and making me yelp again.

'Why not? I can't believe you didn't send me pictures before.'

'I did.'

For a moment, I didn't believe him, but those years he'd had long hair, I'd been travelling a lot for work. Maybe he had sent pictures. 'I'm sorry if I don't remember. I still want to see them.'

'A bit of mystery between us might be a good thing right now,' he said flippantly.

'I told you I wanted to know everything!' That stupid conversation with Florian stabbed me in the brain again, even though I'd deleted it a thousand times from my memory.

'You want to know everything about the guy you're hooking up with and you want him to know everything about you? That doesn't sound like you, Fi.'

'Fuck off, Max!'

He clutched his chin. 'Now, where have I heard that before? A hint of a relationship and Fi fucks off.'

'We don't count!'

'We don't count as a relationship?' he scoffed.

I gulped, wondering how far he was going to push this. 'We count as a *friendship*, Max!' Was that a pleading tone in my voice? I was too damn lonely and unhappy to risk losing him.

Except I'd been happy on Tuesday. And actually, that morning had been pretty good, too.

Max and I were morning sex people because I was often asleep when he came home after finishing up at Snaketooth. He seemed to have endless creative ways to wake me up, from the simple dig of morning wood into my thigh, to this morning's thirsty vampire impression.

'Of course, we do,' he said snappishly. 'I could never get anywhere near a stage with anyone else. I just… kind of want to pretend to be the sexy, mysterious guy you're sleeping with rather than your friend-with-benefits, who needs your help to win the damn money and your hand to hold while we walk on stage.'

'Max.' I caught his eye in the mirror. He was wearing his grey eyeliner again, his hair stiff with gel and I had to think that anyone who went for tall, dark and mysterious was missing a trick, or they hadn't seen Max in eyeliner. I had this mantra on repeat in my mind: *you are the best guy in the whole world and I could cry at how much I like looking at you.*

Instead, I said, 'You could do this without me. You can do anything. You were always wonderful, that's not what I mean – wonderful, like my favourite human being. But you've… come into your own. It's hot. And I don't think you need me for any of this stuff, as much as part of me wishes you did.'

His hands froze in my hair and he stared at me in the mirror, such a broken expression of shock on his face that tears pricked my eyes. My heart hurt. I couldn't keep up with all this change or stop worrying he was moving on without me, but I couldn't help but be proud of the man he'd become. More than proud, if I was honest. Terrifyingly more than proud, borderline disastrously more than proud, like these feelings could lead to so much worse than the numbness of the past couple of years, like I would throw that promotion, my entire career to stay here and let him braid my hair.

Then what?

'You're right,' he said softly, and his words hurt, even as they vindicated me. He agreed that he didn't need me. I was surplus to requirements. When I left, he would still be whole, whereas I— 'I could probably manage this on my own. But I'd much rather be up there with you. It means a lot to me that you want to support Snaketooth. But it means more that you're willing to do these stupid challenges with me.'

I snatched the comb out of his hand and stood, yanking on his suspenders until he came close. He held onto the beginnings of my braid for another moment, before giving up and cupping my head instead. I kissed him, rough and raw, until his fingers tightened in my hair and a groan started up in his chest. Then I tugged him towards the bed.

If I kept kissing him, if I made him feel so good he had to squeeze his eyes shut, he might not see how close I'd come to crying.

* * *

We were nearly late for our own performance. Tanya hissed her disapproval when we rushed up, rumpled and panting, my hair very much *not* braided.

'Stefan was wringing his hands.'

'Shit, seriously? He was *wringing*?'

Max poked me in the back in punishment for my rampant sarcasm, and Tanya scowled. 'Ryan and Marco will go first. Then you two, and Isobel and I will go last. The band leader told me to check with you that the song you suggested was definitely the right one.'

I snorted. 'It's the right one.' There was only one song with that title and I could imagine the band leader being a little thrown. I gripped Max's hand. I was nervous and the noise of the crowd seemed to echo in my fizzing blood, but I was also almost looking forward to it.

Florian caught my eye from where he was sitting at a table with a bunch of portly, middle-aged men with moustaches and green felt hats. He raised his beer in my direction and I flipped him off.

Waving down a harried Stefan, Max quickly reassured his old boss that everything was ready to go with the afternoon's questionable entertainment. Judging by the exodus of horns and trumpets down one side of the tent, the traditional Blaskapelle, the brass band, were taking a break and the Wiesn-Hits were about to start.

The band leader switched on his microphone and waved to the punters in the tent. The answering cheer was deafening and after half a minute of sound checks, the crowd began to drone the guitar riff from 'Seven Nation Army', the classic drunk-man anthem, along with the electric guitar up on the dais.

'We should have sung that,' Marco shouted over the clamour. 'I know White Stripes and the football song!'

'Too late now!' Ryan yelled back.

Without much introduction, the electric guitar started up another riff that upped the chaos factor in the crowd even further. Max grimaced, but he couldn't seem to help moving his feet as the introduction built with drums and bass.

'It's "Wahnsinn", a Wiesn classic, and older than we are.

Schlager, of course.' I rolled my eyes along with him. We'd learned about Schlager together in Freiburg, trying to understand the Volksmusik programmes on TV while pretending we were way too cool to bop to the sentimental pop music that made the Germans inexplicably happy. I didn't remember 'Wahnsinn', but the crowd obviously did.

Vaguely tuneful shouting filled the tent, heads bobbing and beer sloshing. When the band reached the chorus, Max joined them, raising an arm a little sheepishly and chanting, 'Hölle, Hölle, Hölle, Hölle!' at the appropriate moment.

'The number of times I heard this when I worked here,' he groaned into my ear.

'Did all the guys try to chat you up? Or the girls?'

'What happens at Oktoberfest, stays at Oktoberfest,' he said, wiggling his eyebrows, then breaking into a laugh. 'There were a few sexual advances over the years, yes. As well as that time I had to stem the bleeding from a leg injury, the time I broke my index finger because I was carrying too many beers – and came to work again the next day – not to mention the security incident with the guy who wouldn't take his coat off and turned out to be naked underneath.'

'Not a very glamorous job, I take it.'

'Behind the scenes, definitely not.'

The band finished up the song to another deafening, football-stadium cheer and Stefan beckoned frantically at us and the band leader. Ryan looked stricken and Marco was decidedly green.

'Meine Damen und Herren, ladies and gentlemen!' the band leader announced. 'This afternoon we welcome to the stage the contestants of the Wiesn-Chellenge, for Hit-Karaoke!'

The crowd whooped, but Max and I exchanged a look that

suggested we both knew the enthusiasm would be short-lived. Luckily our stage performance would be too. Max slung his arms around Ryan and Marco as they headed for the stairs at the back of the stage, patting their shoulders and murmuring words of encouragement that didn't seem to dim Ryan's panic. The whites of his eyes would be visible from the balcony.

'Welcome, Ryan and Marco, singing "Country Roads"!' More cheering, which at least covered Ryan's dumbfounded shock at where he'd found himself. He stood at the wooden railing and gaped at the thousands of expectant faces. The band leader thrust a microphone into his hand and he fumbled with it, but caught it before it sailed over the railing.

The guitar and harmonica had to play their introduction twice before any sound emerged from either Ryan or Marco. The crowd, now clued into the drama, quieted expectantly. A blow-up unicorn bobbed in one corner and Ryan's gaze latched on it as he pulled himself together. The next time the band gave him his cue, he began to sing the first verse.

I gave him credit for being mostly in tune. He jumped when the band leader joined him in the second part of the verse, singing harmony. After a few deep breaths, Ryan recovered and even managed a smile.

The performance was gripping, like those shows where you watch contestants try to imitate amazing baking and fail spectacularly, but the crowd loved it. They all joined in for the chorus with a resounding, mispronounced 'Vest Virginia.' Marco warbled something during the chorus – just enough not to get them disqualified – and that was probably for the best.

Everyone knew the words except me. By the time Ryan reached the second chorus, the punters were up on the benches waving their arms. When they finished, Ryan looked as though he was about to faint.

'Uhm, thank you!' he called out. 'Danke schön! Ich bin ein Münchner!' he mumbled, imitating JFK. That earned him a laugh and we all enfolded him in a hug when he stumbled off stage. A waiter shoved beers into their hands and Ryan chugged so much that I got worried he was going to choke, since he hadn't breathed enough in the past few minutes.

'Fucking hell!' he whispered. 'I mean, crap and… stuff. I can't believe I did that.'

I squeezed his shoulder. 'You did great.'

Max tugged on my hand and my skin went cold. Ryan and Marco hadn't sucked – or, they'd sucked in a good way. I was pretty sure Max and I were simply going to suck.

'Unser nächstes Paar, our next couple from the Wiesn-Chellenge has chosen a very… interesting song,' the band leader called out. 'Some of our band members are very enthusiastic about the chance to play this, but others of us… you'll see. We are fans of 90s nostalgia, but not usually this kind. Anyway, perhaps the crowd will love it! Come on up, Fiona and Max!'

The whistles and cheering pierced my brain and all the eyes were on me and I truly regretted that we'd ever developed a hashtag. Neither of us moved. Someone shoved us from behind, but we stood stupidly.

'Max? Fiona? Anyone coming?' the band leader asked with a laugh.

'We're going to look like idiots,' I murmured, squeezing my eyes shut. 'But at least we'll look like idiots together.' He nodded stiffly, his jaw clenched, and then he allowed me to drag him up onto the stage.

'Welcome Fiona. You know, *I love beer*, too!' the band leader said, to giggles and cheers from the crowd. While I still wished they'd all get over that stupid video, I got a little thrill out of being cheered as the 'I love beer' woman.

I tried Ryan's trick of focussing on the blow-up unicorn, but it swam, out-of-focus, before my eyes. My forehead was cool with sweat and someone had started up another chant, thousands of feet stamping on the wooden boards.

The keyboard tinkled to life in the instantly-recognisable opening strains of the song we'd chosen. And I made the mistake of lifting my head to the balcony, where there were VIP tables with clean, checked cloths and less harried wait staff.

Dollersen was there, staring down at me. I'd managed to pretend he didn't exist for a few days while I didn't have any work commitments at the Wiesn. I whirled, my feet demanding the exit, but I landed against Max's chest and his arms slipped around me.

'Can you do this?' he asked me earnestly and I knew if I said 'no', he'd bundle me out of here and make me a blanket fort where we could stay and ignore the world. He would forfeit all of that money and never even try to talk me into it for his own sake.

But for him? 'I can do it,' I muttered.

Chapter Twenty-Nine

An enthusiastic clarinet player from the brass band joined in with the keyboard and winked at me when I turned to look. The drummer gave us a nod, holding his sticks ready. I grinned at Max.

'We're really doing this,' I murmured, clutching the microphone I'd barely noticed.

Max held my gaze, swaying subtly as he waited for the cue to sing. He took a deep breath and, still looking at me, he opened his mouth and sang, 'Karma police,' with all the bleak ennui of Thom Yorke himself.

Certain areas in the crowd cheered immediately and joined in singing, but by no means everyone. The result was relative quiet in the tent as Max's unsteady voice crooned the first two verses, mumbling the line about the woman with Hitler's hairstyle with an apologetic wince.

I snort-laughed into my microphone. We were really here, up on stage in a beer tent singing Radiohead the way we'd sung it while drunk in my dorm room in Freiburg.

The first time I'd ever met Max was because of Radiohead. Jetlagged and slightly overwhelmed by my first solo trip to another country, I'd run into him in our shared kitchen at six in the morning. He'd been bleary-eyed, full of weird energy and making himself a vodka espresso. Dragging me to his room, he'd made me watch him download the new album, *In Rainbows*, which had just been released.

At the time, the experience had seemed surreal, between the early hour and my fuzzy head, the magical album download over the slow internet connection and the skinny boy with puppy-dog energy and a deep, groaning crack of lonely vulnerability. And then we listened to the album and we both tripped, even though there was nothing stronger in our systems than vodka, caffeine and jetlag.

The rest of the student exchange year had been punctuated by Radiohead, the album chosen according to the occasion. And then we'd seen them live at the Southside festival in the summer of 2008 and that had been another substance-free high (except for all the alcohol and the trace amounts of whatever in the festival mud).

How many Max-induced highs had I experienced over the past two weeks? After worrying that I'd forgotten how to be happy, I couldn't count them all. I was in another one right now, joining in to sing the cheeky and kind of spooky bit about getting what comes to you.

The last line of the chorus became ours, about not messing with *us*. Max held my gaze as his smile widened and we sang with a lot of fierceness, but not much skill. The music wound down for the second verse, where Max sang alone again, as we'd decided.

He eyed me as he sang the line about being on the payroll and I thought about Dollersen, in the crowd watching me, and it didn't matter. I was here as a private citizen. I didn't want to sit at that table and postulate and judge and act like someone else. Today, I wanted to be Peter Pan with Max.

The drummer went wild, smashing the cymbals and waving the sticks around as he built up the beat for the bridge, the enthusiastic clarinettist keeping up with the keyboard and now joined by a sudden blast from a trumpet.

Max caught my gaze and leaned close. 'It's really high for me and the bridge is worse,' he said, covering the microphone.

'I've got it,' I nodded, grinning. When the key changed, even though my voice was nothing to write home about, I let it soar, belting out the line about losing myself and trying not to cry as I realised that's what had happened to me over the past four years. I should have trusted Max would always find me again.

As the song wound up, the brass band joined in for a last hurrah and the weirdest version of 'Karma Police' in history came to a close to cheers from the crowd. I grabbed Max around the neck and wouldn't let go, tears threatening.

'I've got you, moppie,' he whispered, as though he knew what was going on. 'Remember when we first met and I made you listen to *In Rainbows* about ten times until you fell asleep on my floor?'

'I'd forgotten I fell asleep,' I mumbled into his neck. 'But I remember everything else.' *I remember how different you were from anyone I'd ever met, how I knew in an instant that you'd be my best friend.*

'You've been my family since then, Fi.'

I smacked him on the shoulder. 'You know exactly how hard I'm trying not to cry right now!'

He pinched me in response and I squealed into the microphone. 'You know exactly how much I lo—' It was unfortunately clear to me what he'd almost said, what he would have said without a second thought two weeks ago.

Pressing a kiss to my cheek, he took my hand and we left the stage together, waving to a rippling cheer of our hashtag: 'Fi loves Max! Fi loves Max!' They knew not what they were doing.

'How does it feel?' Max asked, drawing me close and kissing my jaw once we were out of sight. It felt pretty good, actually, being kissed by Max as though he wanted to lick me in public.

I huffed a laugh. 'Amazing. I feel amazing. We got up there and did our thing and… it's like I'm back.' Max's grin was as wide as mine felt.

'I loved watching you, being up there with you,' he murmured.

I love being anywhere *with you.* My thoughts had gone completely off the rails. I'd finally dragged myself up out of the last, desolate few years, but there was still something new up here and it kept taking me by surprise.

Florian sidled up and kissed my cheek, shaking Max's hand enthusiastically. '"Karma Police"? Where do you kids get those ideas? You certainly made me repent and think about mending my wicked ways.'

'That's not exactly the point of karma,' I said.

He leaned close and whispered in my ear, 'What about all the good karma I've earned by pushing you two together instead of keeping you apart?'

And, shit, he burst my bubble. I should probably tell Max about that drunken conversation Florian kept hinting to me about, try to explain in some way that made me sound like less of a horrible person, but it was so far from what I felt now that it would be difficult to describe. If Florian wanted his karma, surely he'd leave it alone.

Tanya and Isobel took to the stage before I could obsess

any further and I whistled loudly enough for Florian to cover his ears. Isobel tripped on the top step, but covered it with a wobbly curtsy. She looked pale, but I couldn't imagine that getting up in front of the crowd was a problem for her. Isobel and Tanya had been the loudest to sing at every party in Freiburg.

The song began with drumming, a syncopated beat. Tanya started singing – in German, the bloody teacher's pet – and the crowd cheered. I didn't know the song, but Max burst out laughing and Florian nodded, impressed. When Isobel performed a short rap in Spanish, I had an inkling of why they'd chosen the song.

The tent came to life in the chorus, many tables singing along and ripples moving over the crowd as they danced. I caught the word 'arsch', meaning exactly what it sounded like, and snorted a laugh, clapping as Max gave up pretending he didn't know the words and sang along.

The song was a little lame, mixing languages and going on about moving your 'arsch', but Germans are weird about music sometimes and the crowd hopped up on their tables and enjoyed themselves. Tanya shook her shoulders and aced the German parts of the song and the mood in the crowd ramped up. I guessed they would get a lot of votes for it. By the end, even my arsch was moving all on its own.

Max cheered and clapped. 'That was a football song about ten years ago,' he said with a laugh.

'A good choice,' Florian commented. He lifted a brow in my direction. 'Perhaps a little better than Radiohead in a beer tent. Lucky for you they carried the team today.'

I leaned closer to Max. 'Shit, I didn't even think we might have screwed up our chances to be the final team!'

'It was worth it,' he murmured into my ear, bringing back my epic wobbles of a few minutes ago.

We raised our hands and applauded Tanya and Isobel as they waved for the crowd. Isobel appeared to be drenched in sweat, even though the dance routine hadn't been so over-the-top. She stumbled once, groping for the railing and I took a step forward instinctively. Then she dropped the microphone and toppled into the drumkit with a clash.

Chapter Thirty

I arrived back at the Fuchsbräu tent in five minutes flat, gasping for breath, two paramedics jogging behind me with a stretcher. Ryan burst out of the doors with Isobel limp in his arms. She was still unconscious as he set her carefully onto the stretcher. As she was rolled away to the first aid tent, we stumbled after her, everyone talking at once.

'Didn't she say her neck was hurting before?' Ryan asked.

'She said everything was hurting, but I thought she was just recovering from the race on Tuesday,' Tanya said, her usual restraint slipping.

'Perhaps we should call her husband. Do you have her bag?' Max asked Tanya.

'What can her husband do? He has the children. If she's sick, she has a holiday in hospital.'

'A holiday in hospital?' Marco repeated in disgust.

'Yeah, my wife would probably like that,' Ryan agreed weakly. Tanya just rolled her eyes.

'But what if she's really sick?' I asked. 'She looked feverish.'

We arrived at the first aid tent to a disapproving expression from the paramedic. He spoke in German first, repeating himself in English. 'How long has she been like this?'

'She only just fell over—' I rushed to explain.

'I mean this fever. She should not be at the Wiesn with a temperature of 41. And if she wants to leave the baby, perhaps she should take the milk pump, hmm?' We all looked at him blankly.

'What?' Tanya snapped.

The paramedic pointed to her breasts, above the frills at her neckline. Even I could see there was something very wrong with one. It was mottled and swollen.

'Alcohol and breastfeeding do not mix,' the paramedic said so firmly that we all nodded, even though Isobel wasn't guilty of what he suspected. 'She has the mastitis, infection in the milk glands, for some time now, I suspect. Do not let her feed a baby now, with too much beer. She needs antibiotics quickly.'

'Actually, she's… sober.' My voice trailed off. There was no way the paramedic would believe us and another a woman in a dirndl had just arrived, bleeding freely from a cut on her cheek.

Max took charge, calling a taxi and shepherding Isobel inside. She had regained consciousness, but she was delirious, calling Max Andres as he propped her up in the taxi and asking after the children, sometimes in panic.

Less than two hours later, Isobel was installed in a clinic, attached to an antibiotic drip after the doctors were worried she'd developed an abscess. Her mumbles of, 'Andres,' continued as she struggled to settle in the bed and Tanya rummaged in Isobel's bag until she found her phone. Holding Isobel's fingertip to the reader, Tanya got it unlocked and searched for Andres, but nothing appeared.

'It could be anything,' Ryan said with a grimace. 'My wife is in my phone as "Pookie".'

Marco blinked at him. 'Pookie?'

'She calls him Tarzan, right?' Tanya suggested, but there was no entry in her phone for that either.

'What about 'amor'?' Ryan suggested, but that also turned up no results. We Googled Spanish endearments, but also drew a blank on 'cariño', 'mi cielo' and 'mi vida'.

Tanya stamped her foot. 'What's Spanish for "good-looking"? That's the only thing I know about Andres.' She turned the phone around to show us the background photo and I had to agree.

'Good for Isobel,' I commented. Max poked me and I slapped his hand away. 'Aesthetically pleasing,' I said drily, 'not "get dirty with me" hot,' I finished, looking him up and down pointedly. Max blushing was one of my favourite things.

'Bello, bien parecido, atractivo, encarado, guapo,' Marco said, reading from his phone screen.

Tanya tapped furiously, before exclaiming, 'Guapo! That's it. At least I hope that's him.' She dialled the number and we all waited in tense silence. 'Hello? Is that Isobel's husband? Yes, something's happened.'

He seemed a little confused at first, but when he understood what had happened, his agitation was audible, even though the call wasn't on speaker.

'She is unconscious. I will call you as soon as we know anything else,' Tanya said, ending the call.

'He seemed really upset,' Ryan said.

Tanya shrugged. 'I hope it's not just because she can't come home and take the twins.' Ryan admonished her for being cynical, but I couldn't fault her for it in her situation, especially as she'd now lost her partner for the challenge, and all hope of winning the money.

A nurse bustled in and bustled all of us out and we collapsed into a row of chairs in the waiting room, staring blankly at the public-health posters about the effects of alcohol.

'This is *not* the reason I expected to find myself in the emergency department,' Marco said.

'Mastitis was not foreseeable for you,' I snorted.

'I have not even been drunk yet.' We all blinked at him. Perhaps alcohol affected his memory. 'Not as drunk as I expected, anyway.'

Max gave him a friendly slap on the shoulder. 'Don't worry, amico. We'll get you properly drunk at least once.'

Marco grinned at him. 'Thank you – all of you. I didn't believe we would still be friends like this.' He glanced at Ryan, who looked ready to blubber. 'And I don't believe you call your wife "pookie". The poor woman.'

'What did you call your husband, when you were still together?' Ryan asked.

'I called him Angelo, of course.'

'Aw, you called him your angel?'

'No, his name is Angelo, stupido.'

'Don't call him stupid,' Tanya snapped in a tone I imagined injected steel into the spines of her children. 'Do you have Fi as "moppie" in your phone, Max?' He gave a sheepish nod and pulled up the contact, with an unflattering picture of the two of us on a rollercoaster at Ferrari Land in Spain. My face was in front, distorted, with my tongue hanging out.

'What am I in your phone?' he asked. 'Max? Or even Max Brouwer?' he asked with a huff.

He was right, damn it. I showed him the contact called 'Max Brouwer' in my phone. 'I could change it,' I said defensively.

He snatched my phone. '*I* will.' I rolled my eyes, but got

distracted when a nurse approached us to explain that Isobel was resting comfortably and seemed to be responding to the intravenous antibiotics already. That was how I ended up with a contact called 'Miracle Dick' in my phone.

As we were leaving the hospital, Tanya staying behind until Isobel woke up and understood what had happened, Florian rushed up the front steps, concern shadowing his face.

'Is she all right?'

'It looks that way,' I said.

'Is Tanya still in there? I need to talk to her about… the challenge.'

'I really don't think now is the time—'

He eyed me and I had the sudden suspicion that he knew more about what was going on with Tanya than I'd given him credit for. 'We've only got three days until they announce which team is through to the final. We have a really good chance. I need to talk to her. I have an idea.'

I gulped, a thousand unwelcome thoughts about the end of Oktoberfest swishing through my mind. It was great that we had a chance to compete for the money on the final day. But then we'd have to face off *against* each other. Competitive spirit was all well and good until it crumbled in the face of such a dilemma.

I sighed and gave Florian a nod. 'Send Tanya a message first though. She's in with Isobel.' He just nodded, no flash of a shit-eating grin or a tasteless joke.

The other reason I was dreading the next few days crowded my thoughts. The Wiesn wrapped up for the year on Tuesday and I would get on a plane on Wednesday. It didn't seem real that this reunion-out-of-time would come to an end, but I knew returning home would feel uncomfortably real.

Even though Sydney was already ten degrees warmer than Munich at this time of year, it would feel so damn cold in my bed and New York wouldn't be any better.

* * *

I told Max I wanted a quick nap before coming to Snaketooth that evening and opened my laptop, my fingers hovering over the keys. I tried to ignore my emails, but I couldn't and spent an hour shooting off easy replies and wondering if what I'd said to Max counted as lying.

I couldn't tell him I was thinking of imploding my life to stay here with him in Munich. Although I knew I meant a lot to him, he'd still tell me to fuck off, like he had when I'd tried to help at Snaketooth. But maybe there would be a career opportunity here and he couldn't argue with that.

Dragging myself away from my work before I got bogged down, I opened up the global intranet and searched out what I was looking for. I didn't know why I'd hoped there might be a job in marketing at Fuchsbräu, when I knew it was part of the stable of brands administered out of Amsterdam and even they had no openings. There was a junior admin position, which I would be tempted to apply for anyway, despite the embarrassing drop from VP to entry-level dogsbody, but I'd never get a visa for that.

You could ask him to marry you...

I cradled my head in my hands. He probably had no idea how many times I'd thought about him quietly and calmly saying I only had to ask. It was tempting even to break the law by lying to the immigration officials so I could stay where he was and work out what came next for us. But if sleeping together had muddled our friendship, what would an immigration-based marriage do?

I shot off an email anyway to a manager I'd met at a conference in Los Angeles last year, asking if she knew of any openings or anyone who might do me a favour. It was a risk, openly expressing what I really wanted when a promotion was on the table. Max thought I didn't take risks, but maybe it was something I should try more often.

When I arrived at Snaketooth, the place was quiet and I was asking myself if frolicking through the centre of Munich wearing only a sandwich-board bearing the Snaketooth logo would help. Florian had been planting these stupid ideas. I would tweak my low-budget social media ads later and finish up the new designs with the photos I'd taken of Max and Jan instead.

Max waved through the windows of the brewing room, where he was busy with Andreas at one of the big silver cones, both of them in sexy hygiene get-up. Jan waved me to the bar and set a plate of Spätzle with mushrooms in front of me. My mouth watered and I wondered how he'd known I loved the worm-like German version of pasta. It tasted so good I didn't care what they used instead of eggs and butter.

I opened up my laptop as I tucked in. Maybe it was because I was working with photos of Max, but a couple of hours disappeared without me even noticing I was working and I was pumped about my plan to tweak the ads. I even had the beginnings of a report on metrics that was exponentially smaller than what I was used to, but infinitely more exciting. Plus, I got to look up whenever I wanted to watch Max skipping happily around his tiny brewing room.

They were still busy at the vats as the last customers left, so I helped Jan clean up and close, drifting into the brewing room as Max was cleaning the equipment with a hose. Andreas had already gone home. 'Hey, moppie,' he said with an enormous smile and hopped down from the ladder to plant a big kiss on my mouth. 'I'm nearly finished.'

'Whatcha makin'?' I asked. 'Aside from "beer",' I said, pre-empting the joke.

'I'm no good at keeping secrets.' His arms snaked around my waist.

'What?'

'I'm making you a kriek beer.'

I squealed in a manner quite unbecoming of a thirty-six-year-old, but I hadn't had a Belgian-style cherry beer in years. More than my anticipation of drinking it again, I was touched that Max was willing to break his beer purity laws for me by fermenting it with sour cherries.

'But you won't be able to taste it until the next time we see each other.' My smile must have vanished too quickly because Max squeezed my hands and dipped his head to catch my downcast gaze. 'It has to ferment. To be honest, it might be awful, but it's called our Moppie anyway and you'll have to come back when we open the barrels and bottle it. Or… I'll bring you a few bottles if you can't come. It'll only take a few months. It was supposed to make you look forward to the next time—' He swallowed. 'Did I screw up? Are you upset?'

I shook my head vigorously and asked myself how many times that day I'd cried. 'I don't want to go yet,' I blurted out. 'I don't want to leave *you*.'

He gathered me up, as though collecting the splinters of my emotions. Ushering me into the cupboard that operated as an office, he clutched me to him, pressing my head into his neck, where I enjoyed the delicious smell of his old-man cologne combined with the fruity tang of cherries.

He swallowed several times before he opened his mouth to speak. 'I don't want you to go either,' he murmured. 'But we'll see each other sooner, this time. If I have to stow away on a cargo ship and land illegally in a canoe, I'll get to Australia. And you might be in New York by the time this is ready anyway.'

'Even one month apart would be too long,' I complained, watching his brow draw low.

He grasped my face with both hands. 'I promise I'll come when I can, but it won't be so hard this time. We'll video call like we always do and make plans for our next trip. We always wanted to go to Costa Rica to see the sloths, right? Let's do it next year. I should be able to afford something if I stop buying cigarettes completely,' he joked with a lopsided half-smile.

He didn't understand. He thought we were just banging each other for fun, an interesting phase of our friendship. It was a shit time to realise I *was* looking for a long-term relationship. Even more shit was the realisation that I'd probably have to give up Max to do it. I couldn't love someone else with my feelings for him so tangled.

That's why this hurt so much. We couldn't just go back, like Max seemed to think – at least *I* couldn't. I was afraid I'd never get to taste my beer.

'Don't look like that. You're amazing. You'll get that promotion and shove it to all the male bosses and transform the company. And when you have a spare minute, you can call me and we can have a beer together. I'll ship you some.'

I scowled at him through tears. 'Do you have any idea how expensive shipping is?'

He cocked his head and studied me. 'I realise. I sent you that case of Tannenzäpfle in 2009 and it nearly cost me a month's rent.'

'Tannenzäpfle is worth it,' I murmured, making him smile. Our local beer in Freiburg would always be a bit special – and almost impossible to get outside of Germany.

'I could send you Tannenzäpfle instead of my beer?'

I wrapped my arms around his neck. 'Don't you dare.'

'It's not the end, moppie,' he said fiercely, but so quickly I almost didn't hear him. I hoped he was right. 'I promise.'

'Just kiss me, Max.'

That was an instruction he followed thoroughly and enthusiastically – just as enthusiastically as he urged me over his desk afterward and pushed inside me, each heavy thrust insisting we could be together like this forever, his body curled around me and mine accepting him.

But it never lasted forever. At some point I was wound up so tight, so overwrought, that I couldn't take it any more. While the shattering was beautiful, the way he linked his fingers with mine and squeezed, his hot breath on the back of my neck, the low groans as he travelled with me, it was too beautiful to be anything but fleeting.

Perhaps that's how it was meant to be for us.

Chapter Thirty-One

Tanya and I visited Isobel bearing gifts the following morning, before I had to head back to the Wiesn for more work drinking, in the day this time. We'd brought a jam doughnut and a fresh pretzel, as well as Mozart Balls, her favourite chocolates (which she of course called 'Mozart's Balls'), but she was being prepped for surgery and had to fast which made her grumpy in the extreme. I quickly shoved the bakery bags behind my back, but not before she saw them, her eyes bulging.

'There is an abscess,' she said irritably. 'Now they do not even bring me food.' We sat with her, letting her vent for an hour, until our stomachs were rumbling which only made Isobel's mood worse.

During an awkward silence when Tanya's stomach creaked and I was dreaming of coffee, the door burst open and a tall man with floppy hair and a distraught expression rushed to Isobel's bedside.

'Mi amor!' He continued to splutter in Spanish, grasping her hands and then wrapping his arms around her.

A smile touched my lips as I witnessed the man, who must be her handsome husband Andres, expressing a satisfying amount of love for my friend. He kissed her, all completely

PG and more tender than ravishing, but that was somehow worse for my confused heart.

No relationship was perfect and some were downright unhealthy. But some were proof that love could grow in a patch of weeds, that people could be imperfect, but still loved.

Like Max. Like *me*?

Tanya and I said goodbye and slipped out as unobtrusively as we could. 'He came,' she commented with a sigh.

'He loves her,' I mumbled.

'What was that? I expected a joke. Have you changed your attitude?'

'No,' I said defensively. 'It's nice for Isobel and I'm sorry if it's making you sad to think your marriage is not like that,' I added quietly.

Tanya humphed. 'You *are* different. You are in love with Max.'

I didn't have the strength to deny it. 'But I'm not different. I'm just finally ready to open up a bit.'

'To Max? To stay together after the beerfest?'

The shot of fear down my spine was cold and sharp. 'There isn't really a way and I don't think it's what he wants.' He'd promised our friendship wouldn't change.

'If you're not sure, then you're not sure,' Tanya said with a shrug.

'How did you feel when you decided to marry Carson?'

She eyed me. 'I was too young. I thought marrying someone my family found for me would be easier than working on a relationship – simpler. But you can hurt people by not loving them just as much as you can by loving them.'

That made me gulp. 'Seriously, if there's *anything* I can do to help.'

'I am sick of being reliant on others, Fi. Besides, perhaps I will win the challenge after all.'

'What did Florian say yesterday?'

'He will be my partner for the last round. He already spoke to the organisers and in the circumstances, they've agreed. He seemed genuinely upset about Isobel. Perhaps he is not the dick we all remember. What do you think might have happened if you'd slept with him instead of Max, hmm?'

It was a strange thought, imagining my friendship with Max as it had always been, oversharing the embarrassing details of sex with Florian – I did remember Florian's weird habit of narrating everything in the third person as it was happening, things like, 'Hmmm, she likes that, what if I try…' which was more disconcerting than hot.

Imagining talking to Max about sex with other people made me nauseous. Imagining telling anyone else that it wasn't a boob day made me shrivel up like the husk of one of the many rotting walnuts littering the pavements around Munich at this time of year. Was this the autumn of my sex life? So soon after the glorious summer?

'Can we not talk about me, please?' Wow, I *was* changing my tune.

'You've got your career, your apartment, a healthy cynicism about relationships. Our thirties will be over soon, and we can start living again.'

Wasn't that supposed to be a mantra to combat intrusive thoughts: *it won't always be like this*? How did that work when you wanted things to stay the same, but knew they couldn't?

* * *

We met for lunch on Saturday for the last round of velvet-bag truth-or-dare – our final chance for points before the winning team was announced the following morning.

Isobel had come through her surgery well and was happily bickering with her handsome husband in the hospital, enjoying Mozart's Balls, but she certainly wasn't up to the challenge, so Florian sat in as one of us at our usual table in Snaketooth, oddly chastened, or at least acting that way.

'We have a good chance for tomorrow,' he announced earnestly. 'We've had lots of comments about Fi and Max. Tanya and Isobel got bonus points for crowd reaction to their song and we gathered a lot of tips in waitering,' Florian continued, belatedly catching my arch look at his use of the word 'we'. 'What are we drinking? I invite you all this time – shit. That's not right in English, is it? I mean I…'

'It's your shout,' I supplied for him. 'I recommend the pils.' I winked at Max and he slung his arm around me.

Florian ordered the tasting paddles – why did every word inspire dirty thoughts when I was tasting Max's beer? – and Jan delivered the wooden boards holding small glasses of each type. I was satisfied to see Florian photographing everything for his socials. He'd better be saying Snaketooth was the best new venue in Munich, after filming us all making fools of ourselves and only joining in himself at the last minute.

'This is a bit different from the "other side",' he said with a nervous laugh. 'Who will ask the questions?'

Ryan reached for the bag and dumped out the last two slips of paper. 'I hope they're not dares. We don't have much time left.' He unfolded the first one. '"Get down on one knee and propose to the person on your left",' he read flatly, crumpling up the paper in a hurry.

I kept my gaze trained on the table, but I could feel Max *reverberating* next to me, the air between us warping and expanding. He was on my left. I gulped, thinking about all the conversations we'd had trying to puzzle out the institution of marriage, its psychological effects, defects and its social hang-ups.

Max's parents were so stiflingly *married* that they somehow forgot he was part of their family, too. And my parents' marriage had been an exploitative disaster that my dad was still paying for – with his emotions, if no longer his paycheque.

Then there were those words that sometimes still echoed in my mind: *I've been waiting years for you to ask.*

'At least it's easy,' Tanya said with a huff. 'No insult meant to your wife,' she said gently to Ryan, who sat to her left.

'Thank you,' he smiled at her, sitting up straighter. 'I miss her like applesauce sometimes,' he said wistfully.

'That's nice,' Tanya said, but somehow, I thought she meant it. I wasn't the only one losing my cynicism the closer we came to the inevitable parting.

'Eh, we have applesauce – on the Kaiserschmarrn. It's vegan already,' Max said with a smile. 'I'll get you some afterwards.'

'Thank you, bro!' Ryan said and I couldn't tell if we were being silly or completely earnest any more. Ryan took a deep breath. 'I suppose someone has to go first.' He pushed his chair out and kneeled behind Marco. 'Marco Bianchi, will you do me the honour of being my husband?'

The air crackled and I couldn't look away, even though I knew Ryan was happily married and any attraction he had for Marco was a sort of hypothetical that didn't have to mean anything.

Marco grinned at him. 'No,' he said with a chuckle. 'But

that was the nicest proposal anyone's ever given me.'

Ryan stood and threw a fist into the air. 'That was actually kind of fun.' He slapped Marco on the shoulder. With a sigh, Marco took up the position and repeated the proposal to Florian, with a lot more awkwardness.

I clenched my jaw when it was Florian's turn. He smiled at me too graciously. Dropping to his knee, he took my hand and I wanted to snatch it back with everything inside me. 'Marry me, Fiona Butkus,' he said, his voice gruff with emotion.

'Seriously? That's the best you can do?' Max muttered.

I patted Florian's hand, a strong suggestion that he should move it. 'Thank you, but I'll decline,' I murmured. My throat was so dry, I wasn't sure how I was supposed to get *any* words out, let alone a marriage proposal to my best friend.

The scrape as I pushed my chair back seemed to ring out in the entire restaurant. I was suddenly panting as I dropped to the floor, like that one time I'd tried to do a parkrun even though I always feel like I'm dying when I run.

I couldn't look at him but managed to get the words out without choking. 'Maximilian Gerard Brouwer.' I said his full name like the sweet sound it was. 'Will you marry me?'

A tight cough and a sort of gagging sound were not what I expected to hear after those words, although I never thought I'd say that in my life to anyone, let alone Max. I grimaced and peeked at him. He grasped my hands and plonked me back into my chair, as though the sight of me in that position made him uncomfortable. Of course, it did. That was the point of the dare.

Then he spoke. 'I know you're joking,' he began, his voice raw, 'but… name the date.' He winked at me, but his smile seemed a little forced. He did not really mean he would marry me, right? *Right?*

'I expect the invitations next week,' Florian said, and I'd never been so thankful for one of his jokes.

Max and Tanya got through their mock-proposals and we all took a long, long gulp of beer.

'I have to say,' Florian said, suddenly looking more than his thirty-seven years, 'this game has been very different from when we played it in Freiburg.' He glanced at Max, who immediately dropped his gaze, as though they were communicating something I didn't understand. My head hurt with all the subtext, tonight – or I was just paranoid.

'Shall we get the last piece of paper over with?' I asked with a sigh. The way Florian looked at me... I wasn't paranoid. Something was going on.

He released a breath on a huff and reached for the last slip of paper. 'There was no getting around this dare,' he began, making my heart leap into my throat. Glancing between Max and me, he leaned on his elbows and continued, 'It's time to tell the truth, you two.'

He placed the paper carefully on the table, where I read, *'Tell your partner the secret you have been keeping'. The* secret. Florian was ratting on me. He didn't need to tell me that if I didn't admit it, he'd tell Max himself what I'd said while drunk two weeks ago. I suspected he'd rigged the little velvet bag for his own purposes. Why now? Why had he kept quiet in the first place if he always planned to make me spill?

My stomach shifted painfully as I realised that if Max had known what I'd said two weeks ago, we might never have slept together, never have... created whatever this was that we were about to destroy again, just as I'd feared. I froze, staring in horror at Max, but he was glaring at Florian.

CHAPTER THIRTY-ONE

'Go on, Max,' Florian said gently. 'Tell her. You know you need to.'

Chapter Thirty-Two

'If you tell me not to freak out, I'm going to freak out.' I grasped Max's sleeve and closed the material in my fist. 'What is going on? What couldn't you tell me?'

'It's about the challenge,' he muttered. My skin prickled, wondering if this would mean I'd made a fool of myself.

'It was all Max's idea!' Florian blurted out. I froze, processing all my emotions in the wrong order.

'Why would you…? You *wanted* to do all this stupid stuff? Just for the money, right?'

'No,' Florian said. 'Max wanted to make *you* do all this stupid stuff.'

'What?'

'It wasn't quite like that,' Max defended, but his tone only confirmed that whatever he had to say would not make me happy. 'Flo contacted me about it. He was invited to suggest ideas for the events that would appeal to a social media audience.'

I wished it didn't make so much sense, but I could feel it in my cold skin that Max had been hiding this from me. The Stockelschuh-Rennen? That even sounded like something Max would suggest. 'Why didn't you tell me? And why did you make me do it when you knew I didn't want to?'

His sigh was long and hitched. 'You obviously thought it was a lame idea, so I didn't want to admit it. But I thought it would be good for you… for us to… I made Flo check that there wouldn't be anything too bad like his usual stunts.'

'He's suddenly your best friend "Flo"?' The word 'best friend' tasted sour.

'You enjoyed it,' he insisted gently. 'Don't say you didn't. I knew you needed something to snap you out of your…'

My throat closed up. 'My depression? That's what you can't say, right? This is all about Fi's sad, self-centred life? Is that what the sex was too? A dose of happy hormones to fix me up, slap me on the arse and off I go?'

'You know that's not what it was. I made a mistake, forcing you to do this under false pretences, but I was doing it for you.'

'Do you even need the money?'

He gave an eloquent shrug. 'Of course, it would be helpful. We are struggling to stay afloat, but… we have options, especially since the investor seems serious.'

'Did you do something to get that video of me onto social media?' I asked in a small voice.

'No! I wouldn't do anything like that.'

'You'd just encourage me to embarrass myself in public.'

'Fi,' he said darkly, 'you didn't embarrass yourself. You found yourself, right? You were amazing!'

'Annnd now might be a good time to explain your reasons for keeping Max in the fuck buddy department and nothing more,' Florian prompted. I stared at him in dismay. The table was all wide-eyed enthrallment. 'I remember how charming she was that first night, drunk and angry and irritable and begging me to kiss her.'

Heat flushed up my chest. That was me this trip: drunk and angry and irritable. Of course, Max had been desperate to snap me out of it. I was miserable company – *depressed*. But he hadn't needed to go so far with the 'cheer up grumpy Fi' project.

'She said a few interesting things after she fell on her arse in the spinning walkway of the LachFreuHaus.'

I shook my head at him urgently. Tears pricked my eyes and I was certain that life at thirty-six, with a good education and a great career, was not supposed to be this messy.

'Shall I show him?' Florian asked.

'Whaaat?'

When he pulled out his phone, the dread seemed to suck all of the blood out of my heart.

'I didn't tell you,' Florian began, almost apologetically, but that can't have been right. 'I have it on video, everything you said.'

My stomach dropped and I wanted to drag the future back in before it could unroll and make me hurt Max. It was the one thing I wanted to avoid above all else, and I'd still done it, with this stupid, sudden attraction to him. I'd known it would ruin our friendship, but I also knew I should have admitted what I'd said sooner – told him I'd been wrong – and not let this fester in the back of my mind.

I'd made a mistake while drunk that would hurt him badly. I didn't hold much hope that he could forgive me. Too many people had treated him poorly and I hated that I was now one of them.

Florian thrust his phone in front of Max and I lurched forward impotently. I couldn't warn him or defend myself. I wasn't sure I had a defence against what I'd said and I certainly didn't have the energy to utter it.

My drunken drawl sounded through the speaker on Florian's fancy phone. I didn't need to watch it again to know that I was sprawled on the floor of a strobe-lit, novelty tube that flashed purple, sliding on my butt as the tube rolled and swayed.

'*...a great place to pick up a guy, right? You guys are all hopeless, you know. Can't give fucking orgasms. I don't know why I keep trying,*' I slurred. '*Only Max... It's so much easier to be me with Max.*'

'*Max?*'

In the video, I sat up, swaying, with my hair all over my face. Then I suddenly said, '*Kiss me, Florian.*'

He only laughed. '*I'm not sure you're in a state to be asking me to do that, Fi,*' he said, surprisingly gently.

'*You have to kiss me! I'm so confused right now. For some reason I keep thinking about jumping Max.*'

The others all stifled a snicker. In any other situation, I might have laughed along with them, but I knew what was coming.

'*Are you secretly in love with Max?*'

Yes! Just say yes! I squeezed my eyes shut, because yelling inwardly at my past self wouldn't help anyone. '*Ha!*' me-from-two-weeks-ago said on the screen. '*I love Max to bits, but he's... a disaster. He looks everywhere for love because his parents don't accept him. He's a great time – the best – but... he's not "in love" material.*'

I couldn't look. How could the words sound a hundred times worse now than they had when Florian reminded me of what I'd said the following morning? So much had changed in two weeks. Some deep truth about my words, those words I would bury under a concrete sarcophagus for the rest of time if I could, tinkled in the back of my mind as well.

'It was before,' I began weakly. 'It was when I arrived. I was wrong – and afraid. I didn't know—'

'You didn't know exactly how great a time I was?' His huff of a laugh crippled any further defence I might have attempted. 'Okay. I've seen it. I understand. It's not really… surprising.'

'It's not about you!' I tried one last time, the words losing strength as something in that sentence struck me with a hint of the truth.

He sliced me in two with the rough look he gave me, his glasses amplifying the disappointment, the hurt and the hint of panic. He was Freiburg Max again, ready to bolt, to blame himself for everything and drown in his sensitive feelings – those beautiful feelings that I'd always loved, even though they scared me.

'How is this not about me?'

'I didn't *see* you – not the way you are now. Maybe I never saw you properly.'

He squeezed his eyes shut and shook his head with a sigh. 'No, Fi. The problem has always been that you see me too clearly. You're right. All of it. Nobody knows me as well as you do, so how could I have expected…?' He took off his glasses and rubbed his eyes with the ball of his hand, shaking with jitters. 'I-I need some time… space. Just— Let me go.'

No.

He whirled and took off for the kitchen, probably headed straight for the staff entrance, where we'd kissed sweetly only a week ago. I opened my mouth to call out after him, but my thoughts swam.

It's not about you! It was about *me.* I was the one who looked for love everywhere, even as I used cynicism and sarcasm to pretend I didn't. *My* parents would never understand me, let alone accept me. I was a disaster – and I wasn't even a great time. And I most definitely wasn't 'in love' material.

But I'd still loved Max – as a friend and… I'd still loved him. And he'd loved me, in one way or another – until I'd said the stupidest thing in the world on a purple strobe-lit rolling tube on the first night of Oktoberfest. I had to do something.

I stood to go after him, but Florian stopped me.

'He told you to let him go.'

'I can't! He might do something stupid.'

Ryan stood and looked at me with concern. 'Weren't you angry with him for telling you what you needed?' I felt suckered, glancing frantically between my friends for some kind of confirmation, but of what, I didn't know.

'Do you really think he'll do something stupid?' Tanya asked. 'The only stupid things I remember him doing in Freiburg, you did with him. If we'd had these phones back in 2008, I'd have a lot of videos of you two climbing inappropriate objects while drunk. It's a wonder either of you made it through that year without broken bones.'

It wasn't news to me that both Max and I had been complete messes that year. I'd thought I was okay, when really… Max had always known I wasn't. I'd let off a childhood's worth of steam in nine months and he'd allowed me to do it without judgement.

Of the two of us, he was stronger. The Max of today was stronger, still. Tanya was right, he wouldn't resort to self-destructive behaviour, as he had previously on occasion. He knew himself better now. But whether he'd still have the patience for me, I couldn't be sure.

'I'm… Fine, then I have to go, too,' I said, pushing past Florian to head for the main door, but he followed me and what he said, as I shoved my arms into my jacket, I had not been expecting.

'I'm so sorry, Fi.'

It was enough to make me turn back. 'You say that now? After you made me hurt him?'

He sighed deeply. 'I *am* sorry. But you also understand that you hurt him anyway. What were you going to do? Keep that secret until you die?'

I swallowed, wishing he wasn't right. 'I'm going home on Wednesday,' I whimpered. 'We could at least have had until then.'

'When you'd let the guilt eat you up and never call him? *That* would be cruel. But we all know there is a bit of a cruel streak in you.' My gasp seemed to echo through the kitchen. 'Don't worry, Fi. I like it. I respect it.'

I shook my head. I was tough and ambitious, occasionally foul-mouthed and secretly broken, but I had never been cruel to Max and I hated to think I was capable of it. I wasn't my mother – or at least, I didn't want to be. 'I was drunk and deluded when I said that stuff,' I bit out.

'You'll have to explain that to him. Better to do that now than after you leave.'

'Don't tell me you did this for my sake! The bloody pair of you!' I threw up my hands.

'It wasn't entirely for your own sake,' he began. 'And this wasn't how I was planning to make you confront this. But you two are so clearly the best at these chellenges.'

'What are you going on about?'

'Tomorrow. Only one pair can win. We both know who

needs this money,' he said bluntly.

I eyed him. 'Tanya?' He nodded slowly. 'And it's just so convenient that you're now her partner.'

'This isn't about me. It would give her a quicker way out.'

I hated that I couldn't tell if he had dickier motives or if this earnestness I'd spied today was real. 'And if Max was only manipulating me into this stupid challenge and I should have satisfied my arsehole boss by now, what reason do I have to continue?'

'None at all,' he said in a satisfied tone that bugged the hell out of me. My stupid competitive streak. I wanted to get back out there, win the contest and rub his face in it, but he was right about Tanya.

'Okay,' I ground out with difficulty. 'But I still need to go and… work out how to make this up to Max.' I deflated as I spoke. There wasn't a way to fix this. I'd hurt him and I couldn't *un*hurt him again. We should never have got so tangled up in a relationship.

Chapter Thirty-Three

I might have been able to let Max go for now, but I didn't go far myself, imagining Max coming back and… No, I didn't know what would happen when he came back. The scared animal part of me thought he'd growl at me and say he'd only ever been my friend out of pity, but our years of friendship were too deeply scratched onto my soul for me to truly believe that.

He didn't answer my panicked phone call, of course. I tried to leave a message, but it came out like, 'Nngh, I— Guh. Fuck,' and I hung up again, terrified of saying the wrong thing and making it worse.

Sitting miserably in the park behind Snaketooth, I wondered what to do with myself until I was shivering and damp in the chilly afternoon. Tomorrow was the first of October and I could kind of see why they'd moved the Wiesn to the middle of September. It had definitely become jacket weather over the two weeks I'd been there.

I couldn't remember if Max had taken a jacket and it bothered me immensely to think he was wandering the streets, shivering, the way several nights out in Freiburg had ended when he'd left his coat somewhere.

Crap, I could give the guy some credit for remembering his

own jacket now he was thirty-five. I was such a shit friend.

By the time I went back inside, the others had gone. I snagged my coat off the antique hook, staring at Max's, hanging next to it. On a whim, I took his, too, and wandered miserably back to his apartment, calling him repeatedly.

As the afternoon dimmed into evening and I had only had beer for lunch, I cooked some pasta and ate it in Max's room. The photos stuck around the place made my heart trip. Framed by the bed was a picture of us sitting on a stone wall somewhere in Italy, chilling a wine bottle between us in a packet of frozen chips. We'd been twenty-six, but we looked about sixteen.

Taped to the window was a more recent photo of Max and me at a rooftop bar in Kuala Lumpur, the cityscape opening up behind us. It was the last time we'd seen each other before I'd got caught up with work and cut off from the world by the border closures. The restaurant had sent someone to romantically serenade us and we'd felt so bad, we'd just thanked them and handed over the expected tip – and then howled with laughter when they were gone.

I didn't remember any awkwardness back then. He'd told me all about the couple of months he'd been with an older woman called Elena before she dumped him for an even younger man. He'd already met Ben at that stage too, so I'd heard about the great sex, but questionable duration of their relationship. I hadn't rolled into a ball of raging jealousy upon hearing that.

Pulling his wardrobe open, I searched out the really old photo stuck inside the door. It was a poor-quality print and probably about a single megapixel because it was from 2008. But it showed our younger selves in the kitchen in the dorm, Max cooking something to feed everyone, while I stood around with a beer.

My memories of those weekly parties in the dorm were so strange now. Meeting so many fascinating people, united by our determination to see the world, I'd talked and laughed more than I ever had in my life. But I'd also been constantly low-key afraid that everyone would hate me, that they'd see through me to the self-absorbed person underneath. How quickly Max had become my comfort zone in Freiburg, a safe place to let myself out for a while.

Staring at our baby faces, I realised I had to do everything I could to make this right again, even if it meant turning the clock back to before we'd slept together. I needed my Max, as we'd been before, a team against whatever life threw at us. I needed to find a way to switch off the sexual undercurrents that had sprung up suddenly and made me think these stupid thoughts about relationship disaster areas. I would grieve what we'd become for two beautiful weeks, but that was a sacrifice I had to make for the future.

Max had promised nothing would change between us. He'd probably be relieved to see the end of this weird phase of my life and go back to how we'd been before. That was probably part of the reason he'd come up with this stupid scheme with Florian. I was fairly certain I'd overreacted to that piece of news and would forgive him more easily than he'd forgive me.

My phone beeped and I snatched it up, just *knowing* it was him. A flood of questions and concern made me realise how badly I'd been wallowing in my own self-interest. How badly had I hurt him?

The message didn't answer any of my questions. Whether

he was so angry he was sulking or simply too cold to take his hands out of his pockets, all he'd sent me was a dropped pin on a map. I pushed my half-eaten pasta aside and grabbed my coat – our coats.

Jumping onto the train without stopping to get a ticket, I popped up again at the main square, where only four days ago he'd hefted me into his arms at the start of the biergarten race and carried me through one of the happiest days of my life. That sense of loss rose up again, insistent grief, but I had to shrug it off. We could still do dumb shit as friends – even more dumb shit, probably.

Following the map on my phone, I took off down the pedestrian mall and raced for the Frauenkirche, the Church of our Lady, with the two knobbles on top which I tried desperately hard not to equate with nipples, because that would only remind me of Max again, in a way I wasn't supposed to be indulging.

The square was lit with lamps, turning the leaves of the trees fluorescent yellow. I found Max sitting by a stone water feature with little illuminated mushrooms, staring into space, as still as I'd ever seen him.

My heart cracked in so many places, I panicked and rushed down the uneven steps, nearly ending up among the mush-rooms in the fountain. He didn't see me until I effectively landed on him, clutching his shoulders.

Getting a grip, I shoved his coat at him and he muttered his thanks. 'That was quick,' he said mildly. He looked up at me, his eyes wide and a little sad, but he was otherwise calm. What did that mean? Was he still mad? Why couldn't I tell? 'Are you all right?' he asked.

'No!' I choked out. 'We argued and you disappeared for

hours and you can't do those things to me, Max!'

He grabbed my hands and hauled me down beside him and my thoughts worked double time, wondering if he used to touch me like that or if that was something that had to go, too. 'I know. I flipped out. I didn't think I could still behave like a hurt teenager, but apparently I can. I've calmed down now.'

He had? That was weirdly not what I wanted to hear. 'I'm so sorry,' I rushed on anyway. 'I meant it when I said those words weren't about you. I was afraid what would happen because I was suddenly attracted to you. But it was always my problem. *I'm* the disaster area. I don't know what's come over me these past few weeks.'

His speculative look made me even warier. 'What do you mean?'

'We don't fight. We just don't.'

'Yes, we do. Remember in Berlin, you were so mad at me going off the rails that as soon as I was myself again, you left the hotel with your bags and told me you weren't coming back. You were out all day.'

'You knew I was coming back, though,' I insisted.

'And the time you hooked up with that guy and forgot to come to the tattoo place in Bratislava for my appointment? I was so angry with you I nearly fell in the Danube.'

'I'm still sorry about that, but you got over it.'

Ouch, the fierce look that flitted across his face made me want to kiss him and drag him to bed. I had to stop seeing him like that. 'What's the difference?' he asked. 'Why didn't you trust that I was coming back today? Why do you think I'm not going to forgive you?'

'Because *everything* is different!' I insisted. 'We have to go back to how things were before. We accidentally made some kind of *relationship*, without setting any boundaries or anything! You told me our friendship wouldn't change, but it did and now these lies hurt so much more!'

He clutched one of my hands and wrapped his other arm around me and suddenly I was crying and leaning my head on his shoulder. 'I'm sorry,' he said softly. 'I should have told you I'd spoken to Florian. I screwed up,' he murmured. 'Things were different between us before we ever kissed because so much time had passed. I tried not to, but I doubted you and that's what got us into all this trouble.'

Those words hurt more than his confession that he'd manipulated me. 'Were you really so worried about spending time with miserable moppie that you had to trick me into it?'

'No, you can be as miserable as you want!' His hand fumbled for my face and it felt so good and I was too tired of working out what was allowed and what wasn't. 'I never doubted how important *you* are to *me*. I know how much I love you. I doubted how important *I* am to *you*. I wanted to do the challenge because it seemed like good advertising for the bar, but I hated the idea of missing out on time with you, if you didn't take part too. I did think you'd enjoy it, if you gave things a chance...'

'I would have done it for you, if you'd just asked.'

'I realise that now. I shouldn't have doubted. And I did ask Florian to check out the challenges first. I wouldn't have made you do anything really bad.'

'It was me who made us do something bad too,' I said with a sigh. 'I wrote that stupid dare about kissing your partner.'

His jaw fell open. 'That first Saturday? You wrote that? I suppose you didn't think *we* would have to do it.' I was tingly with guilt for not confessing everything, but all this weirdness would be over soon, and he didn't need to know how much I'd thought about kissing him before we ever got to it. He dropped his arm from around me. 'I'm still not sure why you ever let me kiss you and… everything else.' He swiped a hand over his mouth in a gesture I recognised as nervous Max reaching for an imaginary joint.

'It was a mistake,' I said on a rush of breath.

'That much is clear,' he said softly.

'Max, I have too much riding on this. You're the only person in the world who knows me – honest shit and all.'

'And that's a problem because…?'

'Like I said, I'm a relationship disaster area. And for a few hours there, I didn't have you any more and it hurt too much.'

'Are you trying to say that you don't want to sleep together any more just because you're scared of what will happen when we break up?' he asked, his tone speculative, rather than hurt. The situation felt a lot more complicated inside me, but I managed a silent nod. 'Are you sure it's not because I'm bi and I have albinism and you've seen me vomit and shit my pants and even my parents don't think I'm worth anything?' he asked quietly, followed by a little huff.

I nearly screwed up and kissed him there and then. 'Of course not! You're like a part of me, Max. I already loved you!'

'Yeah, but not like… that.'

'I loved you just as much, and it was…' I nearly said less selfish, but that word would only make him misunderstand again. Perhaps I really meant 'less terrifying', but that platonic love had been just as deep. 'I can't lose you.'

He gripped both of my hands hard. Had I ever seen such resolute lines on his face? 'You won't. I'm sorry I ran off. It was immature. I should have stayed and talked, but you never lost me and you never will.'

'I hurt you,' I said flatly. 'I can't live with that.'

'You'll have to. It happened. I would have been hurt even if we hadn't been… together like that, although maybe not as much.'

'Max, I'm sorry,' I said, my nose stinging. 'I really didn't mean it. You've worked life out and even if you hadn't, you have to believe I loved you anyway – I always have.' As a friend. I didn't think I needed to say it for his benefit, but the reminder was for myself. 'All this time, I thought I was the one who knew about life, but I don't even know if I want this promotion. It's selfish, but you're my comfort zone and I need that.'

'It's not selfish,' he said gently. 'Calling it selfish is your mum talking.'

I looked up at him sharply. The tingles at my hairline were trying to tell me something here, in chorus with my heartbeat and my animal brain. It was something like, *He's right. Listen to him. Florian is wrong, too.'*

'Fi, if you want to go back to how everything was before, then we can do that.' I slumped against him in relief and he brushed a hand over my head, mussing my hair and it could have been us returning to normal. 'But what happens when you find a real relationship? What if *I* want a relationship?'

'We've had relationships before and it was fine.'

'No, we haven't,' he said with a snort. 'We've had romantic dysfunction. But I suspect that's over, now – for both of us.'

Part of me wanted him to shut up and let me pretend he wasn't right, but another part was reaching for something – maybe even for a *family*, even though I'd only ever seen shitty ones of those.

'Romantic dysfunction is exactly what I don't want for *us*! I don't want to hurt you and then you hurt me, too, just because mid-thirties hormones are weird,' I insisted.

'I've talked you down from tears enough times on the phone to know exactly how passionately you can blame yourself,' he said, his voice deceptively quiet. But I'd definitely never seen such a fierce look in his eye. 'But this isn't all on you. I don't have the excuse of hormones,' he muttered. He took a deep breath and his next words only delivered another shock I was unprepared for. 'Maybe I'm wired differently, but I always knew it could be like this between us.'

Chapter Thirty-Four

Ohhh, shit. I bolstered my nerves carefully against that bombshell. What did it even mean? He'd always wanted to sleep with me? When we'd cuddled in bed in that cheap hotel in St Petersburg he'd found me attractive? When I'd changed clothes in front of him in our beach hut in Koh Samui? The naked sauna? Those days in our single beds back in *Freiburg*? Was he trying to destroy all my memories?

'Why didn't you… say anything? *Do* anything?' I asked before I'd thought it through.

'I was pretty sure it wasn't what you wanted. But you understand the feeling of not wanting to risk our friendship. I've loved you for just as many years as you've loved me, even though you like to forget that.'

I stared at him with the suspicion that nothing would make sense ever again. *I've loved you…* I knew the 'as a friend' was implied, but that distinction didn't seem so clear any more.

He took my hands again, the punishing grip keeping me on this planet. 'I didn't want to end up here, questioning and doubting and arguing instead of enjoying our time together. We're better friends now than we would have been if we were exes as well. But don't run now, moppie. We can just be friends. I'm used to ignoring it.'

I wasn't used to knowing it! A fresh ripple of panic shot down my spine. I was ready to run, to take off over the little mushrooms sending their glowing light over the water feature in front of us. But Max had already told me not to. He'd told me it was safe. By some miracle – or by the grace of fifteen years of friendship – I trusted him.

'I promised our friendship wouldn't change,' he continued, his voice low and smooth. 'You are still more important to me than anyone else in the world. Maybe I made mistake to push you now. I can't… I don't really regret it yet. You felt that something had changed and I was terrified you would decide you finally wanted to stop fooling around with dickheads you'll never fall in love with and get a real boyfriend and I—' He paused and licked his lips. 'I panicked.'

The lightheaded feeling returned at his words and was I swaying? The towers of the church, illuminated against the slate-grey night sky, blurred before my eyes as I stared at them, waiting for answers. What I'd interpreted as scepticism in Max's expression that first, jetlagged night had been panic. Far from a public service orgasm, he'd seized the chance to be with me in a way he'd wanted for years.

But he still thought we could go back to being friends afterwards, that he'd wave me off to New York and we'd watch shows together across the ocean and only see each other a few times a year for a cuddle. I wasn't sure I could compartmentalise like that. If I let my feelings continue down this path, it would be all or nothing for me and I wasn't sure either of us could ever do 'all'.

If we were exes… He was right. It had always been safer to stay friends, but we'd busted that one well and truly.

'I don't want to freak you out,' Max said gently.

'A bit late for that.'

'But I also don't want you to think this is all your fault.'

I grabbed the crosspiece attached to his suspenders in my fist, my palm over the little embroidered edelweiss. 'Are you seriously telling me you were attracted to me all this time? Since Freiburg?'

His brow was eloquent with something that looked suspiciously like frustrated hope. 'Not exactly Freiburg. I thought you were beautiful. I always liked your mouth. But I was… working myself out that year.'

He liked my *mouth*? I shook him by the lederhosen. 'When, then?'

He bit his lip. 'That time in Morocco, sure. You bought that woven hat that you liked and when you smiled…' He gave a little apologetic shrug.

'Max, that was the year after Freiburg.'

'So? I told you I'd had a long time to get used to this. I know you haven't. I'll understand if it's all too much for you.'

'What does it mean though?' I asked with a sigh. 'We're friends who live on opposite sides of the world who find each other attractive? In what universe does this end well?'

He covered my hand with his, pressing my palm into his chest. 'In this one, moppie.'

'What?'

He brushed the backs of his fingers along my temple, the gesture so affectionate it quieted all of my confusion. For once, I just listened. 'We just take everything as it comes. Nothing's a break-up because we'll always be friends. You're not going to lose me. Sydney, New York – wherever you are, you mean too much to me too. I'll come and visit. If you don't want to sleep together again, that's fine. But let's not waste the last few days this week arguing. There's still time.'

Time for what? To plan our next visit, which would be too short and make me hurt again? But he was right about one thing. 'I don't want to argue,' I agreed softly. My eyes had been staring blindly at his pecs, but I switched back on, noticing the rise and fall of his chest, the beat of his heart under my hand.

We only had four days. All this time, I'd thought I was the brave one who went out and succeeded at life, but Max had taken chances and got hurt and *lived*. On those trips we'd shared over the years, I'd lived too, only to snuff out again when real life returned, because he was the only one who made me feel *enough*.

But these visits might not be enough any more and I only had four days to find all the solutions to life and love and everything in between.

I tugged on the leather to draw him to me, slipped a hand into his hair and kissed him. The instant our mouths met, I knew it had been foolish to think we could go back.

* * *

Although we'd had sex that morning, it felt like a lifetime ago and we didn't stop for anything after we got back to Max's apartment. I wanted it all, which was new for me. I was used to being touched the wrong way, to expressing displeasure in sex as much as pleasure, but even when Max sank his teeth into the underside of my thigh, it was somehow exactly what I'd needed. He knew me, he cherished me and I trusted him.

When he tumbled onto his back on the bed and pulled me on top of him, I put my own teeth to good use, making him jerk and gasp when I grazed his nipples, loving the familiar flavour of his skin on my tongue.

He already had a condom on and it took no effort at all to take him in, my eyes crossing at the way he flexed and thrust beneath me. He lifted himself enough to bury his face in my breasts, his fingers tight on my hips.

'That time in the river,' he said, panting. 'You're so beautiful naked, Fi. You're beautiful clothed. You're beautiful in my lederhosen,' he chanted under his breath.

He was beautiful, too, but I'd already told him that and he hadn't believed me. Instead of telling him, I showed him, slowing the frantic pace and drawing out each rock of our bodies together until our gasps were in unison.

'Turn around,' he muttered and I obliged with a giddy smile, sinking back onto his cock slowly, enjoying the press of the new angle and the way inarticulate blabbering burst from his lips. I worked him slowly, leaning forward and coming down hard, teasing both of us with just a touch too little friction. He sat up and gripped my boobs, scraping his mouth along the back of my neck until I pitched forward with a groan.

A moment later, my face hit the blanket and he hitched my hips up and thrust in hard. 'Fuck, it's good,' he groaned, tight and low.

'Smack me,' I blurted out, not quite believing I'd actually said it.

A second later, his palm connected with my butt – not hard, but firm enough to send a stinging shiver through me. He hadn't hesitated, as though I hadn't surprised him. His hand ranged over my cheeks, his thumb pausing between.

'You can have it,' I murmured, remembering our conversation after we'd first had sex. 'I want to make you feel good.'

His hands moved away and landed next to mine on the bed. His face dropped close and every inch of my skin tingled to have him over me. 'Maybe next time. Right now, I'm enjoying being with you like this,' he whispered against my cheek. 'Because it's all new – it's all just us.'

I understood what he meant. Everything was different, when it was his hands on me, his breath on my neck, purring soft praise.

He paused, his lips skimming my shoulder blades as everything inside me turned to mush. *Enjoying* was too mild a word for how I felt about us together like this. It was *necessary*. The brush of his skin over mine, the weight of him behind me were imprinting onto my soul.

I pressed up, seeking more, and he pushed back, harder. When he sank his teeth into the back of my neck, I could only moan – high-pitched and strange. He pushed again, curled over me, and I could tell by the way his arms shook that he was losing it. And then the friction washed through me in spades as he let loose with a grunt, pumping hard.

It was better than winning – even the money I would have liked to win for Snaketooth. Max fucking me, his cock solid inside me and his breath ragged against my neck, was the answer to the universe in that moment.

His moaning gasps, the way he was trying not to lose it before he'd got me off was so hot it was probably what tipped me over the edge, whimpering and thrashing as he groaned into my ear with his own release.

So this was make-up sex.

He flopped next to me on his stomach, his hair standing up and his face smooshed into the blankets – as mine must have been, but there was no way I could move right then. We were the wrong way up on the bed, staring at each other as our breathing slowly returned to normal.

My gaze met his and held. I'd thought we were as close as two people could be, back when we were friends, but we were so much closer now. There were things about him I hadn't appreciated before. He'd understood that. I was working out how he needed to be treasured and loving every moment of discovery.

As though he sensed how close I was to tears, he rolled onto his side, stroking my face and my hair. He was so good at affection. So many life skills I'd never learned – or only begun to learn from him.

'We don't have to get up for the challenge in the morning, since we kind of publicly quit,' he said, pressing lazy kisses all over my face.

I stilled, sluggishly remembering everything Florian had said to me earlier. 'You know he did this on purpose,' I said, trying to shake myself back to consciousness. 'He was trying to get us to drop out.'

'What? Why?' Max asked with a sigh.

I sat up, my stupid competitive spirit still firing, although it was a weird feeling, getting ready to conspire with my boobs hanging out. 'Annoyingly, he has a good reason. He's going to help Tanya win the money.' Of course, I'd already told Max about Tanya's situation. 'It doesn't hurt that he's now on Tanya's team.'

Max sat up too, running a hand down my spine and pressing a kiss to my shoulder. It was almost enough to distract me. 'You find that… disappointing?' he prompted. I could feel his smile against my shoulder.

'It's your fault.'

'I know,' he agreed far too quickly. 'I awakened fierce Fiona. I'm sorry. You don't want to hear this, but—' The sneaky bugger knew exactly what he was doing, stroking my skin, my hair, and letting his breath tickle my cheek as he spoke. 'You enjoyed some parts of the challenge.'

He shot off the bed before I could poke him for that, dashing to the bin to throw away the condom and then grabbing his glasses.

'I did,' I begrudgingly agreed when he slipped back onto the bed, hauling me into his arms. He was the only one who could get away with telling the unfortunate truth to me like that. I took a deep breath. 'I loved the challenge – when I got over myself. You knew I would.'

'I hoped. It hurt to see how closed in you felt over the past few years. It will take more than a tattoo to recover from the shock, moppie.' Did he realise that I'd been closed in for a lot longer than the last few years? He only ever saw me when I was flying.

'I really underestimated you,' I whispered. *I love you so much.*

'You underestimated yourself, too,' he said softly. 'We won those challenges, against all those brawny guys. You and me, Fi.' *Stronger than ever.*

I leaned back against him, enjoying the feel of his fingers skimming down my arms. 'We nearly won the whole thing,' I said with a wistful smile. Wait… I jerked upright again and turned to him. 'We can still finish the challenge,' I said suddenly. 'Not win it because if you have a solution lined up, then Tanya needs the money more. But we could finish – for our pride.'

Max grinned at me. '"Our pride – our beer"?' He made a stage-musical gesture with his arms.

CHAPTER THIRTY-FOUR

'Pride is your brand. We can't pull out now.'

'You want to finish the challenge, even though we don't have to? Even though we could just stay in bed having sex all day?' His voice went high at the end.

I crossed my arms. 'You think you could keep getting it up all day?'

'Is that… a chellenge?' he asked with a snort and I slapped him on the arm.

'I'm serious. We need to finish the challenge. It's exposure for Snaketooth and closure for me. You were right. I needed something to get me out of my rut. Now I want to finish it and I need you to do it with me.'

'Okay,' he said with a tilt of his head. 'Tomorrow, we fight.' He held up his hand in a fist and I bumped mine against it. 'But today, we cuddle.'

Chapter Thirty-Five

Max and I, Ryan, Marco and Tanya marched into the Theresienwiese the next afternoon, kitted out in leather, hemp and silk and ready to take over the world. Florian raised an eyebrow at me, but I just gave him a curt nod. Let him squirm.

The teams gathered under the statue of Bavaria for the organisers to dramatically unroll their scroll and announce the team that would participate in the final day's torture. It was early afternoon, but there was already someone passed out on the ground a few metres away and a group of young men taking turns to fall over in the mud.

The same guy who'd outlined the route of the biergarten challenge cleared his throat to make an announcement. 'The scores are remarkably close!' He looked like a town crier in his embroidered shorts and felt hat. Someone should have given him a bell.

I'd taken a peek that morning to see Florian had edited together some kind of video from yesterday, but I didn't want to know how much the world knew about my argument with Max.

'Overnight I tallied the responses,' the guy continued, 'the comments, likes and shares, and added it to my scores. The winners of the group stage, with an outstanding lead at 116 points, are the 2008 Freiburg International Students!'

Sportsmanship obviously wasn't strong with the beerfest challenge, because the applause was limp at best.

'Uh, yay?' Ryan tried.

'Yay,' I echoed with a curt nod. It was time to get down to business.

'The three pairs from that team will compete today for the grand prize, awarded by our panel of judges rather than social media interactions.' A group of grim officials with clipboards as well as feathers in their felt hats nodded to the group.

'First, you must… drink a Maß!' he announced with unnecessary fanfare. 'Then, you will confront the Devil's Wheel! Whoever can stay on the longest will win the points for their pair.'

When Max merely snorted, I assumed it wasn't the horrible whip-you-around ride with the piles of vomit on the ground underneath.

'And after another beer, the Toboggan! Whoever can stay standing will win the ten thousand euros!'

Florian eyed me at that, but I just gave him another nod. Since he already thought I was cruel, he could suffer, thinking I was about to ruin his plan to win the challenge.

'What is all that stuff?' I asked Max out of the corner of my mouth.

'The Teufelsrad, the devil's wheel, is like that thing in the children's playground that spins around fast, except this one is on the ground and has no railing. The last one to stay on wins. There is a technique to this.'

'Good.'

'The Toboggan is a big slide, but it's more famous for the

conveyor belt that takes the drunk people to the top.'

'That sounds amazing.' I grinned at Max. He grinned back, giddy with something like excitement, although I was certain he'd done both of these attractions before. He pressed a kiss to my cheek and I realised that smile was for *me*.

After saluting the organisers with our upturned mugs to show they were empty, I hauled Tanya to her feet and squeezed her hand as we stumbled away from the table.

The Teufelsrad was housed in a striped tent with a gaudy plastic-and-neon façade. Above the entrance was a repre-sentation of the wheel itself with four mannequins perched on it, looking like enormous sex dolls with suitably vacant expressions. Inside were bleachers, five rows high, for spectators to witness the indignity and flashing of knickers occurring on the wheel below. My stomach turned just looking at it and I had to blink to clear my vision, willing away the surging alcohol in my blood.

As we arrived through the turnstiles with our tickets, the announcer roused the crowd to a cheer and then called, 'Alle Männer ohne Ledahosn! All men with no lederhosen!' Over the padded barrier came a rush of men of all ages, squashing into the middle. To the sound of shouts and laughter, the wheel started to spin.

'You can all have some practice turns, but when he calls the contestants of the Wiesn Chellenge, it's crunch time,' the organiser explained, 'and we'll see who stays on the longest.'

I really could have skipped the practice run. It was difficult to stop myself imagining the effects of centrifugal force on vomit.

'You want to be as close to the centre as possible,' Max whispered in my ear. 'And keep your feet flat to stop you moving to the edge. When you are the last one, get on your stomach. No sex jokes.'

I gave him a mock frown. 'Spoilsport. But aren't we *trying* to be thrown off early?'

'I figured you'd want to put in a good effort in the test runs,' he replied with a grin. The man knew me well.

In the middle of the tent, the wheel had already thrown off three men, like a rodeo bull, except flat and less suggestive. A few minutes later, only one man remained. I jumped in astonishment when a giant spongy ball swung down from the ceiling, clobbering the man on the head. Two attendants flung ropes across the wheel and, even though the poor man dropped into commando stance, the wheel always won and he slid off like the puck in a game of air hockey.

'This is utterly ridiculous,' I muttered to Max.

'And you can't wait to go on it,' he said with a smirk.

A grin broke out on my face. 'You're absolutely right, you dope.'

The announcer called for all the women wearing yellow and I searched and searched, but couldn't find any in my outfit. Even the middles of the little embroidered flowers on my apron were orange. Tanya had some yellow piping on her bodice and headed for the wheel, steeling herself with a crick of her neck.

Florian stood still next to us, watching the action closely. Tanya wasn't quick enough to nab a spot in the middle and it wasn't long before she slid off into the barrier. Lucky it was only a practice run.

'Alle Männer mit Turnschuhe von Adidas! All men in Adidas sneakers!' That was oddly specific, but I didn't even need to look to know it applied to Max. Tempted to smack a kiss onto his lips for good luck, I resisted, shoving him forward instead. He shouldered his way to the middle – I knew there was a reason his shoulders were my new favourite thing.

The wheel revved up, throwing the men against each other, and I closed my hands into fists, willing him on. The first few men tumbled off, but Max was unflappable, unrepentantly grabbing another guy as a counterweight.

A persistent buzzing from my little felt bag distracted me, but I ignored it – at least, I ignored it until it sounded again and again and pissed me off. I tugged my phone out, intending to reject the call, but I saw it was Dollersen. I froze. I was on leave and he'd given his blessing for this contest. It wasn't unusual for someone at my level – or at the level of the promotion I was supposed to get – to be called in while they were on leave. But surely he could wait three days.

My stomach turned at the thought of returning to normal life in three days – what passed for life when I wasn't with Max. Grinding my teeth in annoyance and a good dose of dismay at my dewy-eyed feelings, I pushed to the back of the crowd, pressed a finger over my other ear, and connected the call.

'Ah, Fiona, it's good I caught you.' His words only made me wonder if I'd made myself too available. It sucked being a woman in this stupid, corporate minefield – and at this beerfest on steroids. I took a deep breath to clear my head. When would the alcohol start wearing off?

'Hi, Mr Dollersen.' I grimaced. When would I start calling him Bram? It all seemed false to me now – a construct designed to make me feel small and young and incompetent, although the 'young' part was a nice change. I narrowly avoided asking him how I could help.

'I've managed to sneak some time in with de Bruin tomorrow. I was lucky, given how everyone is courting them right now.' He reminded me about de Bruin as though I would have forgotten the Beerhemoth's next takeover target since the last work junket.

I restricted my response to, 'Yes, I know.'

'They want to see the global marketing forecasts.'

That's a nice change, a company that values the role of the female-dominated marketing team. 'I updated the reports before I went on leave, including the presentation. There are current figures accurate to the end of August, the graphs and metrics too.' *Now, leave me alone.*

I glanced over my shoulder to see Max and his new friend on the wheel clutching each other desperately as a giant, stripy ball clonked them on the head.

'I need September included in those reports and I need you to brief me before the meeting tomorrow.'

I froze, biting off more of the filthy words I hadn't needed to censor over the past couple of weeks. Clutching my forehead with my hand, I managed to say, 'I can update the presentation tonight.' If I didn't drink anything after my second Maß, I might manage to do a decent job.

'I need you to meet me tonight – with the presentation.' He sounded as though it was completely reasonable to ask me to drop everything and do his bidding. I was too much of a millennial for this!

'Mr Dollersen, I'm—'

'I realise you are probably filming for that marketing stunt,' he said, his voice flat. A shiver of misgiving zipped up my spine. 'You must have enough material by now. Think about your priorities, please, Fiona.'

Oh, I was thinking about my priorities and Bram Dollersen was right at the bottom, although my promotion still hovered somewhere up there. 'It will be finished this afternoon,' I began, hating the weakness in my voice.

Dollersen's heavy sigh came down the line very clearly, despite the rowdy cheering behind me. I glanced over my shoulder in time to see the other man shoving Max off the wheel, sending him crashing into the barrier. I took an involuntary step towards him, but he hopped up, brushing off his trousers.

'I was hoping I'd be able to overlook this,' he began and the cold tingle turned to icicles. 'Not only have the incidents over the past few weeks shown questionable judgement, you've been filmed supporting a competing product.'

'What? You told me it was a good strategy to join in with this challenge.' And what did Dollersen mean about competing products?

'Yes, when I thought you'd be using the opportunity to get a jump on our competitors and turn this "I love beer" nonsense into something positive, but you've been supporting Snaketooth Microbrewery,' he said slowly. 'A quick search on the internet and I have footage of you wearing sponsored products.'

I scrunched my eyes shut. *Stupid.* I was a hopeful marketing VP. Even on annual leave, I should have been more careful. But supporting Max was far more intrinsic to me even than the job I'd poured my life into for years.

Something broke inside me when I realised my employment contract prevented me from supporting Max. Even the photos and the ads I'd done up for them probably went against the terms of my non-compete clause, although it wouldn't be easy for Dollersen to prove anything. Was I *married* to the Beerhemoth? Had I given up my right to a private life for money and responsibility?

It wouldn't have mattered so much a year ago, when I hadn't had a private life, but now… I felt another 'I Love Beer' moment brewing and I didn't want to fight it.

My head spun as those priorities switched around more quickly than the scoreboard at the end of Eurovision. There was no reason to stick around and see out the challenge, not when I didn't want to win anyway, but when I looked back at Max, ambling over the barrier from the Devil's Wheel, his hair mussed, I found a whole lot of reasons.

'I'm disappointed,' Dollersen continued, 'but I've worked *so hard* to develop you for the VP position, Fiona, that I'd gladly overlook it this once, but I need to be certain of your commitment.'

Apparently, he thought I *was* married to the job.

'I need those reports by six, and I need you to meet me at my hotel tonight to brief me. Will that be a problem?' *Will you be a problem?* After he'd worked *so hard* to develop me, like I'd been a great big mess before Bram Messiah-syndrome Dollersen had picked me and turned me into his automaton.

I'd spent my whole life trying not to be a problem. With the promotion dangling, it had felt like it was working. I looked back at Max. He stood watching me questioningly. I gulped, wondering if he could tell how close I was to doing something exceedingly stupid.

'I'll meet you at six,' I murmured.

'I'm sorry, what was that? There is a lot of noise on your end and you spoke very quietly.'

'I said, I'll meet you at the hotel at six.'

'Good,' he said emphatically. 'I knew I could count on you, Fiona. Your friend's business isn't going to last much longer anyway, I'm afraid. I did some research and found out they're alarmingly in the red. The market just can't sustain boutique beer prices at the moment.'

I tried. God knows, I tried, but there was no way I could keep it in. 'You're wrong, Mr Dollersen,' I blurted out. He spluttered something in response. 'Boutique beers are a growth market. Snaketooth just needs time.' Heavy silence greeted that pronouncement, but I wouldn't back out, now.

The announcer from the Devil's Wheel called out, 'Alle Frauen mit braunen Haaren! All women with brown hair!' and that was my cue to hang up on Dipshit Dollersen.

Chapter Thirty-Six

I didn't hesitate. Shoving people out of the way left and right, I pushed through the crowd to the wheel, tossing my phone to Max as I ran. I landed with a bump, but I snagged the last spot in the middle, squeezing my butt between two other women.

I glanced back at Max, who took a puzzled look at my phone. His brow furrowed and when he met my gaze, I could tell he had suspicions about who had called me. What would he say if I told him Dollersen wanted me to blow off the challenge to work? Would he tell me to get my butt into gear and do the work, earn the promotion? He was always my biggest cheerleader – which was a gorgeous mental image I kind of wanted to see in the flesh one day.

It was juvenile. I was definitely tipsy. I was making a big mistake not rushing off to do Dollersen's bidding, but making Max happy felt suddenly more important than anything else in my life. As I pressed my palms and the soles of my feet onto the slippery wheel and it began to move, I stared up at the spinning ceiling and allowed myself to imagine a stunning marketing campaign, turning Snaketooth into the popular destination it deserved to be.

Would he let me? Would he trust me with his dreams, his *pride*? He thought he had something to prove to me, but he needed to trust himself, believe he could succeed – *we* could succeed.

I was imagining a lot more than a marketing campaign now. As my blood surged and my thoughts scattered, all I could see was an image of us in a kitchen somewhere, Max with his incorrigible smile on his face and his hands all over me. It was *our* kitchen.

My head spun. Sure, my whole body was spinning, but that image messed with me big time. When I'd thought about a serious relationship, it had always been something vague, the opposite of my loneliness, a complete fantasy where there was no cost and no risk, like a polite housemate. But this… what I pictured with Max was a mingling of souls, sharing fears, hurting and being hurt, healing and being healed.

Was that what he truly wanted, even if he wasn't ready to admit it? Neither of us would ever be ready, but being screwed up together was what we *did*.

I searched for his face in the crowd, but the crowd was little more than a blur. Shit, we were spinning really fast. Feeling the outward pull, I groped for the woman behind me and locked my arms with hers. I couldn't get off this wheel yet. My brain was working on something bloody important and I hadn't figured it out.

'Is that "Ms I Love Beer" on our wheel today?' called out the announcer. 'Good for you! We're all about equal opportunities for women here at the Devil's Wheel – equal opportunity to fall off!'

I was so distracted, I didn't even have the headspace to come up with a cutting retort about putting male blow-up dolls on the outside of the ride, if they were so big on equal opportunity. I was thinking too hard – feeling too hard.

Afraid that I already had everything I'd ever wanted with Max, I couldn't believe I'd nearly given it all up, assuming that, after one argument, we were through. *I* was the problem. I didn't know what a healthy relationship even looked like, but if Max wanted me, I would give up a lot more than a promotion to make it work.

The truth knocked me over the head like… actually, that was the stripy ball from the Devil's Wheel. It knocked me onto my back and Max's words came back to me, reminding me to roll onto my stomach. Where had the other woman gone? Something slapped my butt limply and there was a strange rhythm to the colours swirling in front of my eyes.

I had been reaching for something, so close to understanding. What was it again? Everything felt fuzzy and I wanted Max more than I wanted my stupid competitive spirit. I shuffled towards the edge and the centrifugal force took hold of me so quickly, it sucked me off the wheel and shot me out like a ball in a tennis machine and it was a blessed relief. I blinked at the bright blue padded barrier that still looked as though it was moving, although my eyes didn't agree with my stomach.

I felt horrendous.

Strong hands hauled me to my feet and I hoped like hell it was Max. If the brawny announcer was dragging me out of the ring, I would die of embarrassment. When his arms came around me and I recognised the rough wool of his cardigan, the fine white hairs on the backs of his hands, I released a long breath and slumped against him.

'My hero,' he whispered in my ear. 'You stayed out there for ages.'

'I was…' *Trying to work out if this is love, if I believe in it after all.* 'Really dizzy.'

'It'll be all right in a minute. Was it a call from work?'

I hesitated, not wanting to hear his reaction. If it was anything other than, 'Screw him and spend time with me, because I bloody love you, moppie!' I would drown in disappointment. My head already felt as though it was underwater. I managed to nod, hoping he wouldn't ask me anything else.

'Bad news?' His arms tensed around me.

'Not… exactly.'

'Was it something about the promotion? When will you have that confirmed?' There was a catch in his voice, but I was too woozy to work out what he could be thinking. 'Fi?' he prompted, skimming his lips up my neck to below my ear.

'Don't want to talk about it,' I mumbled.

'Fi,' he said more firmly, his mouth on my skin, 'is something going on?'

'No?' I squeaked. *I'm just quietly freaking out because I think I want to be with you forever like this.* My head had finally stopped spinning. I turned in his arms and wrapped mine around his neck.

'Alle Wettkämpfer der Wiesn-Chellenge! All contestants of the Wiesn-Challenge!' the announcer called.

Max was gone in an instant, fumbling for my hands and tugging me after him. Ohhh, shit, I had to get back on. He bustled me onto the wheel before him. 'Try to keep Tanya on,' he whispered in my ear. With a nod, I took deep breaths and ordered my stomach to stay where it was.

All six of us landed in the centre of the wheel like a Looney Tunes cartoon, a jumble of arms and legs. I gave Tanya a strategic shove, earning a glare, but she ended up right in the middle, the rest of us making a deformed circle around her.

Sharing wary glances, we waited for the wheel to start.

'I don't like being on a different team from you guys,' Ryan blurted out.

'Don't worry. The others won't hesitate to beat us,' Marco added with a grunt as the wheel began to spin. 'But please don't vomit on my shoes.'

'I'm not very good at… aiming with my vomit,' Max said with an apologetic smile.

'I bet it's not the announcer who has to clean it up,' Tanya added between gritted teeth.

'Nobody's going to vomit!' Florian grumbled sharply, looking green.

'If the contents of your stomach flies off the wheel, does that count as part of your body?' Ryan mused, making Florian groan.

'He's not going to vomit up his entrails,' Max joked a little too gleefully.

'All right, focus everyone,' I said sharply. I was worse-for-wear myself and Florian was sitting right next to me.

The crowd was already a blur and I just wanted to get off this thing, but Max and I had a plan which didn't involve me bailing. We were all too polite to shove each other, so it was the big stripey ball that took the first casualties, sending Ryan skittering off like a cat tumbling from a fence. Max and I closed ranks around Tanya, grabbing onto Florian as well. Marco rolled his eyes and elegantly gave up. Max and I had set everything up to lose.

'Ready?' Max called.

'Yes!' We didn't even need to count. We let go at the same moment and went sailing off, leaving Tanya and Florian in the middle. I met Max's gaze across the wheel, as the ropes were flung and the stripey ball swung between us. We were a team. And I was just about ready to let go of everything else and jump off my life after him.

Maybe I wouldn't be meeting Dollersen after all.

* * *

My second Maß settled heavily in my stomach. Max had fed me part of a pretzel to soak up some of the alcohol, but that had settled heavily, too. I was a bloaty, fuzzy, tipsy, swoony mess that only Max could love.

He was unsteady on his feet too, his eyes glazed. I knew this because I stared into them whenever I could. He kept asking me if I was okay and I kept avoiding the question. The flashing neon lights and echoing shouts of Oktoberfest were not the best place to blurt out the sensitive questions I had for him – for both of us.

Our efforts on the Devil's Wheel had pushed Tanya and Florian into the lead. All Max and I had to do was fall down on a conveyor belt and the job would be done. That didn't sound difficult at all.

I squinted up at the colourful toboggan, strung with lights. It looked as though it was made of Meccano. In one squat tower was the entrance and the twirling helter skelter slide looped around another tower. In between, on a sloping walkway, was the infamous conveyor belt.

We stood as a group, our faces turned up to the grey sky, gawking at the punters making their way to the top of the slide in varying states of drunkenness. A man fell onto his knees and the thing had no mercy – it just zipped him up to the top like that, an attendant holding him upright by his collar. The obligatory drunk girl in a tiny dirndl arrived at the bottom and lasted less than a second, before she was flashing the world, heading up with her legs in the air.

I could do this. One undignified trip to the top of a slide – and presumably down again – sober up, and make a fucking decision like an adult. But first priority was a trip to the little girls' room. I handed Max my bag out of habit and dashed for the nearest toilet trailer. When I arrived back, the others were lining up for the toboggan – and Max held my phone to his ear.

I froze in alarm, tiptoeing back to Max and shaking my head furiously.

'I'm sure she will have everything ready. Here she— Uh, thank you.' His brow deeply furrowed, he shoved my phone at me. I grabbed for his arm before he could turn away, holding my phone to my chest. 'Answer it!' he hissed under his breath. 'It's Dollersen.'

'I know it's Dollersen!' I whispered back, joining the queue.

'Then talk to him! He thinks you're working on some kind of report!'

'Well, I'm not,' I replied rather stupidly – or rather, the beer replied.

'Why not? He's expecting you at six! Do you know what time it is?'

'I have no idea.'

'It's four o'clock, Fi! I don't know what you're still doing here!'

The fledgling hope I'd developed on the Devil's Wheel took a knock, but I was tipsy enough that I didn't let it stop me. 'You think I should drop everything – drop *you* – and do my boss's bidding when I'm on annual leave?'

He took my arm as we shuffled further along the queue for the toboggan. 'I know it's shit, but what about the promotion? It's your *career*.'

Okay, it seriously sounded like, for once, Max was on an entirely different page. Maybe he wasn't thinking of us staying together after I left on Wednesday. *We still have time…* Had he just meant we'd had time for some more great sex? 'What do you care whether I'm in New York or Sydney?'

'New York is a *lot* closer.' His voice had that undercurrent of steel again that I didn't remember from previous trips.

'That's right, you want me to get the promotion so you can visit me?'

'Exactly,' he confirmed, his eyes suddenly huge with a mix of dismay and hope. He hopped up on the first step to the toboggan and took my face in his hands. '*Yes!*' he repeated, one palm sliding down the side of my neck. It felt so good, my eyelids drooped. 'Don't go to sleep yet, moppie,' he said softly. 'Did you want to throw your promotion just for this stupid contest? You deserve this job.'

I shook my head. It was still too fuzzy for my liking. My skin prickled with the awareness that this was a conversation that should not happen with so much alcohol in my veins, with cameras for the challenge everywhere and the impending carnival ride mishap that we had to stage. 'Not for the contest,' I murmured. 'For *you*.'

His hand dropped from my skin so fast, I had to grab for the metal railing behind me. 'What are you talking about?' His expression was hard. But I'd gone too far and had drunk too much beer to stop now.

Chapter Thirty-Seven

'Bitte schön. *Bitte schön*,' the attendant called and I suddenly realised I was at the front of the queue for the conveyor belt. The line behind us had grown. I couldn't go back, I could only stumble up the steps, groping for Max. In front of me, the belt flapped and grumbled and zoomed off at an unpredictable pace.

'Get on!' Max urged me.

'Are you annoyed with me?'

'No!' he insisted. He totally was. 'What are you waiting for?'

'*You!*' I cried.

'Fine!' he said, taking my hand and barging onto the conveyor belt, ignoring the attendant's cries of protest that we were supposed to go one at a time.

Max hauled me onto the thing and it took off so fast, we crashed right down onto our butts. I grappled for the railing, but the belt jerked, and I was knocked over. Max appeared above me, his arm outstretched, but a sudden kick of the damnable thing had him toppling over, right on top of me.

There was an attendant somewhere, trying to untangle us. The belt kept shooting us upwards. Max tried to push himself off me, but there was nowhere for him to put his hands and he tumbled into my cleavage. Then his fingers were on my boob.

Somehow, he'd ended up nestled between my legs. He lifted his head, his glasses askew, and his eyes were full of fearful questions.

Everything went still. I lifted a hand to his cheek, smoothing my thumb over the fine lines of his cheekbone and jaw. He didn't understand, yet.

'Visits won't be enough,' I said softly. His face contorted and I realised I hadn't expressed that properly. We were a disaster area of fears and vulnerabilities.

I didn't register the urgent shouting until the weight on me suddenly doubled and a tipsy stranger with a beard and an unsettling smile grinned down at me from over Max's shoulder. 'Oof,' was all I could manage to say.

Someone hauled the stranger away and we struggled to our feet.

'Keep moving, please!' called the attendant, when Max and I would have just stared at each other as the bodies piled up at the top of the conveyor belt. Max turned me around and marched me to the bottom of the stairs.

'What do you mean visits won't be enough?' he bit out. 'If you were in New York, I could come five times a year. And maybe…'

I turned to face him. 'Maybe what?'

'Maybe you could visit me here… more often… sometimes.' He stepped up to me, nearly brushing his lips against mine, but not quite. 'In Sydney… I missed you too much. I always missed you too much. When I heard about the promotion, I thought this could be a chance.'

I could have kissed him where he stood. I knew that feeling of missing someone in my bones, in the nuclei of my *cells*. Why had it taken me this long to realise what that meant? But would he accept what felt, to me, like the only solution? I needed him to trust me in his life for more than visits. 'You thought it was a chance to see each other five times a year?' I prompted.

He inclined his head. 'Well, it could be ten times, if you… you see.' I pictured it, flying back and forth, keeping things between us alive.

'You're right. It could work, but it's not—'

'Wir war-ten!' called an impatient man at the bottom of the stairs. I glanced up to see I'd created a bottleneck.

'It's not what I want, Max!' I called over my shoulder as I hauled myself up the steps. The moment was slightly surreal, climbing high above the festival grounds, with a rollercoaster roaring by on one side and the faint sound of a brass band playing 'Ein Prosit' from the nearest beer tent.

'What *do* you want?' he called back, an edge to his voice. When he spoke again, the wind whipped his voice. 'I've been trying to tell you… show you… what you mean to me.'

As he uttered those last words, he came up behind me, his lips near my ear. We'd reached the top of the steps. Only the slide down remained. My fuzzy brain whirred back through all of the moments of unbearable tenderness I'd endured over the past three weeks, wrapped up in his arms, freezing cold in a river, and right back to that first hug at the airport that had put me back together again.

He *had* been showing me – so slowly that I didn't realise what he was doing, slowly enough that I hadn't run in panic. But how much could I mean to him if he wanted to see me ten times a year in New York and he was scared to let me get involved in his life?

'I promised our friendship wouldn't change,' he said, his

voice firm. 'I still mean that. I meant it for me, too, Fi. If you're suggesting you can't be friends just because we hooked up—'

'No, Max, I—'

'Can the man and woman arguing at the top of the slide please make up or break up and get moving! Our guests paid for a ride, not a soap opera.'

Max gave me one last, troubled look and headed for the slide, shrugging me off when I grasped his arm. He said, 'Don't make me regret something with you for the first time in my life, moppie,' and swung deftly onto the narrow toboggan slide, shooting off on the woven mat.

I rushed after him, grabbing the sides and leaning down. 'Don't slide off in the middle of a— I fucking love you, Max!' I yelled. 'Even when you're a lily-livered shit-for-brains!'

Someone behind me gave me a nudge. 'That would have more effect if you say it to his face.'

I drew myself up and turned to face the guy. 'Oh, would it?'

'Can the woman causing a disturbance at the top of the tower please just slide down and put us all out of our misery?'

'Come on, Fi! You can still make it by six!' I heard Max's voice from the bottom of the ride, rising dimly on the breeze.

'I'm not moving to New York!' I yelled back. 'Screw the promotion!' Whoa, apparently that was that. No VP for me. My stomach rolled and my head felt worse-for-wear after the beer, but... that was my decision. I wasn't going to New York. I just had to get Max to see we could throw everything into this little family we'd already made.

'If you expect me to come visit you in Sydney, then...'

I waited for the hurtful words that would land like a slap. He'd misunderstood me, but he was still being obtuse, thinking I wouldn't move here for him, thinking I couldn't feel that much for him. I waited for him to push back.

But he didn't. When he spoke again, he said, 'Fine! I'll get a credit card,' in an oddly tight tone. 'You can't get rid of me that easily!'

'I'm not trying to get rid of you!' I cried. 'I mean I'll move here for good, you gorgeous idiot!'

As though the entire Volksfest had heard my impulsive declaration, everything fell silent, except a low ringing in my ears. It gave me a moment to listen back over what I'd said. Beer and life decisions really didn't mix. Had I truly decided to throw over my hard-earned promotion and move to a country where I had no prospects and not even the right to work?

Yes, yes I had.

Shouldn't I be thinking of how disastrously this could all end? No job, no rights, no best friend. Perhaps I should think about that, but I was drunk enough to ignore it, to release the little piece of my heart that only ever peered out from behind the safety of my lonely existence.

That piece had always belonged to Max.

With an odd sensation like a zip yanking closed, the sounds of the festival whirred back to life around me and I heard Max's voice, yelling, 'Fiona Jade Butkus, get your delicious arse down here, right now!'

That was enough for me. I dropped my delicious arse onto the mat and went flying down the slide. The festival lights blurred; shouts and bursts of music rose up to me; the cold air was heavy with moisture, cutting through my grey cardigan as though I was only wearing the little blouse. The breeze picked up my hair and whipped away my howl of surprise.

And suddenly, I was at the bottom, warm hands grasping mine and hauling me up and straight into the best place in the world – tucked against Max. His grip was tight, his breath unsteady. 'I don't think I heard you right,' he said, gulping down breaths.

'I called you shit-for-brains and an idiot,' I murmured against his neck.

'*That* I heard loud and clear.'

'I didn't mean it,' I began, pulling back, but he tucked me firmly into his neck, his hand on my head.

'I know you didn't mean it.'

'But you are being dense,' I insisted. 'If you heard me calling you names, then you heard the rest, too.'

'You… your job is important to you. I don't want to take that away from you.'

I poked him in the ribs until he flinched and nearly let go of me. 'Not as important as you. It's not a sacrifice. I don't want to be without you for hundreds of days a year and I want to be part of Snaketooth.'

'What part of "we're losing money" wasn't clear?' he asked, his eyes flashing.

'Get over yourself, Max!' This time, when I gave him a shove, I didn't dive straight back into his arms. 'Businesses lose money at the start. You've made a fantastic place. The only thing holding you back is *you*! Do you even believe it will work – do you believe *we* will work – or is this another "I think I'm going to die young" thing that only pushes away the people who love you?'

I'd knocked the wind out of him. His Adam's apple bobbed convulsively. I swayed on my feet, my skin tingling and my thoughts like molasses, as though I'd drunk some magical beer that operated as a truth serum *and* a bullshit detector.

He turned away, a hand running over his hair. I reached for him, tears pricking my eyes and fifteen years of a love I'd been too stupid to recognise came flowing out. 'I love you. I *love* you.' I found his hand and twisted my fingers with his, as though I could knot us together so we'd never have to untangle.

'What if we're not ready,' he said quietly, not looking at me. 'You called me a disaster. There's a good chance you're right. In fact, I know I'm not ready for you, for the things you make me feel, for the things you make me want.'

His words only increased my certainty. How had I not seen until now that he was the best human in the world for me? Perhaps the only one who could see me, appreciate me fully? 'I don't know about being ready,' I began. 'Perhaps we never will be – perhaps no one is ever ready to love someone else. But you taught me to be brave and, ready or not, I'm standing here, asking you not to make me go.'

Chapter Thirty-Eight

He turned back like lightning and curled an arm around me, his forehead dropping to mine and his hand sliding up the back of my neck. He was still breathing hard, his eyes wide and bright. I wanted to kiss him, hold him, but I'd taken this step, ended the first act of our relationship, and I needed him to say we could start the next.

'You're right,' was all he said at first, his voice shaky. 'You're right. The things that mean a lot to me… I push them away. Snaketooth… you're *right*. I have to start believing it will happen. And *you*…' He paused, rolling his forehead against mine and clutching my neck. 'You mean the most to me. It was hard to say goodbye, every time, but you were safe – safely away from me – until this time.'

'Don't push me away,' I murmured. 'You know I'll push back.'

His breath escaped on a huff. 'I love you so much, Fi – so much I would have ruined it, if you weren't… *you.*' A cheer sounded dimly and it took me a moment to realise it wasn't inside me. A small crowd had formed around us, watching the awkward car crash of our tender feelings.

'Aaaaand finally, the saga is resolved and they can go and be boring together!' Florian said with a clap. 'Ryan? Marco? Up you go!'

Max drew me to one side and, with the crowd distracted by what sounded like a messy trip up the conveyor belt, he reached for me. 'Are you serious? You'll give up New York? For me?' His lips brushed mine as though he couldn't hold off any longer.

I clutched his neck to hold him where he was, returning the kiss with a little more agitation. 'It's for me, too. I'll be happier at Snaketooth – if you'll let me be part of it, debts and all.'

'You're already part of it,' he murmured against my mouth, before kissing me again with a groan and pulling me tight against him. My fingers tightened in his hair. 'I wanted you there so badly. Before you arrived, I kept picturing where you would sit and what we would say and I nearly lost it, looking forward to seeing it happen for real.'

The kiss turned slower and, inevitably, hotter. I could barely remember the time when the smell of him, the feel of his skin didn't turn me to mush. He drew away to give me one last wary look.

'But what about immigration? What if you have to marry me?' He couldn't quite stifle a little smile that made me lightheaded.

'I didn't think you were a fan of marriage.'

'I'm not, but I am a fan of you staying here.'

I had to pause to launch myself at him again, kissing him fiercely. 'We can try to sponsor me, but if that doesn't work… yeah, we could get married.' I bit my lip. I probably looked twice as goofy as he had at the suggestion.

'You want to marry me for my bar?' he asked with a chuckle. He was eighty percent joking, but that twenty percent was still too much doubt.

I shoved him and then drew him close again. 'Looks like I have a few things to prove to you.' I kissed him, hard. 'Snaketooth might not be forever, but *we* are. You promised our friendship wouldn't change, but I promise that, even if things change, we'll be together, working it out, married or not.'

He grinned against my lips and our kisses grew clumsy and perfect. 'We're not too drunk to be making these decisions, are we?' he asked against my lips.

'We're just drunk enough,' I assured him with a smile. 'Dutch courage,' I said with a chuckle. We both knew how many times I'd explained that expression to him while drunk.

He clasped both of my hands in his and it was just as overpoweringly intimate as the way he held me close. 'Maybe we can talk honestly without alcohol sometime.'

I gave a wobbly shrug. 'We can try. And until then, you brew beer, so we should be good.'

'Did you decide to stay when I brewed you a kriek?'

'That was when I started looking for a transfer to Munich,' I admitted.

'You… what? You didn't tell me!'

'Well, you didn't tell me that you liked my *mouth* for fourteen years!'

'I won't do that again,' he said with a snort of laughter, before dropping his voice and continuing, 'I love your mouth. And a few other things, too.' The little zing up my spine told me exactly where his thoughts were going. It was strange that I'd never known he brought the A-game when it came to dirty talk. It made so much sense, now I knew. 'Look, there goes Tanya,' he said, gesturing behind me at the toboggan.

I cupped my hands to my mouth and cheered, hearing Max's shrill whistle behind me. Taking a deep breath and squaring her shoulders, she stepped quickly onto the conveyor belt, holding her hands forward. She wobbled and shot a hand out, but recovered her balance like a contestant on *Gladiators* and waved her arm with a flourish.

Florian zipped to the bottom of the slide with a whoop and roused more cheers for his partner. 'Top marks for style on the conveyor belt! Have you ever seen such dignity?' He shot us a dry look and I grinned back. Max and I sprawling everywhere and holding up the queue should be enough to lose the chellenge. When Tanya arrived at the bottom, holding both fists up, I was pretty sure her dignity would win them enough points to get Tanya on her way.

We'd thrown the contest. I'd blown off my boss. And I'd never felt so proud of myself.

I rushed to Tanya and wrapped my arms around her, before the awkward pat on my shoulder reminded me she wasn't a hugger. 'What's going on, Fi?' she asked. 'Did you lose today on purpose?'

'Don't be mad,' I began. 'Max has other financing options for the brewery and I couldn't take the money anyway, because of conflict of interest.' It was probably still true even though I would be quitting. I took a glance at my phone, annoyed to be thinking of Dollersen. I'd missed three calls since I'd declared my love for Max. I might show up at the meeting later, but only to hand Dollersen my resignation.

I'd never been a good people-pleaser, so it was with relish that I shed the last feelings of responsibility towards the Beerhemoth and followed the group of contestants towards the statue of Bavaria. Dollersen had a good report. He could either present without the September figures or he could find a solution himself, because I was on leave – and I would hopefully be on gardening leave sooner rather than later.

The organisers of the Wiesn-Challenge announced Tanya and Isobel/Florian as the winners after their brave showing on the rides – and the last-minute collapse of the rest of the team – and all six of us won a case of beer, which Max and I politely declined, citing conflict of interest rather than lack of interest in a case of industrialised beer-water when the delights of Snaketooth awaited us.

Tanya appeared numb and I knew she had the hardest part of her fresh start still ahead of her. She met my gaze with a small smile and I promised myself I'd keep in better touch with her in the coming years – with all of them.

Ryan and Marco shared a backslapping hug. I had to admit that the stupid contest had done some good. Looking out over the flashing lights and elaborate tents of the Oktoberfest with Max's hand in mine, I was satisfied with my last, drunken stunt of the beerfest and looking forward to our next chellenge.

Chapter Thirty-Nine

Farewell hugs are one of those bittersweet things you have to do to remember you're alive – like watching sad films or reading the news. They hit you in the stomach.

As I allowed Ryan to wrap me in one of his enormous, American hugs before he got on a train for the airport, I leaned into the feeling for once. 'Take care of yourself, my friend,' I mumbled into his shoulder.

'You, too, Fi,' he said, giving me an enormous, American smile. 'I'm glad you finally worked things out with Max. You're good for each other.'

'Thanks. Maybe one day I'll get to meet your wife and kids.'

'Don't make it so long this time!'

'Definitely not!' I agreed.

Marco gave me and Max a quick squeeze in farewell before dashing off for the drive south, back to Italy. Saying goodbye to Tanya and Isobel was difficult. Isobel was discharged on Tuesday, the last day of Oktoberfest, and cleared to fly home to medical supervision back in Valencia.

'I want to watch that video again already,' she said to me after a long hug that probably would have been a squeeze on my side, if I wasn't so wary of hurting her. 'It was the sweetest thing I ever saw, you yelling at Max that you love him! Andres said he wanted you to get together right from the start. He's such a sweet idiot. He should have told me! I took too long to see you two had sparks jumping! Max took your challenge to get an orgasm, huh?'

'Come and visit us, Isobel,' I blurted out, my eyes stupidly moist. 'And I'll come and meet your kids.'

'Ha, if you do that, you will babysit. Just a warning. But I'll visit. I promise! Now I know Andres can find babysitting so easily, I am free as a bird!'

'The babysitting isn't even putting me off,' I said, fairly certain I meant it.

Andres whisked her off towards their airport train, complaining about something in rapid Spanish, but his arm around her was achingly gentle.

When it was Tanya's turn, I travelled with her all the way to the airport, even though we didn't say much. She even let me hug her for longer than usual.

'You don't even have to say it,' she said curtly, giving me a slightly wobbly smile. 'I know I can ask you for help if I need it.'

'And hopefully, you won't need it,' I finished for her. 'Keep in touch, if you can.' As I waved her off, I suspected it would be a long time before I saw Tanya again and it made me cry into my pillow that night – my pillow being that spot on Max's chest that was now officially mine.

'I've had some kind of weird mid-life crisis,' I mumbled into his pec.

'Since we're both going to live until we're ninety, it's not quite the middle of your life yet, moppie,' he replied gently. His response earned him a kiss, which I fumbled rather close to his nipple, which led to me moving on from my pensive crying jag rather quickly.

Florian came to Snaketooth the following day to say good-bye, his expression unexpectedly sober. 'How's gardening leave?' he said to me in greeting. 'I enjoyed your "I Love Beer" video challenge. Suits this place, hmm?'

I was so happy with how my little social media campaign was running that I didn't even mind Florian's tone suggesting he'd had some part in our success.

'When's the wedding?' he asked with a wink. 'I'll be your witness for the immigration department.'

I had already rolled my eyes before I realised he was being serious. 'Uh, thanks. We might need that, actually.'

After giving me a brief hug, he said, 'I never expected you two to turn out quite like that when you agreed to join the challenge.' He rubbed his chin and his smile was almost genuine. 'Naked swimming, sex in the toilets, a drunken declaration of love on the toboggan.' He chuckled. 'I thought you were just a couple of weirdos, but I'm impressed.'

'We are just a couple of weirdos,' I said. 'And you're still a dick.'

He grinned. 'You might have been better off with me, but… happier with Max.' He shook Max's hand, clasping his forearm even as Max gave him a scowl. 'I'll come to Snaketooth whenever I'm in Munich,' Florian assured us.

'You'd better!' I scoffed.

Max squeezed my hand in reassurance. 'You'll have a free beer whenever you visit, Flo.' I watched as understanding flashed between them. They were friends. Perhaps not the closest or the deepest, but Max extended the olive branch and Florian accepted it gratefully. It appeared even dicks needed friends sometimes.

Part of the reason all of those hugs sucked was because they were all reminders of the one I was dreading the most. I'd stretched my time in Munich to seven weeks, instead of three, since Dollersen had luckily banished me from work the instant I'd handed in my notice, but I had to go and pack up my life.

'This is not fair,' I insisted at the airport, trying not to cry.

'You've left me at least twenty times before,' Max pointed out.

'I was an idiot,' I said, burying my face in his neck. I was just starting to trust in this closeness and I had to go again.

'This is the last time you have to leave,' he said softly into my ear, smoothing my hair back. 'And we get to kiss goodbye.'

'You have a point,' I agreed with a sigh. 'A small one. It still sucks.'

'But do you know what I love most?'

'Hmm?'

'The hugs when we see each other again,' he said. 'You always feel like life itself that first time I have you in my arms.'

'Only six weeks,' I breathed, waiting for the prick of emotion to subside again. 'Six weeks until you become Mr Butkus,' I joked to cover a sob.

'No, six weeks until I become *your* Mr Butkus,' he replied, wrapping his arms tighter around me. We wouldn't actually change our names, but the sentiment was there. We would be the Brouwer-Butkuses before the law, inseparable, even in the face of immigration policy. 'I love you, moppie,' he whispered.

Those were words I heard countless times during our video calls as I feverishly sold off all my stuff and faced up to how little I had to leave behind. I'd wasted so many years, trying to untangle myself and the past and ultimately finding no way into the future except a job that could never be fulfilling. My imminent departure made my parents and sisters more tolerable company, although I was never letting my mother anywhere near Max.

Although I'd worried about the time apart, it turned out distance was a different construct when you loved someone freely and they loved you back. We talked a lot, discovered that phone sex was difficult without a tripod and it was almost like we were back in the dorm in Freiburg, learning what it was like to have a soulmate – except we weren't stuck inside our own insecurities any more.

When I finally stepped off the plane six weeks later, I was even more certain, not less, that we could do this. And the hug…

It was a long breath out, a little tear, a tremor of longing and relief. I was home.

Also by Lilo Moore

Berlin Calling

Rose writes twee pop, smiles a lot, and believes in magic and rainbows. When the cheesy love song she wrote is chosen for the European Song Contest, her luck seems to be turning around – especially when a chance encounter leads to the hottest one-night stand of her life. It's almost too bad she'll never see him again.

But then Rose discovers it wasn't a chance encounter. The hot German DJ with the sexy deep voice is her rival for song contest glory.

Grumpy Emil is incredibly talented and the song he spins with his sister could be a winner, even if he doesn't appreciate the playful spirit of the contest. As the continent falls in love with Rose and Emil's competitive banter on social media, they must hide their history from the press or risk losing credibility – and a future songwriting career.

With an anonymous gossip out to ridicule the colourful contestants and a plot to undermine European public broadcasting bubbling under the shiny surface, Rose must be strong in the face of criticism and stand up for everything the contest means to her.

If this Canadian girl can save the contest, maybe she can believe that her feelings for Emil are the real deal.